Love
At the End
of
Everything

A Novel by

D.D. Williams

Ixtab Media

First paperback edition, Ixtab Media, 2020
ISBN: 978-1-8382045-4-9

Printed on demand through various distributors, see inlay for details where applicable.

Cover art by Adriellen Aragão, aragao.carrd.co
Cover design, typesetting, and the rest of the fun stuff by Intern #4

Ixtab Media is based in Newcastle-Upon-Tyne, England
www.ixtabmedia.com

20% of each sale will be donated to local charity Live Well with Cancer, a regional well-being and outreach program.

For those I love, have loved, and will love in the future.

Love at the End Of Everything

South
3 Void Avenue
The Universe
August 3rd, 22 Billion CE

Alexandra:

~~Please find enclosed~~ No, too formal... You'd have thought after all this time I'd know how to write a letter. It was never really my forte. Anyway.

Hi.

A wise writer once said, "Start as close to the end as you can." Personally, I don't think this was the best advice, what with me being the only thing left in existence and all, but here we are: the end of the universe. There isn't a whole lot to do in space other than think about the past. Of you.

Did you know my first memory is of my fist ramming into a full-grown stegosaurus? No idea how I got there, or what the stegosaurus did to deserve a punch in the mouth. It's not a child's memory either, because I was already a developed adult when I was doing it. I think. What followed was a mess. There were so many things I never had the nerve to tell you. And now it is far too late. But! That's why I'm writing this all down. I want to remember how we met. I want to confess my sins. I want… I want something to do up here.

And I know just what you'd say to all this. It doesn't take any effort to conjure up that voice of yours, even after all these years. "But hey," you'd say, "It's a good few billion years too late to be writing your memoir. Why couldn't you have done it when we had that big-money offer? This is some serious procrastination, buddy. You've got the entire universe to yourself and this is the best you can come up with? And just who is going to read this memoir, anyway? You wiped out your entire readership ages ago."

And to all that, all I can reply is:
A) There are only so many things to do up here, sweetheart.
B) Pretty sure you told me not to take that book deal.
C) Since when is an avid Marguerite Young fan concerned about readership?
D) I miss you, love.

But here's the real reason I'm writing this all down now: All the things you couldn't allow yourself to hate about the world are dust now. Less than dust. The only memory in existence is mine, and what's mine is, has been, and will forever be yours. I want the last thing ever created to be a memorial to the woman I loved. Still love. Will always love. Once I am finished with this, with as little fanfare as possible, I guess I'll just float here while what's left of the universe tears itself apart.
So, make of this what you will, my love. This is a confessional, a shrine, a gift, the tale of how a mere mortal dragged an ancient being out of the pits of nihilistic despair and showed him the light.
And it starts, as all the best stories do, with gratuitous nudity and violence.

Much Earlier:

Back when humankind was only just starting to make a name for itself, Earth had an eighth continent. Zzyzx. Very few people have ever heard of Zzyzx because, for reasons that will soon become clear, someone plunged it into the ocean long before anyone bothered to invent geography. As continents go, it was a small and lonely one, a dollop of rock out in the ocean somewhere between South America and Africa. Zzyzx was a blossoming, green land with verdant, majestic forests, and immaculate coastlines all beautiful and pearl white. If it had survived only a few more hundred thousand years, it would have made an excellent tourist location for about a decade, and then a very depressing one for another three.

In among the trees, a kaleidoscope of floral colours sprung forth, a spectrum of fantastic shades nestled in among the greenery. The wildlife, too, was diverse and bountiful, with many a gracious beast roving the land and flocks of graceful birds flying overhead. From one side to the other, Zzyzx was a quilt of natural splendour, abuzz with the music of life unending.

There were human progenitors there, too. Small tribes of naked humanoids had adapted faster than those on the other continents. They were already living in crude mud huts, or up among the trees in makeshift shacks. As pre-humans went, they were a humble, resourceful bunch who only ever killed precisely what they needed to, which tended to be each other.

As vibrant as life on Zzyzx was, there was a dark heart in the centre of the land. A place devoid of life and hope. The people there called it nothing because they hadn't learned about nouns yet, but if they could have named it, they would have probably called it Scary Death Mountain of Death. Scadmood if they were realtors, or the author trying to write less. Scadmood's border began where the trees fell limp and darkened, giving way to an infertile plain of ashen soil. A trail of skeletons made a path to Scadmood's two hills, behind which, depending on the direction you came from, was the jagged and black mountain itself. A stillness claimed the terrain, as if death itself governed the land. No birdsong, no grazing animal, no emboldened children, not even the carrion birds who would have found an ample banquet waiting for them. It was usually quiet.

Blood soaked, salted, and burnt, Scadmood was a sacred patch of land visited only by the pre-humans on very special occasions. For centuries, warring chieftains had settled arguments under the shadow of The Mountain God. Tribes would stand atop opposing hills and declare their grievances to the disinterested pillar of augite. They would perform intricate, sacred routines in an attempt to win the approval of their god, then they would run down into the valley between the hills and try to beat their enemies to death.

A fierce sun hung at high noon as one final ceremony began in earnest. The shadow of the mountain's sharp peak cut the valley below in half. Each tribe ascended their hill in silence, finding favourable symbolism wherever they looked. Even before humans were humans, they had a knack for finding positive signs where there weren't any.

On one hill a tribal leader, more muscle than man, stood before his soldiers. His serpentine penis slapped against his apelike calves as he swung a massive oaken club above his bulbous head. He gyrated as if born to do so, firing pelvic thrusts off toward his chosen enemy, spat upon the ground with a theatrical flourish, and defamed his rival as best he could with his limited vocabulary, his voice a roaring baritone. His name was Ian. Unkempt and furry, his band of marauders stood behind him, grasping clubs of their own. They stomped in rhythm upon the spoiled ground and chanted insults. It sounded like this:

"Agh agh ragn,
Gah gah gah!
Mnrgggg thlgrgjrn,
Nah, nah nah!"

Over on the other hill, Mavis and her ragtag band of insurgents stabbed at the air with pointed slabs of rock. In unison, they swung their hips with lascivious glee. Their pendulous breasts clapped together with some regularity as they performed an intricate song-and-dance number they'd spent weeks rehearsing. Before their holy mountain, these irate women sang of their enemies' lacklustre lovemaking abilities and poor hunting skills. It went like this:

"Kama go go kama,
Ratschs shshs gal nag!

This went on for some time.

With the sun moving off toward the ocean, Ian and Mavis let out battle cries, united by a sudden frenzy. They charged down their hills toward each other, savouring the promise of impending violence. Even at the picturesque beaches, people were poking their heads up to see what the fuss was. As they neared each other, a bright flash interrupted their assaults. Festivities ruined as the ground between them glowed.

Someone had tossed a fireball down from the mountain into the valley from above. Struggling to stop their momentum, the tribes clattered into each other. Some tripped and rolled with terrified screams toward the green flame. Others contorted their bodies into a halt. Fireballs had never been a part of the ceremony. At once, the tribes looked up at Scadmood's peak and saw two figures leering down at them.

Two beings, ancient even then. Populations the world over knew to fear them, even the primitive race of sex maniacs cowering beneath them. Their existence predated oral history; their dangerous nature instead etched into the marrow of all living beings. North, the magnificent She-Beast, a wild-eyed destroyer cloaked in ethereal green flame. South, the cleanser of souls, from whom all storms were born. With elegant dives, the two immortals fell from their perch and landed with catlike grace at the feet of the huddled proto-humans. No longer warring tribes, these lesser beings, unified instead by the sudden certainty of their own extinction.

"This land is surplus to requirements," North said, already bored. "Your experiment was a failure and you shall all be purged."

Before the annihilation began, South was almost sure he saw Ian and Mavis hold hands. A last act of compassion; one variable The Creator had not considered. In an instant, he saw a vital part of human life had been over-looked. But continental destruction was bureaucratic even then, and before he could fully rationalise his thoughts, a ball of fire was forming beside him, the crouched mortals looking at their end with teary-eyed ambivalence, and then

"Oh, hey man, you're burning the chips!"

The John Muir Inn, Whitby — 20__ CE:

Hot oil flicked up and out from the boiling vat as Jimmy shoved Edwin to one side and yanked out the smouldering basket of chips. Small spots of boiling liquid hissed against Edwin's forearm. He felt nothing, heard the sizzle, remembered humans were supposed to feel pain, and pantomimed mild discomfort. "Ow," he said, in a performance not worth giving.

"You've been working here too long to make this kind of mistake, pal," said Jimmy, salvaging what he could from the smouldering wreckage of HMS Chip Cage. "This isn't exactly rocket surgery. If you keep messing up like this, I'll have to dock your pay."

"What pay?"

Jimmy nodded absently, focused on the surviving chips, and trying to determine who among the waiting customers would be least likely to complain. Then, dropping the uptight boss facade, he observed Edwin with as much concern as a sleep-deprived and lonely man could muster. "Are you doing okay?"

Edwin wasn't ready to answer that question. It was almost time for him to do it again. To leave. And once he admitted as much, there was no resetting the clock. The moment he uttered "I'm done," it was impossible for him to focus on the human world until he began his next life. His mind would be elsewhere, running through the unused names he still had on his list, the small towns he had yet to visit this century, the ever-shrinking number of jobs he could hide behind. In the final moments of each alias, he was all but spectral, a minimum wage Janus focused on everything but the present. Life, for Edwin, was how one feels at a much-hated job after handing over your two-week notice, but before leaving for the last time, in perpetuity. So, he stalled on replying to Jimmy.

Instead, he dug up a handful of frozen potato slabs and tossed them into a fresh metal cage. The cold starch sizzled as he dunked them into their bubbling damnation. It was a trivial thing he enjoyed, one he wanted to say goodbye to properly.

"Listen," Edwin started after submerging his last batch of potato prisoners. "I think this is my last day. I quit. I'm going home. You can keep this week's wages if you need to."

Almost by accident, this statement had become a litmus test for Edwin. Whatever response he was given, it always told him exactly what sort of person he had been dealing with. Most would react out of spite, their true selves cracking through a thin veneer of amicability, paystubs withheld, vague threats of violence and insults to manhood doled out. Those found reacting this way strived to prove the adage *shit floats* in any way they could. Others revealed themselves to be cowardly weasels, denying they owed any money to begin with, but more than happy to promise on any number of graves they would look into it. They never did. A few brave souls found enough human decency to muster up an indifferent platitude and a final wage. Fewest of all would act, in those final moments of a working relationship, like the men and women they pretended to be, so when Jimmy dug into his front pockets and replied "Nah, mate, I've got you. I've seen where you live, remember?" Edwin experienced more gratitude that the situation deemed necessary.

Jimmy, of course, had no idea that this basic gesture had reignited Edwin's flagging love for humanity. He always assumed Edwin was an underachieving burnout or struggling artist or post-grad in the midst of a thesis-related breakdown. Any of which suited Edwin just fine – in terms of wasted potential, failed author was far more romantic and far less depressing than the truth: reclusive, immortal entity who has given up.

Edwin finished the shift. It was a gesture and concession he made only once before.

Out by the fire exit, leaning against an over-full dumpster, Edwin sipped his warm farewell beer while Jimmy counted out his paltry share of the tips. Seagulls circled above them, waiting for a chance to return to their feast of mushed potato skins and rotting haddock. Behind the incessant squawks, Edwin could hear the summer's first tourists milling around the crowded streets, their ancient tour buses idling with audible purrs in nearby parking lots.

"Here's an extra twenty, buddy. I know it's not much, but maybe it'll get you a train ticket or something."

"It's been a while since you've taken a train, I'm guessing. But thanks, Jimmy, I appreciate it. Not a lot of people in your position would do that."

"All the more reason to do it, then. I, uh –" He scuffed the ground with his cracked leather boot. "I'm impressed you stuck with this job as long as you did, mate. I know it's nothing to be proud of, but you stuck with it longer than most. A smart guy like you wasting away behind one of my chip pans? Heh. Glad you're getting out of here, honestly. I just hope your next adventure is a little less greasy."

"You know, I'm not as smart as you might think, Jimmy. I've turned down —" *God-Emperor, the first Hamlet, Cleopatra's side piece,* "—I'm where I'm supposed to be. It's been a good stay, Jimmy. Thanks for everything. You're a good man, and I say that as someone who doesn't meet too many."

Jimmy's eyes betrayed flattery even if the rest of his face remained neutral. "If there's one bit of advice I can give you, Ed, it's this: You choose your own fate."

Edwin drank the dregs of his tepid beer and tossed the glass into a container. They shook hands and said farewell.

Edwin's daily routine since arriving in Whitby had largely involved hiding in either a cramped studio apartment or a cramped kitchen. His time outside has as brief as possible. With it being his last night in his current incarnation, he decided to take the long route home. The next time he would see Whitby would be in an unknown future century, and by then the town would find a way to become unrecognisable. Perhaps he would find the town half-submerged in irradiate seawater, torn asunder by a nuclear blast, or else replaced entirely by a hive of futuristic condominiums and vertical farms. However he found Whitby in the future, it wouldn't be the same Whitby. Just as nothing remains unchanged for long. Every time is the last time. And so, he decided to take his time walking home.

As he ambled down the seafront, he pushed against the tide of struggling day-trippers making their slow escape back home, sunburnt and poorer for the experience. He would stop when the mood took him to close his eyes and breathe in the sea air, to feel the breeze and saline mist find his face, hear the rolling crash of incoming waves. He wanted to remember everything, his mind a library of forgotten history. More often than intended, he would stop and look up at the ruins of the abbey. The last time he had visited Whitby, long before weather, crooked kings, and time itself had stripped the walls, the abbey had been something to behold. Even there, surrounded by the din of the twenty-first century, he could still visualise what no longer was.

On the busy, visitor-friendly streets leading uphill, families were struggling to return home. Children whined about things without having the words to express how they felt. Small injustices beyond name and description their psyches would carry into adulthood. Dazed parents stood as if in mourning, resigned to the prison that was the next twenty years of their lives, looking on with defeated eyes, their bodies betraying resentment for their progeny, their lovers, themselves. Friendly pubs were besieged by rows of picnic tables, clutters with empty glasses, cardboard plates, and unfinished food. Less friendly pubs stood protected by surly old men with bulldog jowls and uninviting stares.

Edwin registered it all with the indifference of a historian. Smelled the spilt beer, dead crabs, coconut-scented SPF-15 lotion, fried food, stagnating seaweed. Watched gulls swoop down on fallen ice cream cones, the former owners of which stood by, releasing impotent, frustrated tears as the world looked on. Why did the beach blush? Because the seaweed. He saw visitors stop to take uninspired photos they'd forget about within five hours; locals wrestle looks of contempt and desperation as groups of punters flitted by their empty souvenir shops. Felt the jostle of movement as the stop-and-start foot traffic of the oblivious and slow dictated the pace for a thousand strangers. Pangs of half-forgotten misanthropy as people he had never seen before and would never see again became accidental obstacles, the whole walk at once descending into a panicked exercise in restraint for a being who once levelled mountains.

He reached his apartment without succumbing to the whisper of old ways. His home a squalid cube of tangerine walls bearing the mottled markings of black mould. In one corner, a small kitchen made up of recycled appliances, in another a small, hard bed. Little more than a prison, which was wholly the point. Good thing he never had visitors. The only real company he had was the tiny television set he'd mounted on a stack of old books. As with most of his possessions, the television was an antique, complete with a useless wire hanger antenna and twisty knobs beside the screen. Again, it was a good thing he never had visitors.

Edwin had to ram his shoulder into his front door and lift it a half-inch before he could lock it. He wrestled the locks into place before plodding over to his bed. From underneath, he dragged out a battered army chest and looked inside. A growing layer of grey silt covered the bottom, all that remained of a thousand mementoes lost to the ages. He went through what remained: a barnacle-encrusted sacrificial dagger, the rusting Cattleman revolver taken from one of Galton's boys, leather pouches filled with obsolete currency, the stone head of a fallen angel taken from Notre Dame, bundles of fading letters written by long-dead friends, two Fabergé eggs, the completed first edition of *The Epic of Gilgamesh*, parchments advertising concerts and speeches, Leonardo's naughty drawing of two women and a chalice, The Florentine Diamond, the cap of a young chimney sweep, a signed photograph of a monarch in flagrante delecto, business cards from insane billionaires, Jack the Ripper's handwritten confession, Egill Skallagrimsson's silver, the DVD box set of *The Wire*. To add to his collection, Edwin tossed in Jimmy's crinkled twenty. He smiled standing over his loot and then pushed the chest to the door.

In the morning, he would begin again as someone new. Lugging the heavy chest out and into his hidden crypt was the least of his problems. Finding a new town, creating an identity from scratch, getting a steady, anonymous job, these tasks were becoming more difficult with every new incarnation. But those were tomorrow's problems. Before then, he thought, rolling into his stiff bed, still dressed, time to enjoy the final sleep of Edwin Hego, deep fat fryer extraordinaire. May flights of pimpled angels sing thee to your oily rest.

Sandy Vale Retirement Home, Cullercoats — 20__ CE:

"She doesn't get many visitors, Nell. You may even be the first. Hard to believe she once…" the cherubic carer drifted off mid-thought, huffing as they walked up the five flights of stairs. The building had once been a mansion, its regal past life hidden under framed motivational posters, sterile paint schemes, and low-budget MDF-based remodelling. A medley of confused whimpers and solipsistic soliloquies hung in the air. The fifth floor contained the VIP suites, each belonging to someone with enough money to be taken care of. It was quieter up there.

The carer opened the door to room 51 without knocking.

In a pastiche of old LA diners, the walls of Nell's room were hidden behind a shell of framed black and white photos. In each crisp image, a supernaturally attractive starlet stood with the same rehearsed expression, her confidence and beauty radiating from behind the glass across the room. She stood posed with lithe grace in a thousand locations with a thousand people. Arms draped around the likes of Bergman, Grant, Sud, Hepburn, and Gable. Embraced by a hundred actors whose good looks weren't enough to save them from the vacuum of the past. She stood beside smug society girls, all vying for the attention of the camera with eyes full of both promise and resentment. In small numbers, there were photos of her sitting with anonymous screenwriters, who seemed about as scared of the camera as they were of a strong female lead. She sat in the laps of a dozen ghoulish directors whose proclivities had since become career-enders to all but a handful of well-related scions. Somewhere among the blur were photos of her with two different celebrity horses, one of whom was a suspected zebra and communist.

The gallery of her life was up there somewhere between MOMA and Getty in terms of content, and in real life she sat facing the longest wall in a large, leather recliner, surveying her legacy the way some people watch Kurosawa films, i.e. with misty-eyed gratitude. It was clear, to her at least, her own memories were better than anything on television. Especially at 3PM on a Tuesday.

South and the carer stood in reverence for a moment, Nell was unaware of their presence. She tilted forward, looking at a photo near the floor. "Oh, Humphrey," she whispered. "Humphrey."

With deliberate, loud clicks of their heels, the carer stepped forward. "Nellie," they blurted out, waiting for Nell to respond in some way. "You will never guess what, but you have a visitor."

South could all but hear the tendons crack and her starched clothes crinkle as Nell "Lil Nellie" Campbell turned to face her uninvited guests. A brief ripple of shock as she recognised South, her heavy makeup accentuating her raised eyebrows and slumped jaw. "Claudio," she called out, struggling to stand as she did so. With the calculated, meticulous, almost imperceptible glance of a seasoned dilettante, she examined her old friend.

"I'll leave you to it," said the carer.

The reunited pair stood in silence until they were sure the carer had walked down the hall. There was so much to say. So many years had passed them by, and it was impossible for South to pick the right way to start a conversation. A simple hello didn't seem to be enough.

"You've put on weight," said Nell, sitting back down with audible relief. "How are you going to make any more films looking like that? You know how shallow they are. And they're even worse these days."

South looked down at his waist. He didn't notice any change. "I'm not in the pictures anymore, Nell, remember? Besides, I think I look good for my age." He crouched beside her and hugged her with what firmness his conscience would allow.

"If you say so, love. I've just booked a supporting role in a film adaptation of something or other. So…" she looked over at the photos of her with noted actor Claudio Sud. "… Either you were serious about the whole immortality thing or I'm going to need to see that caretaker right about statem."

South grasped her shoulders and flashed his teeth. "Of course it's me, Nellie. How has life been treating you?"

She let out an ambiguous laugh and peered at her gallery. "Well, I'm in here, so make of that what you will. I suppose, though, that I'm far luckier than just about anyone else who has ever been alive. I've outlived all my enemies, which is more than my enemies can say. Oh, but I'm being rude. How about you? It's so good to see you after all these years. Last time… Last time I was more than a little concerned. But, oh, but it is good to see you. I never thought I'd see a member of the old guard again."

"I don't imagine many of them get to Cullercoats often," South said as he walked over to the far corner of the room. Alone and leaning against the wall was a visitor's stool. He wiped the dust off the seat and carried it over to Nell. He sat and clasped her hand.

"Not since Stan Laurel, I guess," she said. "But that's enough about my boring semi-retirement and self-imposed isolation, Clod. What have you been up to since your LA meltdown?"

"That wasn't a meltdown."

"They brought in the FBI. You were the headline story for a month. The hotel is still finding bits of bedframe under the floorboards. Did you know Tod spent half his fortune looking for you? It was a mess, Claude. The whole thing was a mess. I never told anyone your secret, of course. Not that they'd have believed me."

"OK, maybe it was a meltdown. But can you blame me?"

Nell smiled. "Ah, but you must have found some worthy cause to fight for since then. Tell me all about your big adventures."

"Nell, I..." his shoulders fell limp, and he sunk into himself. "I didn't go on any adventures, and I found no worthy cause. I've been running from town to town working meaningless jobs and hiding in hovels. I thought maybe penance was what I was looking for after all."

Nell looked disappointed. "I'm disappointed," she said. "What an incredibly selfish way to handle your self-pity, Clod. Here I am, living in a museum of my own life with only thirty or fifty years left before I kick the big one, and you're out there pissing away immortality trying to flagellate yourself. It's a waste. A huge waste. Frankly, it's unacceptable, Claudio."

"I didn't know what else to do. It's not like I deserve to enjoy the world after the things I've seen."

"No, but maybe the rest of us do. Because your crisis of faith wasn't supposed to be about you, was it? So, look, I'm sorry you feel guilty about your past, but you have an obligation to everyone you've lost or let down, to everyone whose future was snuffed out. Was all the suffering for nothing, Claudio, is that what you're telling me? Did they all die so you could feel sorry for yourself? Am I going to die knowing you're still out there selling insurance to pensioners? You have time in a way no one else will ever have. You owe it to all of us to do something with it."

"I tried."

"Pah. When? Six hundred years ago? Do you have any idea what a woman of my background went through in Hollywood? But I adapted. And I'm a fraction of your age, all evidence to the contrary, *and* I can die. You don't see me making excuses. Isn't it time, once and for all, you stopped moping around in the shadows? It's just a waste. An absolute waste."

She let out a breath and leaned back in her chair. South glimpsed the photo of the two of them sitting at the counter of The Frolic Room, Nellie with her dainty hand pressed on his shoulder, his eyes cold and shell-shocked and sad in ways he hadn't noticed in his reflection. Memories of their old conversations echoed through the corridors of his mind.

"You can wallow in it or use it, Claudio, the choice is yours."

He blew air through his nostrils. "You're right, old fr--"

"None of this *old* malarkey, you decrepit fogey, I'm already mad at you."

"As I was saying, you're right, you young, beautiful, dazzlingly intelligent friend. But I don't know how to start again, Nellie. It's been too long. I'm trapped down here."

"How do you start walking? Take the first step."

South gave a chuckle and looked into Nellie's eyes. His thumb gestured at their candid photo. "You know, for a mortal, you've always been good at this advice stuff."

Nellie smirked. "Darling, what else am I supposed to do?"

Author's Note:

In writing this, I thought it would be cool and trendy to switch between time periods every chapter or so. This is a stylistic choice based on what I think you'd like, Alex, and not the result of dropping the pages into space after falling asleep.

Plus, too, after this long alive you find yourself wishing for non-linear time on an almost daily basis.

A Long Time Ago:

Hovering far above terra firma was a city made of onyx and amethyst and magic. It shimmered in the night sky, floating like a giant, evil disco ball above fledgling civilisations. The people on earth looked at it as an ill omen, a warning from the sleeping gods. Elders spoke of a time when they could hear the gregarious sounds of celebrations up above. But the revelry had long since ended, the palace in the sky little more than a tomb of echoes. It loomed overhead like a threat, but an empty threat made by a forgetful prankster.

In the grand banquet hall of the palace, South and North sat on citrine thrones and thought of past millennia. They remembered the time before the other inhabitants died out or fled. North cast her mind back to the post-genocide galas and tournaments, how the city had once trembled with primal rage, the feet of a thousand immortals marching in unison down the grand halls of the palace toward their next conquest. South reflected on the mortal guests who once filled his tower, now little more than dust and bone and fading memories. The two of them had been sitting on their thrones for a lifetime, awaiting further instructions from The Creator. Their master had slunk off into the city's core many decades earlier. As for the others, most had given up entirely, turning themselves into nothing out of protest. For all the two of them knew, they were the last living remnants of the floating citadel.

"They've been working down there for ages," North said one morning. Breaking eleven years of silence.

"I know," said South two days later, unused to his voice.

Silence fell again for a fortnight. Two weeks is not much time for immortals, especially when there's nothing left to say.

North stood; her body groaned as it came back to life. "I've had enough of this. I'm going to the workshop; I refuse to waste away."

Together, they marched through the winding palatial halls, through a network of secret passages and trapdoors, down into the tunnels and dungeons they seldom used. North pushed open a hidden door and entered the labyrinthine network of hand-carved caverns. South paused, not a huge fan of the tight, luminous space he was about to enter. As they descended into space few knew about, the walls pulsed with green and yellow lights. They were close to the power source.

After what could have been an eternity of walking and crawling through the narrow caverns, the pair entered The Creator's workshop. It was a giant, spherical room filled with levitating furniture, scrolls, and half-finished mechanical contraptions. A glowing orb, the source, hovered in the very centre of the room, spinning with its own micro-orbit and unleashing arcs of neon electricity. South had avoided the workshop for most of his life, but even he could see the source was losing momentum. It flickered like a dying heart, sending rippling shock-waves through the floating city.

The Creator was nowhere to be seen. South and North scoured the room, desperate for clues, the orb above them sputtering all the while. At last, North noticed fresh carvings on a slab of marble, engraved with The Creator's signature chisel stroke.

IF ANYONE IS STILL HERE,
I HAVE GONE OUT FOR A WALK.
PLEASE DON'T COME LOOKING FOR ME.
SINCERELY YOURS,
THE BOSS.
P.S. NOW THAT I'M GONE, THE CITY WILL FALL FROM THE SKY
JUST AS SOON AS THE ORB STOPS SPINNING.
SORRY. START RUNNING.

"No. This has to be one of their weird jokes," South said, searching the workshop with fresh vigour. He was justified in believing this: The Creator had invented the kangaroo, after all. He knew The Creator was hiding in a chest or under a table, or else had left instructions to reset the orb. They wouldn't just abandon their two loyal children. As the orb continued to slow at an increasing rate of decay, the entire city slanted on its axis as it hurtled toward the earth. A sudden, uninvited thought confronted South: he'd never had to think for himself before.

North, meanwhile, stood motionless, a sly smirk growing over her face. She took hold of South and dragged him to the exit. Fleeing the structure became easier when a huge chunk of the floor tore off, revealing the rust-coloured earth far below. She stood at the fresh precipice with one arm draped across South.

"What now?" South asked, defeated, limp, lost.

North surveyed the land beneath them and let out a wounded, bitter laugh. "This entire planet is ours, South. At last."

They jumped together, headfirst into an unknown future. North continued to laugh. South looked up as everything he had ever known crumpled in on itself, engulfed in a thick, green flame. The cleansing fire was as beautiful as it was an omen for bad times to come.

"Do you need a brochure?"
"No thank you, I've been here before."

On the outskirts of town, there was a second-hand book store specialising in occultist literature. A small group of angry Scottish wizards ran it. Angry because the demand in wizards had plummeted over the centuries. Scottish ones in particular. In the store's basement, there was a tiny museum hidden away, unadvertised, and almost forgotten even by the store's owner. As a vaguely symbolic gesture of metamorphosis, South would pop into the museum every few identities. He would sit down in one of the cramped rooms and reflect on his past, reminding himself why he needed to hide away in factories and kitchen.

The reason South did this was because there was a twirling alabaster statue in the centre of the room dedicated to dead gods. Most of the other exhibits, as far as he could tell, were forgeries or old punchlines to forgotten jokes. Thrones and helmets of Hell Kings, bad taxidermy, and supposed ancient figurines made of plastic. The statue, though, was the genuine article. He knew this because he'd carved it by hand many thousands of years earlier. With coarse, eroded features, it didn't look like much–perhaps the tentacles of an eldritch abomination wrapped around a pillar–but it once showed two svelte figures intertwined in an eternal embrace. It used to stand behind his throne in the grand hall.

Quite how it had found its way to the cramped basement of an Edinburgh book store, surrounded by slapdash hoaxes, was a jumbled story and proof you should throw nothing away. South had saved the statue from destruction and carried it around with him for aeons before finally donating it to a group of druids for safekeeping. The druids were engaged in an age-old clandestine battle against a group of sorcerers. Their battles were wild, unbelievable and, frankly, best not repeated. By the time South came back for it, the Druids were gone. This is where things got complicated. One druid wound up marrying a refugee from Atlantis, the statue found its way to a Templar Knight, a shadowy organisation of despots took the statues once the Templars fell, only for it to be stolen once again by a nomadic tribe of libertine bards, the last descendent of whom wound up opening a bookshop and museum in Edinburgh. The current owners of the store knew nothing of the statue's true past or value, or even that they were bona fide descendants of such an interesting group of people. It was a pedestrian, dull tale, from what South could gather, filled with betrayal and subterfuge and sex, and not something the general public would want to read about. What mattered was that a relic of his old life had survived, and he had found it.

Next to the statues was an unhelpful placard. It said:

> *Representing yon snake Azu*
> *Entwined with wyvern Morlax*
> *Birthed hellish terrors all anew*
> *Vampyr, wight, and sore backs.*

The other exhibits had similar strained poetry. They reminded South of the kind of things you would find in an unofficial gift shop just outside a UNESCO site: trinkets, haggard and cheap and almost contemptuous in their gaudiness. And yet, he was sure people would say the same for his statue. Perhaps it was all authentic. Perhaps the polyurethane Bast collar, Yama-Raja's chintz throne, Tezcatlipoca's buck leather funeral mask, and Puck's potion pouch were all the genuine article. Rarely, but on some nights, South would yearn for all the old myths to come true, so he'd at least have someone to talk to. Someone who would understand eternity. Not that Tezcatlipoca or Puck would make good friends.

He stared into what had once been his bejewelled face and was about to drift into daydream when a fake cough rattled behind him.

"Hey, I didn't know anyone else liked this thing," a woman said.

South jolted, frozen with the temporary belief his old partner was back from her fiery tomb and ready for revenge. With a slow turn, fists clenched, he expected to see preternatural rage incarnate staring back at him. Instead, a woman of indeterminate everything stood under the room's low, arched doorway. She looked at him with a half-cocked smile through welcoming, bright eyes. South uncurled his hands. It was clear the only contempt the woman bore in that moment was for her own pant suit. Still buzzing from sensory overload, South stood relieved but transfixed. Glad not so much for who was there, but for who wasn't.

The woman walked around the stationary South and stood nearby, looking at the scarred surface of the statue. Noticing South was frozen in a post-panic refractory period, she turned to face him. "Didn't mean to startle you. I've never seen anyone else down here."

His composure made a slow return. "No, me either. And I've been coming here for years."

"Good to know," she replied, were voice at once on guard, body poised to retreat.

They stood beside each other and admired the statue in tangible silence. South remembering with sobering clarity he'd started conversations three times since 1952; the woman a seasoned expert in not being approached by strange men. Her mouth puttered around with some words. She was weighing up the multitude of potential outcomes continuing to talk could yield. Most weren't pleasant.

"It's nice, though, isn't it?"

"What's left of it, yes."

"No idea why visiting this thing became a superstition of mine, but I haven't died yet, so that has to count for something."

He looked at her, laughed in a way he thought was sheepish but was later informed sounded like an anime villain. "I know exactly what you mean, and I'm not even sure I can die." *Shit,* he thought, *that's why you don't force friendliness.*

The woman chuckled at what any rational person would take as a joke. "See? Empirical proof this statue saves lives. I've always wondered what it is, exactly, though. Maybe that's why I like it so much because I have no idea what it was except that it definitely was something. Unlike the Medusa head over there. Part of me wishes I could find out more about its history, and yet I also don't want to know. There's something about the mystery."

South didn't want to act like he thought he was smart. As a man who spent his life in hiding, he knew better than to show off to a stranger. He pretended to think, looking like a cheap magician pretending he hasn't already snuck a look at the card. "Ah, it looks like it's a man and a woman entwined around an ancient divining rod. Two immortals, maybe, who thought they'd be together forever, but then, I don't know, maybe their creator abandoned them, and she wanted to destroy humanity and he had some reservations."

"Uh," she paused, tilted her head. "If you say so. Not sure I can even pretend to see that. I think this is clearly yon snake Azu pulling down the Tower of Babel."

"That's pretty specific."

"You're one to talk. But yeah, I pulled that out of nowhere. Whatever it is, I think it's a totem. Whoever built it wanted to scare people away."

In all recorded history, there are precisely five occasions in which a man should have said "Well, actually…" but thought better of it. This was one of those times. It was always the ones who should have thought better of it who were too overwhelmed with hubris to do so. Instead of saving everyone some time and telling the truth, South shook his head and said, "I guess I can see that, but I think they're people."

She squinted, knelt, and took a closer look at the statue. To be fair, it had looked like little of anything for over three thousand years. "Where do you see people? Show me."

He crouched down beside the statue and gestured at a section. "This right here? This is two hands clenched together. If you follow either hand up, you can see the arms, the back, what's left of their heads."

The woman all but crawled onto the floor to take a closer look, hands hovering over the vague remnants of shapes in the stone. After several minutes she mumbled, "Huh," and turned to face South. "OK, so I guess maybe it is two people. But still. Who are they? This could be one of those random archaeological finds you hear about on slow news days."

"I'd say they were probably ancient immortals. People used to call them gods. I think. What I mean is, I don't know."

They hovered mid=squat looking at the stonework, resembling in that moment two overdressed beginners following a workout DVD. She was the first to stand, shaking her legs as she did so. "Who are they, then? What era are we talking about, exactly? And why is this statue here in Dean Village instead of the Met where it belongs?"

"Everyone else forgot about them. Would be my guess."

The woman walked around the statue, trying to visualise its original form. "Cute theory, anyway. How did you figure this out? Are you one of those secret anthropologists I've been hearing about?"

He resisted once again the urge to reveal his true nature to her. While he had few friends, and was drawn to the woman's familial glow, and wanted, despite himself, to talk to her for as long as she would let him, he knew any confession, no matter how minor, would end the conversation within an instant "No, I just thought it made sense. It's just always been the impression I got when I look at the statue. You're right, it's a totem or something."

"No, no, I think you hit the nail out the park," she nodded to herself and turned to look at the other exhibits, inspired by a newfound curiosity or else trying to end the conversation.

South watched as she made fleeting glances at the various other Dead God relics. They didn't possess the qualities of the ruined statue, but she continued to look. A knot somewhere deep inside his being untied itself and before he could rationalise or justify it, before he even knew he was speaking, he said, "Hey, could I buy you a coffee? It's just I don't see many—"

"No."

Fair enough, he thought to himself, relieved as the knot reformed.

"I mean," she said, "No, I will buy my own coffee, thank you. Last time I let a guy I met in a basement buy me coffee, I was billed for services unrendered. Not that I'm saying you'd do that. You can never be too careful with strange men and basements."

"Services unrendered?"

"You know… sex."

The word sex hit South with more force than a bullet, and he had been hit by plenty of those. If his physiology were more modern, he'd have blushed. Instead, he recoiled the way a thirteen-year-old boy or male politician does during conversations about menstruation. This was not unnoticed by the woman, whose face widened as South tried to form a sentence. "I would never, I mean, I'm sure you're a lovely, but no, I don't know, I haven't thought about it, and besides which—" was all he could ramble.

"Relax, I'm not accusing you of anything," she said. "We're just getting coffee, anyway, so don't get your hopes up, bucko."

South felt like one of those children taught to swim by an ex-navy grandparent, tossed into deep water and left to their own devices until they figure out how to flap their legs. He didn't know what he was doing or why he was doing it. Wasn't this the thing people did? Drink coffee and chat with each other? "I just thought it would be nice to drink a coffee with you since we both like this statue and I certainly didn't mean to insinuate anything or am planning anything or anything."

The woman looked at South, hoping, perhaps, he was as sincerely no-frills as he appeared. "A coffee would be grand right about now. I have a few hours to kill before I have to get back to the department, anyway, so you can tell me all about those old gods of yours."

Author's Note:

Anthropologists and dating columnists alike would later claim that this was the last ever "meet cute." A meet cute, I am told, was something that happened between the years of 1879 and 2018, when two people would meet, and it would be cute. They went extinct shortly after I met you, from what I've heard, for two primary reasons. The first is that people stopped leaving their homes shortly after 2018 for reasons I don't quite remember. The second is that besides an unwillingness to leave the house, single people were all a sudden adamant in their refusal to settle for anything less than they deserved. "Deserve" and "settle" are two words with a long and violent history. In the long ago, before dating, people would settle on land they deserved and kill anyone who disagreed. Neither word got over their respective smears.

At any rate, the anthropologists are wrong on this count, Alexandra. Our meet cute was in fact the *third* last one. I've done my research. The second last meet cute happened a mere seven hours later in Providence, Rhode Island, when two disaffected millennials interviewed for a job both were overqualified for. Neither got it, but they got each other, and their cumulative student loan debt was commendable. Then, in 2162, a Clem Boop and Oscar Jong's eyes met during a boating tour of the Lower Manhattan ruins when they both reached for the same parboiled thigh.

Meet cutes, I guess, were American by design, even during an apocalypse. Of which more later.

Pappy Café, Edinburgh, 20__ CE:

Whatever chemical imbalance had propelled South into a coffee date abandoned him within five seconds of leaving the book store. Out in the real world, the woman he was walking with became real, and he found himself rethinking his impulsive decision. They walked to the centre of town without much talking, like the strangers they were, both lost in their own insecurities. South was oblivious as to what he supposed was to be doing, evidently, and was convinced he would run out of things to talk about before they even ordered the coffee. Taking his immortality out of the equation, his life was a heady cocktail of alarming red flags, the unbelievable stories only a pathological liar would tell, and the crushing banality of working life. None of which were interesting or advisable enough to talk about for long.

If he asked the woman at the time, he would have learned she had similar concerns, but ones borne out of experience: as an unmarried woman with well-intentioned friends, she was often set up with dull, nervous people with nothing to say and had learned to treat the first thirty minutes of any encounter as a slow release of anxiety. The idea of two strangers sitting in awkward silence, stumbling over sentences and frantically trying to force conversations was something she had lived through fifty plus times before, and an experience she didn't need to have again.

They walked with creeping trepidation, a mutual desire for the other to find an excuse to leave or else find something they could talk at length about. This sensation disappeared the moment they saw the coffee shop and were free from their self-inflicted vows of silence. Now they could talk. Now they could drink the coffee way too fast and pretend to have somewhere else to be they only just remembered and, boy, would you look at the time, I'm going to be late.

The café was congested. Tightly packed sets of sunken tables and benches were packed with cheery, phone-wielding students. Older couples and laptop-carrying writers had commandeered the tables and transformed them into temporary offices, complete, in some cases, with photos of loved ones, binders, and portable printers. A mixture of relief and disappointment fell on South as he scanned the room. He was just about to say "oh, well, guess we tried" when the door closed behind them and revealed an unclaimed pair of stools next to the window.

It was a tight space, one that created a forced intimacy South wasn't used to. He'd been pushed against people in cramped kitchens, mineshafts, and galleons, but never by choice. As they sat, he felt her legs pressing against his thighs and searched for a hint of discomfort on her face. She did not share his prudishness, having been on various forms of public transit and not viewing the touching of outer quadriceps as inherently sensual. Instead, she leaned her elbow against the tight countertop and stared at an old couple passing by outside. She smiled.

"So, these old gods you mentioned, how come I don't remember hearing about them in any lectures or history books?"

"Oh, they were in plenty of history books, they just all got burnt up years ago."

"Ah! That explains it. Of course. How very inconvenient for all of us." She paused, remembering something crucial. "I'm Alexandra, by the way."

Alexandra. The name stirred an aethereal soup long since left to coagulate in the corner of South's cobwebbed mind.

But, *shit.* Thanks to an accumulated wealth of paranoia, superstition, and one too many close calls, South could not use the name Edwin again. Not so close to Whitby, and especially not without performing the necessary ceremonies. The last time he was lax on changing his name, a small fistfight broke out in Limerick. No, he couldn't use Edwin again, but, but—He had said nothing in some time, and Alexandra appeared to notice. Scanning his mind for unused names, he muttered the first thing that came to mind. "Uh, Tacitus Umlaut, how do you do?" He extended his hand. *Nope.*

"That is not a real name."

"You're right, my name is," this was easier alone in the crypt, he thought, as the plausibility clock wound down, "Virgil Rakim Santon."

"Get out! That's my dad's name."

"Wha-Really?"

"No. Why so cagey about using a real name, Virgil?"

"Because I, uh, it's—" he trailed off, mind rebelling against him, spirit defeated. It was as if some part of his psyche knew what was to come if this meeting continues. *Just tell her the truth right now, and be done with it,* it was saying, *she'll probably think you're nuts, but you'll save yourself a headache.*

She grasped his knee and squeezed. *Maybe heartache.* "It's fine, we're just two strangers getting a coffee because of our love of bad museums. If you've got a secret identity, or a wife, or brain worms, that's your business. I mean, it's a little shady, for sure, but what guy isn't these days? Besides, it's not like we're ever going to see each other again."

His visible disappointment confirmed long-held suspicions he would never make it as a professional poker player. Long-dormant parts of him awakened to alien sensations. What was happening to him? What was it about Alexandra that made his stomach turn in on itself? The fibre of his being twinged like the muscles of an athlete fresh off an injury. Was he just lonely? Had Nell's advice resonated more than he realised? Or was he just so unused to talking to strangers on a personal level?

"Oh," he muttered after what felt like an hour, doing his best to appear demure and detached.

"Yes, yeah," Alexandra gave an excited nod, talking as much for her own benefit as his, "I'm heading up a dig in the Atacama Desert for the next three months. Don't tell any of you archaeology buddies, but we think we've uncovered a religious site over there. Shame, too," she sipped her coffee and eyed South, "my standards are so low these days, I was starting to like dodgy men who can't come up with decent fake names."

"I'm sure I can come up with a plausible name in three months. If you're coming back here, that is."

"I am." A tentative smile. That was a good sign. Wasn't it?

"Great, I'll hit up a bookstore and come up with something cool. What about Rock Hardway?"

"Too on the nose. You might as well call yourself Mike Bigcock."

"Wait, so Mike Bigcock is off the table too?"

"I'm afraid so. My ex-boyfriend had the same name."

A pause. "Wait, really?"

"No, his name was Collin. That's twice you've done that. You must be the most gullible liar I've ever met. Well, except for Mike Bigcock."

South considered protesting his innocence but decided, wisely, to move on. "Atacama, huh? I really valued my time over there."

"You've been? Walked the gringo trail?"

"Not exactly. I guess you could say I'm an amateur anthropologist."

"Oh man, that's a shame. I wish there were more amateurs out there when we were looking for volunteers six months ago. Instead, we just got a bunch of people who were clearly just looking for a cheap, photogenic holiday. And Johnny Reilly, who's a good worker, except he thinks he's going to Majorca."

South thought of an era-appropriate phrase he could use. Bites? Blows? Hard? "That, uh, sucks?" he offered, unsure of himself.

"Yeah, well. It's not like anyone around here can translate Kunza or Quenchua anyway, so we have to take what we can get. I wish I could show you some of the rejected applications, but I think it's illegal."

A stunted laugh escaped from South's mouth. He tried to stop himself from talking, but before he even knew what was going on, he'd already said, "I'm pretty good at speaking both, now that you mention it."

A *suuuuuure* glance from Alexandra. The perfect opportunity to not go any further, to pass the whole thing off as a joke and take his hat and his leave. Something between pride and an eagerness to please a woman he'd only just met forced his head sideways into a *no, really* tilt. Her playful gaze waned, transforming into disbelief.

"You're kidding," she said.

"Huq simi mana askhachu yachanapaq, or something like that. I'm a little rusty."

"You could have looked that up this morning. Everyone knows that one. But on the off chance you can, it's a shame we didn't meet a few months ago. We could have used you. Your skills, I mean. My mother used to say things happened for the right reasons at the wrong time."

"Wait, though, surely there are people over there who can help with translation?"

"Plenty, which is why we're not allowed to use them. Higher ups want us pretending we're saving the history of entire continents all on our own."

The rogue need to connect with her slithered up out of his mouth once more. "I'm between jobs at the minute, so I could come with."

"Oh, I bet you would, too, you little creep." Alexandra's voice had a superpower: It lilted upward when she was simultaneously joking and assessing someone with complete accuracy, leaving people charmed rather than offended. It was a rare gift. Her eyes danced to a song only she could hear as she knocked back her cup, realising too late it was empty. "But, you know, I'd have told you to go for it if it wasn't for the visa and immunisation process. And even if we could get all that sorted out in time, I'm not sure my department heads would agree to letting a complete stranger on such short notice, and that's assuming they believe your name is Octavius Dinglehorn, or whatever you settle on."

South didn't have the frame of reference to know it, but he felt almost exactly like people do when receiving a rejection letter: the flowery opening line, the glimmer of hope, and then, wham, a blunt and sudden "no" just as you're daydreaming of spending your new riches. He could have left it at that. He knew, for instance, it would appear desperate to offer his services in a remote capacity, and then did just that by saying, "I can give you my email and I can help from over here, if you want. No big deal."

Alexandra looked as if she had just lost a round of dominoes. "Listen, if this is an elaborate and poorly constructed ploy to get into my pants, you should know right now you're wasting your time."

"The thought hadn't crossed my mind." In that instance, though, at the very mention of her pants, flashes of nubile flesh and parted lips flashed through his mind.

She leaned in. "Come on."

"What can I say, I'm an old-fashioned man. But this is me wanting to help someone because I can more than it is because I'm lonely and you seem nice."

"Man, therapists must really love you, huh?" She paused. Her fingers played a miniature concerto on the table, her mouth accompanying them in a slow waltz. "Fine. Give me your email, and if I don't come to my senses by the time I'm in Chile, I'll get in touch. Or, you know, just give me your number for now, and we'll sort out the rest of it later."

South flinched. "I don't have a phone." *Or, for that matter, an email address.*

"Uh-huh. Did you buy all these red flags wholesale or what?"

South was confident the wrong answer would only cement his untrustworthiness. Which would have been fine, in other circumstances. He'd been accused of being far worse than a liar. The malevolent harbinger of doom, for instance. Still, he wanted Alexandra to like him for reasons a being of his advanced years should have figured out long before humans had fire. The only thing he could really say to save face was the truth.

Unfortunately, the truth in his case involved tens of millions of years, ancient immortal beings, volcanoes, secret identities, and self-imposed solitude. It's a scientific fact only one out of every seven women responds positively to such news. For sure, he could resort to some of his time-tested lies from his colonial days (missionary come home, reclusive writer come home, eccentric millionaire who just escaped Bedlam, etc), but he knew even in that moment he did not want to lie to Alexandra any more than he had to. Instead, he pivoted gingerly in his seat and got ready to leave.

Her hand grasped his knee once more. "I'm joking. You're either an obvious serial killer or so oblivious it's endearing. Fortunately for you, I'm fine with both. What's the email?"

"Huh?" Escaped from his defeatist alternate universe, he saw her holding a notepad and pen. He paused. What he knew about emails could be stored in a muon. The only thing he was confident about was that people couldn't have the same address, so he scrawled statueandlanguageenthusiast1583@gmail.com and prayed the universe would grant him this favour. A sudden jolt of inspiration ran through him, and beneath the email he wrote what was to become his new name: Alvar South. He returned the pad and looked away, staring at the menus on the wall like a guilty school child.

"Alvar, huh? Would have preferred you stuck with Tacitus, now that I think about it. And that's a super specific email you've got there, too. Everything else taken by the time you got there?"

"Something like that."

"Shall we?"

They left the café. South was not one for long farewells, which was just as well because Alexandra let out a quiet "see you later, my dude" and walked away. He stood there watching as she made her way down the sloped path. Not just because he wanted to savour what had been the first coffee date of his long life, but also because, as soon as she disappeared around a corner, he was going to have to sprint off toward Princes Street in search of a phone, an email address, possibly a computer, and whatever else people used to talk to each other. He ran almost as fast as he had in Pompeii, carried to startling speeds by visions of another man registering the exact same email account and being so charming, so debonair, so completely and utterly *not* a shady and awkward immortal that HE, not South, would wind up courting and, after several years of romance, marrying Alexandra.

Imaging this guffawing buffoon in the arms of his sweet Alexandra drove him to sprint faster than he had in centuries. By the time he reached the first phone store, he was so carried away with visions of this fictional louse and Alexandra that he all but kicked the door open. "PHONES," he yelled at an

employee who'd heard far worse that morning alone, "I NEED PHONES
AND AN EMAIL ADDRESS RIGHT NOW!"

- 33 -

Whatever he did worked: Alexandra never got married.

Egypt — 2668 BCE:

Netjeriykhet walked to the edge of the treeline before he bade his entourage to remain still. They hesitated. Strange rumours abounded that the architect Imouthes had resorted to witchcraft to build his gift. The workers were all gone, and nobody knew how the rocks moved from the quarry to the worksite as those who worked in the quarry disappeared weeks earlier.

"Stay here," said Netjeriykhet.

"But he's mad," said Bayek.

"Do as I tell you. If you hear screaming…" he drifted off, looking out into the worksite "It will already be too late."

The trees gave way to dirt and rock. Someone had been busy. A giant rectangular field of stone had been laid down, with markings placed in various sections to indicate where future work would go. Netjeriykhet was in awe. Far more than he had asked for when he made the wager. In the centre of the rectangle lay the beginnings of a structure, one Netjeriykhet could not visualise. The second row of rocks was smaller than the first but larger than the third, too tall to be steps but steps all the same.

As he drew closer, he could see that holes had been dug into the ground, leading down into who knew what. Imouthes was nowhere to be seen.

In truth, Netjeriykhet was not concerned about the rumours of Imouthes' sanity. The fellow was peculiar and ancient, but his intentions were pure. He had to keep all this to himself; of course, were his entourage and advisers to discover his architect had sent away four hundred men and their families to live in freedom elsewhere, there would be civil unrest. Easier to just give the false gossip credence.

He surveyed the grounds once more and noticed a vine-bound slab of rocks were moving toward him as if on their own. Yes, rocks twice the height and width of a grown man were creeping toward him, significantly faster than a beetle moving in the sand. He stood transfixed for a moment, only to back away to scramble up the side of the central structure when the rocks picked up momentum and began sprinting toward him. His screams trapped in his lungs, and he could only let out desperate blows of air. The rumours were true. The mad architect was a sorcerer of the darkest kind. It was only when his screams found themselves trapped in the back of his mouth that a head peeped out from over the rocks.

"Oh, you're early. Or have I lost track of time again?" Imouthes pulled himself up the side of his rock pile and stood smiling at Netjeriykhet. His skin was dusty, and he had no modesty; he also was not sweating, which was not something Netjeriykhet would realise until that sleepless night.

"I just asked for a courtyard," said Netjeriykhet.

"And this is it. When I lose a bet, I pay in full."

"All of this is for me? What is this structure I'm standing on?"

Imouthes laughed. "It serves multiple purposes. First, you know I will miss you when you're gone, and while you may think that's a long time in the future, for me it will come all too soon. It's just how it is. This is a good way to remember you. I'll come here every couple of hundred years to give remembrance."

"That's the nicest, oddest thing anyone has said to me."

"Oh, you'd hear all sorts of strange stuff if you weren't a king. But alas."

"Maybe they know to fear their betters."

With a smile, Imouthes jumped down from his rock pile and hoisted one slab of rock over his shoulder. He carried it over to an open space and slotted it against an identical rock. "You know I can't stand it when you talk like that. Betters? Pah! Who do you think you are? You don't do any work and I've seen children with bigger muscles. Get a grip, buddy."

Netjeriykhet watched as Imouthes carried one cube of rock after the next to the structure and placed them in a perfect line. "Wait," he said, remembering something, "What's the other reason you're building this?"

"What? Oh. I just need a place to hide some stuff. You know I move around a lot and lugging it everywhere I go gets tiresome."

Netjeriykhet looked at his friend. He was speaking a half truth. "You're speaking a half truth," he said.

"Oh, fine, I will tell you, but you have to promise not to ever tell anyone about this, do you understand?"

"I'll take it to the grave," he looked down at the hole in the middle of the structure. "Uh, this grave, I guess."

"You know how I am ancient?"

"Yes, I can't forget if you keep reminding me."

"I like to build oddities all over the globe to see if anyone notices. Sometimes people copy them. Other times, I don't even know yet, but it's something to look forward to when I'm older. I just thought this would be funny, is all."

"So, you're making a joke at the expense of people who aren't even alive yet?"

"Pretty much. Wouldn't it be funny if a bunch of your ancestors built their own structures like this one not knowing it's a joke?"

"But they'd not know it was a joke?"

"It's a private joke."

"But I'll be dead."

"Private between myself and myself."

"And others like you, I suppose."

Imouthes face turned sour, pained. He looked at Netjeriykhet's eyes with an earnestness never given to a man of his self-proclaimed stature. "If you ever meet another like me, you must promise not to listen to them. They might kill you, but death is sometimes better than the alternative."

"Ah, then there are others like you. I knew that must be the case."

"Somewhere out there. Byblos, last I heard. But promise me you won't listen to anyone like me. They mean only bad things. The worst things."

"I'm not too worried about it. Anyway, you build these weird things all over the land. Anything I might have heard of?"

Imouthes sat down on the top tier of slabs on the structure, Netjeriykhet sat just under him. They looked down at the courtyard and out into the wilderness all around them. What a land they lived in, so beautiful that a simple stroll could yield rapturous tears.

"Now some of these places you haven't heard of, so please try to pay attention. The first place--"

"C'mon, c'mon, c'mon. Please."

Various — 20__ CE:

Throughout the annals of human history, people have done reckless, impulsive things when manipulated by even the faintest promise of romance. Young men would turn down their first-choice university because their unrequited crush mentioned possibly going elsewhere – a delusional and short-sighted mistake for a litany of reasons. Women would stay at soul-destroying jobs because they were worried that leaving would ruin their blossoming-but-doomed relationship with a co-worker, the prospect of starting *again* too much to handle. People binge watched television shows they didn't enjoy, got meaningless tattoos, spent hours at the gym, or otherwise wasted hours on things they did not particularly care about, all for the possibility of it impressing someone they found attractive. At least one naïve and lonely man did all the above on more than one occasion, never quite learning whatever lesson the Fates were trying to teach.

South had no frame of reference to know it, but he had fallen into the same trap. There he was, unattached to anything and without a future planned out, and a woman had *smiled* at him? Held his knee and accepted his fake email address? Even before Alexandra was sitting on the first of four flights, South was planning on establishing a life in Edinburgh. Just in case. Giddy with anticipation over the vague idea of getting to know her.

Before he could do anything else, he returned to his hidden crypt and retrieved blank passports, banking information, pawnable antiques, and just enough loose jewellery to get started. Handing people purses full of gold coins and gemstones hadn't worked for him in decades, and every time he switched identity it became more difficult to pass off his documentation as authentic, so he had to play it smart. There were brief flashes in his mind of going out to a restaurant with a newly returned Alexandra, only to be arrested for fraud or illegal immigration. A definite mood killer, and not a good basis for a blossoming relationship.

With everything else acquired, he set up his first bank account. He entered with anxiety and a violent exit strategy, only to leave half an hour later with a new account and aggressively one-sided interest rates and terms.

Alvar South found himself a modest, no questions asked apartment on the outskirts of the city. A big, half-empty building run by human slugs, people interested in making the most money for the least amount of work. On the plus side, they didn't ask for past addresses or referees, only cash, sweet, unearned cash. To the average human, it was a glorified hovel run by a slumlord with a vanity phone number, but to South it was a stately manor. There were rooms separated by walls and electrical sockets. It even came with its own bathroom; a utility South had gone without since 1964. If decades of living in squalor was good for anything, it was accepting more of the same.

With a home and a bank account, South tried to fill his new rooms with furniture. Not just any furniture, either, but the kind of sofas, armoires, and apothecary tables he imagined Alexandra would like. One benefit of starting from scratch this way was that he could decorate his apartment in her image. The only real downside was the fact that he knew nothing about her, so ultimately his rooms were a hodgepodge mix of styles and colour schemes, a shotgun approach to interior design that only worked on the gambit she had to like at least one chair, be it Art Deco or Gothic Revival or the florescent surrealist monstrosity he'd paid too much for.

To say South was carried away by his excitement was an understatement. Alas, he was as carried away as any number of offensive metaphors involving natural disasters or marauding Vikings. A child's helium balloon floating off into the sun had a better chance of coming to its senses and returning to the crying toddler's hands. Once the furniture was in place, he filled his walls and shelves with art and literature with the same slapdash sensibilities. Walls overcrowded with Duchamp, Guyton, Manet, Goya, fake Banksy, Warhol and Vermeer.

Bookshelves fast became a confusing collection of panic. The books were arranged chronologically not by year written but by the slapdash, neurotic order of South's purchases: *Infinite Jest* but maybe too male so *Ain't I a Woman* but maybe too radical so *White Teeth* but maybe too popular so *Ars Amatoria* but maybe too old so *2666* but maybe too male so *We Have Always Lived in the Castle* but maybe too obvious so… And on it went, all conceivable genre and market share accounted for, like an overgrown media conglomerate's itemised list of properties. An entire wall filled with books placed in an order Turing would have scratched his head at. All based on the ludicrous assumption Alexandra even read books at all, which led to deeper rabbit holes of anxious logic, and buying habits South had to drag himself out of before his apartment became fifteen identical living spaces existing merged into a single entity.

Then there was the matter of employment. He was going to need a proper, provable job—not just reliable cash-in-hand mercenary work for kitchens or factories. From what he had heard from younger co-workers in his recent lives, a job was a big deal for the romantically inclined. Females, as teenage boys would hiss, would pick a boring doctor over an exciting and completely imaginary pastry chef. But he didn't have time to become a doctor. Or, for that matter, a pastry chef. Career prospects, he was beginning to see, were a minefield for those who had never seen what a literal minefield was capable of. Scary hypothetical outcomes, all the same. Lounge around too much and Alexandra might suspect he was a drug dealer, a crook, a charlatan. Live off his stockpiled wealth from centuries of misadventures and the wrong sort of people would come sniffing around, mainly the government looking for their cut. Wealth, he had learned time and again, especially when unexpected, raised too many eyebrows, so even if being an affluent man of leisure was something Alexandra liked, it would only be a matter of time before militant tax agencies would come looking for him. The only people who didn't pay any taxes were those who made careers out of complaining about paying them. There was only one solution: get an anonymous job and live within his means in a run-down apartment, so nobody asked any questions.

It turned out, though, that a lot had changed in the world since the job searches of the 1940s. Corporate offices didn't put up Help Wanted signs in their windows like coastal chip shops. He couldn't just walk into a major Hollywood studio with a handshake and a smile and expect a high-paying job. There were entire departments with quotas to fill and background checks to run and friends to hire. Beyond those hurdles, there were unrealistic, phantasmagorical job criteria to be met for even the most useless of middle management jobs. He could tell after the first few attempts that finding a "real job" was going to be far more difficult than even forging fresh passports. How did the humans do it without going mad? Struggling to make ends meet and being constantly reminded you weren't considered good enough for even the most basic of entry-level positions, all while banks and countries alike were run by professional failures.

All of which was beginning to feel moot for South after three weeks of expeditious activity. Despite having an over-decorated apartment, a carefully curated false identity, and dozens of pending job applications, Alexandra had yet to send him an email. Had he got ahead of himself? He could sense the initial spur of giddiness from meeting her fade, and at nights he would often wake up convinced he met a phantom or else been tricked by a cruel mirage designed to trap him in a cluttered Edinburgh apartment of his own making. Early in the morning he would wake up with a start and stare up at the ceiling, embarrassed and rejected and alone, replaying every potential error made in their one conversation. He couldn't have known at the time, but this was a flaw in partitioning himself away from human life; there was no way for him to know he was experiencing something millions of other people had gone through. Nobody ever bothered to tell him that as bad as things could seem, they were always worse in your own head. And inside South's head was a horror show of humiliation borne out of millennia of nightmarish experiences.

Another issue brought on by his coddled ignorance. He didn't know to suspect any job offered too quickly. He accepted an immediate position at an ambiguously named call centre—JobEx, WorkLife, ErgoCall, or something—the kind of business that would talk about how they were a family in one breath and fire six people for not meeting sales figures the next. Pride flag and heritage festival tickets on the weekends, dead naming new hires and mocking accents by Wednesday. He was happy to take it; their positions came with impressive-sounding and meaningless job titles like Outbound Telephonic Acquirement Engineer and Liaison for Electronic Customer Conversational Exchange Officers. What caught his attention was the fact that, unlike most jobs, they didn't seem to care about anything beyond his ability to show up to an interview.

After only a few shifts spent enthralled in tangible boredom, South missed backbreaking labour, war zones, and prehistory. Even as a man who had spent centuries under the sea, the level of detail-orientated-but-useless information he was expected to parse was a fresh level of banal pointlessness. He had to familiarise himself with procedures that only existed to exist, secret backdoor grounds for termination some smarmy HR rep would use when someone did something unconscionable like report sexual harassment or complain about nepotism.

He stumbled into a world where department managers sat convinced they were the lead character in a classic machismo film, but succeeded only in coming off as old, anti-West propaganda. Then there were the team supervisors, failures at every turn in life, who had remained secure in their blankets of smugness, oblivious to their own ineptitude. The rest of the workforce, while nice enough, were mostly fresh out of dropping out of university, and so prematurely bored and indifferent and moribund that South couldn't help but think of his days working as a porter in a rehab facility. The job, South realised, sucked, and yet he was supposed to pretend he was part of a family, a team player, selling useless products to people who didn't need them all so someone in an office hundreds of miles away could make more money to not spend.

He was about ready to leave Edinburgh. The experiment at normalcy had failed in infancy and only highlighted how his admiration of the mortal race was blinkered by the truth that so many of them only lived to exist. With bags packed in his mind and a nice Finnish village picked out for his next identity, he checked his emails one last time.

Imagine for a moment your oldest, least computer-literate, most naïve relative getting a new computer and unfettered access to the internet. He clicked on and answered everything he could with the wide-eyed frenzy of a bargain hunter in a sale. A dopamine fiend with unlimited Wi-Fi. The only reason spam emails remained untouched was because he wanted someone else to get the millions from overseas benefactors. In less than six weeks, South's inbox had accumulated over three teraflops of useless information ranging from unsolicited insurance sales opportunities to doomed petitions. He scrolled up and down, recognising too late that perhaps he shouldn't have given out his email address to every website he visited. And then he found this:

To the alleged Alvar South:
 Sorry for the late email. Turns out that jobs expect you to do work. Also, the internet here is questionable. Plus, I wasn't sure I wanted to email you. How are things? Are we settled on the name Alvar? It's not too late to call yourself Bazooka Maximus. I like that one, so make a note. Anyway, here's where I ask you for something: Could you maybe look at these photos? That's

assuming you weren't lying about the whole language thing. Thanks.

And just because I'm worried ending an email with me asking for a favour sends a bad message, did you know that dancing is illegal in San Pedro? I guess they don't want the town becoming a party capital, so people have to go get their groove on out in the desert, which really could mess up our dig. It might almost be worth it, just for the story. If you're lucky, the restaurant you're in will close the shutters and turn the lights down low. Very Footloose. But in Spanish, I guess. "Suelto?" No, that can't be it.

Anyway, there's also this old ruined fortress just outside of town, and I caught myself imagining the sort of bullshit you would make up about it. Funny how some people you can know for all of three minutes and you find yourself projecting qualities onto them. I mean, I'm only about ninety percent convinced you're a patho- logical liar (which I'm used to at this point) and not something far worse (like a tabloid journalist), after all. Anyway, that was my obligatory waffle to mask the fact I was asking you for help.

Hope you're doing well.

Alexandra.

South reread the email several times before falling onto his bed. He had been waiting for this moment, but there was a fresh dilemma. The email had been sent a mere thirty minutes earlier. Despite an overwhelming urge to reply, he worried that answering anything too early could be correctly con- strued as a bit desperate. He needed to wait, if not to portray some false image of aloofness, at least to come up with just the right response. Charm- ing, stoic, just the right amount of self-deprecating, helpful but not conde- scending, a flirtatiousness that lent itself to plausible deniability. Qualities a man like South, whose last love letter was written on a stone tablet, didn't fully grasp. He spent the rest of the night rereading the email, typing up the first paragraph of his intended lengthy response, deleting it, swearing at his own ineptitude. Repeat.

Intellectually constipated, he took a walk up to King Arthur's Seat before the first of the early morning joggers got there. Climbing in the dark felt like walking through someone else's dreams, with vague shadows becoming ruined, looming, and imposing figures morphing into rocks, steep drops transforming into nothing at all. For a moment at the top, everything resolved itself, and he returned home with a perfectly crafted response written in his head. It was the sort of email Shakespeare would have written if he had access to the internet and wasn't a complete and utter phony.

The words he was going to write were neatly arranged in his mind right up until the moment he sat down to type. He sat there grasping at eloquent turns of phrase as they slipped through his synapses. Sentences that earlier seemed so genuine and sweet transmogrified into the inane ramblings of a pleading, lonely old man. Which he supposed he was.

He wrestled his sentences like a rich preacher fights their own hypocrisy. Bashing out an email he wasn't remotely happy with.

```
Hi!
    It will please you to know that I can confirm my name
with ID and everything now. The ID is also real. Happy
to hear from you.
    I think Footloose in Spanish is just Footloose for
the same reason they don't call him Kenny La Talas.
Although Kenny La Talas is probably the best name I've
ever come up with.
    I'll get back to you with the translations.
    Yours,
    Alvar.
```

He stared at the screen after hitting send. For a whole night or more, in fact. He sat there with only the roiling storm of insecurities in his stomach for company as he waited for a response. Momentary pangs of hope as he refreshed the inbox to see new messages, only to see "RE: Job Offer Home Sales" or "This Week Only: Sale on Underwear." By 3AM he was offering up hushed prayers to the gods of computers to usher forth a reply. By 6AM he was questioning the last seventy years of his life and wondering how he'd reached such a point. Then at 9AM:

Ha.
        Thanks. Look forward to your interpretation.
                            Alex.

Which did nothing but yield more questions for South, who had all but turned into a child. Except, at least children could confide in friends and family and had the excuse of being literal children. A child would have someone explain what was going on with handy diagrams and words like hormones and lust. Otherwise, a child would be mocked relentlessly until they knew to pretend to have no feelings at all. Either way, they'd have some understanding, for better or worse. South had none of that, and the fact he was even envying children at all just threw him into deeper despair.

Not only did he have almost nothing to reply to, but feelings of inadequacy and paranoia ensnared him. *Was this it?* Had he done something wrong? Was there more he could have said? As the world went on outside, he reread the exchange in search for hidden clues and imagined alternate realities where he precisely said the right thing. By the time he realised he'd missed a day of work, it was already the evening, and he was trying to astral project across continents to gauge how Alexandra – no doubt probably laughing in the arms of a handsome archaeologist – was feeling.

He lay on the floor wide-eyed and nervous, with the sort of jittery alertness you only get after transcending beyond sleep deprivation. Something was wrong. A distant church bell chimed nine the next morning, and he knew some ancient blood magick had finally caught up to him, penance for one hundred and fifty million years of cruelty. But this presented a fresh set of problems, namely that all the old wizards, witches, and shamans who could have helped him in his time of need had long since been wiped out by overachieving, peaceful missionaries. What hospital would take his claims seriously? Even if a doctor agreed to examine him, the moment the third syringe broke against his impenetrable skin South would be exposed to the whole world as an impervious being. There was no one and nowhere that could help him, which made the whisking blender of emotions in his stomach stir all the faster.

Most of the people who knew his secret were dust, and it was only after mentally thumbing through all potential solutions that he decided to call Sandy Vale Retirement Centre. His slow descent into chaos began when he visited her, so maybe she had a solution, or at least would listen to him without alerting the nearest branch of military. South's thumb hovered a boson's distance away from the end call button and was about to press it when the line crackled.

"Hello?" said Nell.

"Oh, hi again, Nellie, it's me. Claudio." It was at this moment South discovered he hated telephones. Their impersonal, garbled versions of conversations reminded him of an afterlife he would never see.

"Twice in a year, Claudio? Is everything fine? It's a bit late for you to be having a midlife crisis."

"No, nothing is fine, Nell, I haven't slept in two nights. I think I've been cursed."

"Who would curse you?"

"Do you remember that old friend I used to tell you about?"

"Oh, I think so, yes. Is she still around?"

"No, our last meeting was pretty final. But maybe she found a way. Maybe it's someone else. I don't know, I haven't felt like this before and I don't like what's happening."

"OK, well calm down first, South, I can't help you when you're sounding like the third act of a Scorsese film. Actually, I'm not sure I can help you either way. You know I only played a doctor once in the fifties, right?"

"Yes, but I have no one else to talk to about this. Nobody else knows. I mean, there are a few people I think maybe in the Amazon, but they don't have phones. Or at least they didn't."

"Well, I'm flattered, I guess. So, start from the beginning."

"I was fully formed, and my fist was already slamming down on a Ste--"

"Not that beginning. When did you start feeling like this?"

"It's been building for a few weeks. I, uh, met this woman, and--"

"Let me just stop you there for a minute, pal. You met a woman?"

"Yes."

"And you've spent the last seventy years in hiding and a few hundred years before that on a quest for revenge. When was the last time you met someone?"

South had to think hard about this question. He raised a hand to his chin to show just how hard he was thinking, but quickly put it down when he remembered he was alone. "Um, not counting Los Angeles--"

"Trust me, honey, nobody considers meeting people in Los Angeles as an accomplishment. But, sorry, go on."

"I had a couple of friends in London in 1890, and then before that I think I was buddies with a couple of rustlers on the plains. Oh! And my boys on the boat, they were some of the nicest men you could meet. This was about 1720, though, and—"

"Right, so in other, fewer, words it has been a while? And now you've met this woman and you feel what, exactly?"

"I don't know if giddy is the right word, but kind of like that."

"And nervous and anxious?"

"Yeah, it's pretty bad."

"So bad that you would call a ninety-four-year-old woman for advice?"

"Yes. Exactly."

South could hear Nell move away from her phone as she laughed. "Claudio," she said, "It all makes sense. Now that I think back on it, you were always kind of cagey back in Hollywood. Some women spread rumours you were a confirmed bachelor, and some confirmed bachelors spread rumours you had a secret wife out in Scranton or Poughkeepsie or somewhere. But the truth," she laughed again.

"This isn't helping, Nellie, I've been awake for almost three days. Do you know how much I've spent on furniture this past month? And why? To impress some woman I met for all of five minutes. I don't like this. Any of it."

"Oh, hush, Claudio. It's a crush. Please don't tell me that this isn't your first one of those."

"I don't know what you're talking about, Nellie."

Nell's was loud enough to travel through to phone. "Claudio, my friend, you're finally a real human boy. Welcome to the human race. It only took you a million years."

They talked for the next two hours. Nell's advice was simple and easily manageable and applicable to anyone with dating woes. Id est:

1. Don't overthink things.

2. Don't get your hopes up.

3. Remember the other person is a, you know, person, not some prize to be won.

South promptly ignored the first two rules when he decided to use all his government-mandated sick days and spend the rest of the week translating the documents Alexandra sent him. They weren't particularly interesting, just the history of the area, religious texts, and vague directions to a hidden subterranean city. He did his best to ignore the fantasies of presenting the translations to Alexandra and immediately having a girlfriend which was a word South never bothered to learn the meaning of until an evening of asking the internet such questions as "how to tell girl like you" and "what do with feelings have girl have." Hours spent researching online for guides on getting said girlfriend didn't make anything clearer.

In the evenings, he watched a television he paid too much for, bought purely because he read somewhere about sitting with a lover and staring at classic, half-decade old films. Watching the constant stream of propaganda and class warfare had a sedative quality to it, and he found quickly that he could sit in front of the screen without moving. Eight hours spent catching up with a hundred years of television history prevented him from entering daydreams full of flowers, wet kisses, and sunset hikes up mountains. A wasted evening is inconsequential when you're over hundred million years old, but South could see how accumulating them as someone with a shorter lifespan would lead to a pretty lousy deathbed realisation. Nobody dies wishing they'd watched more television. Unless they never got around to finishing Six Feet Under.

There was good news in that Alexandra began to send more emails as her boredom and isolation grew. The emails between them fluctuated between terse and meandering. Sometimes, Alexandra would send something like:

```
Hey,

    Thanks for the translation, Alvar, I'm impressed
you somehow managed to do all that in under a week. It
would have taken our department five months for a par-
tial. Hope you didn't just run it through a random word
generator.
    Alexandra.
```

And other times they would be filled with so many unasked-for details that even South in his boyish daze had a hard time reading the whole thing.

About two weeks before Alexandra's scheduled return, South decided it would be a great idea to ask her out. The phrase "ask her out" had been floating through his psyche since 1993, when two of the other pot-washers suggest he do it to the sous-chef. There was only one issue: he didn't know what it entailed. It was clear that his thoughts on courting, with all the dowries, duels, and even the fact he referred to it as courting, were outdated. Gone were the days he could slap Ptolemy's face and toss a bag of gold on the floor. It turned out that women in the twenty-first century found things like autonomy, self-actualisation, and not being harangued into supposedly romantic activities by complete strangers. The only people who seemed to disagree with this, in his hours of research, were old puritans on their third marriage, joyless puritans on the first marriage, and a dark corner of the internet who collectively decided that women were intergalactic terror monsters driven up through eldritch vortices to wrap their whirring maws around mankind's cumulative soul and bank account. Even South, in all his great-great-great-great-grandfatherly obliviousness, could see that such people needed therapy and perhaps a hobby. Like, for instance, consensual sex, or maybe some better friends.

With his meticulous, often terrifying, research on modern dating finished and no more excuses left on the table, he tried to think of the most neutral way to invite her out. Coffee, according to everyone who wasn't a US sitcom character, was out, as were cinemas, restaurants, burlesque shows, Renaissance Faires, palm reading seminars, frozen yoghurt, and hot-air balloon rides. He settled on the museum, which seemed like a safe bet.

Then there was the matter of composing the email itself, which was more difficult than he ever imagined. Once the verbose, self-deprecating drafts were trimmed down, all the words that reeked of desperation omitted, and the gratuitous oversharing purged, he believed he was looking at the perfect email. It had taken him seventeen hours of uninterrupted work to write.

```
Would you like to go to the museum when you get back?
```

Easy enough, or so he thought, but then the panic returned the moment he hit send. The same feelings of inadequacies he'd experienced in recent months returned to his body with a newfound force, like dragoons on their second charge. He wondered how humans were able to put up with it all, and if perhaps that was why so many seemed to prefer to numb themselves to everything. He understood why some spend their whole lives alone. A rejection, while undesirable, would take all a second to read, but until that moment there was no single reality, instead infinite alternate universes all vying for attention. Possibilities as banal as a "no" to as convoluted as a jet-setting global treasure hunt for lost religious iconography floated around his mind as he waited for the answer. South didn't like it at all.

And then the answer came.

```
Are you seriously asking me out over email? Loser.
```

His heart flipped over and stopped, his eyes blurred, and his knees buckled. This was it. This was why humans wielded cynicism and detachment like weapons: rejection was worse than he realised. To not matter. To be judged unworthy. Your daydreams rendered into ash in a handful of words, your longings as disposable as the seedhead of a dandelion, and your plans just as wishful. Women. Romance. He fought a growing urge to, no, wait—there was more.

Of course. I love that place and I figure I owe you.
Win-win for me. See you soon.

And all was right again. A meadow of possibilities bloomed right before his eyes, and he for the rest of the week he was unable to stop smiling. Perhaps being a bit more human wasn't all that bad.

Author's Note:

All evidence to the contrary, I cut seven thousand words out of that chapter. They were all about the large quantities television I would watch while I would wait for your emails and how, in a sad, strange way they helped educate me on what was, at the time, modern living.

Modern living now, if you're interested, is lots of floating and not much else. So much floating. And spinning in place.

The crux of it all was that while I had been around death for countless years, it was always something intangible to me. An illusion. Not a concept I could get a firm grasp of. Death, for me, was often a violent conclusion, or else some abstract thing that happened while I was somewhere else. Everyone I loved has died now, of course, but back in the day it would only be a century after last talking to someone that I'd have to think "Oh wait, yeah, that person must be dead now."

There was this one sitcom I watched a few times and for the credits of the last episode it showed the cast as they were in the pilot, young, thin, different, barely fully formed. And it hit me harder than it had any right to, because I'd watched these people age over the years. Granted, they became caricatures of themselves, and were fictional, but there was something in that dawning realisation. While life for me has been a slow, indestructible plod, it is so fleeting. And to see how much a person could change in ten or fifteen years. Well.

Always take your lessons where you can.

It was the same with other shows, too. Some didn't hit the note quite the same way, but the more I watched, the more I understood. You can never go back, and neither can they. That scrawny Julliard graduate who can barely grow a beard is there forever in that one episode, but who they became, who they grew to be, is something else entirely.

I understood how parents can miss children they still
have. Miss every one of the infinite iterations of the
same person. The plucky five-year-old who wants to be a
singer is mourned just as the tired, funny teenager
resenting their own development. A development they
can't stop. So many versions of the same person you
loved, all gone, even if they're sat across from you
smiling, the smiling version itself doomed to become
little more than a cherished memory. And you, too, will
die a thousand deaths.

And when you lose someone you love. No. Love. Capital
L. You don't just miss the person who you slept beside
and adored the day before they left for good; you
lament the many facets of them that will never again
brighten yours or anybody else's day. All the potential
Theys they could have been had things been different.
Had you been different. Had the world been a little
fairer, easier, and more understanding. All of them
gone, destined to return to your mind one late, sleepless night like the flashing image of a younger version
of the main character's best friend, the best character, there but not, stirring long-dormant memories you
try to bury deep down, making you almost tear up as you
acknowledge it is all an illusion, and that part of
them, all of them, is gone, rendered little more than
sparking synapses in your brain no matter how hard you
try to wish them back into existence while you think of
them.

So, yes, I watched a lot of television back then.

The Mediterranean Sea — 50 BCE:

In what would, in the centuries to come, prove to be something of a safety hazard, roaring fires burned in metal bowls on either side of the boat. An orange glow in a sea of inky blackness, the nearest coast a mystery, the sky a twinkly slab of wonder. Armed men stood by the boat, looking out at the other boats nearby, their flames already snuffed. In the centre of the boat, a silken tent, red and gold and private, curtains shut, with even an accidental glimpse inside punishable by death. Water lapped against the wooden frame like a lullaby, so the wardens of the boat were used to the noises of light splashes and didn't think twice that somebody was clambering up the side of the boat and crawling under the tent to the waiting empress inside.

Cleopatra lay wide-eyed, arms draped along the sides of her resting chair. This did not last. Flicking her body around, she tried one pose after another, some supine, others standing, none quiet eliciting the right demeanour. She couldn't decide if she wanted to look dispassionate or seductive, and opted instead for a clunky combination of the two, the sort of awkward come-hither drapery only the most beautiful of women could pull off. Fortunately, as already mentioned, she was Cleopatra.

The soaking figure slithered into her room, the guards outside oblivious. In the morning, perhaps they would be punished for their lack of care. Perhaps. To be fair to her bodyguards, they were in the middle of the sea, and it would take a god or mythological hero to swim onto their boat undetected.

She laughed. "You came."

The man stood up, grinning.

"They are going to freak out when they see you again," she continued. "I was quite clear that any many who spent the night with me would be executed, and few would argue that you were executed."

The man shook arms, wiggled, tried to dry himself. "It was quite the execution."

"And you quite the actor. For a moment, there, I was convinced you were lying about your gift."

"Which one of my gifts were you unsure about?"

"Ha." She stood, handed the man a robe, and returned to her seat. "Care to join me?"

The man's face betrayed his ambivalence before he could form an excuse.

"Ah, I see. It is for the best, I suppose. Do you ever wonder what the future holds?"

"I've seen too much future to be too worried about it."

"I suppose you have. I think about it all the time, myself. I wonder what they will make of me. It came to me earlier that it maybe wasn't the best idea to pull off that little prank."

"It was hilarious."

"Yes, but think of the ramifications. I'm not stupid—"

"I never—"

"I'm not stupid, and I know that the lands around me have male rulers, a history of male rulers. I know some of them will attempt to court me, and I know someone will inevitably succeed. Will I, then, become a joke in the future? A smutty reference? A slur? Will I be remembered for what is between my legs more than what I have done with my life?"

The man looked down at her. He looked at the candles, the glint of the gold ornaments surrounding them, the papyrus rolls and maps on the table. He thought for the first time in a while of his old friend North. "I don't see what you are as being different to anything else. Wouldn't the men be judged by what is between their legs too?"

Cleopatra tittered. "For what you claim to be, you sure are naïve."

"I just don't want you to worry about a future you can't control."

"But don't you see, it's the fact I can't control it but can foresee it that's precisely the problem. I know what will become of me, it's something I can feel in my bones. In life I am destined to be a great ruler, but in death? Although I suppose you won't ever have to worry about that."

"No, I suppose not."

They stayed there in silence. The guards outside still oblivious even after the inconspicuous flurry of conversation. The boat began to rock gently. An insomniac bird called out from somewhere up above.

"You could join me, you know," Cleopatra blurted out with the force of a confession. She staggered over vowels and found her footing once more, talking at a sprint. "I mean if you want. Just think of all the good we can do together. What we could do for this country. I wouldn't have to seek out liaisons with strangers or worry about the future, because we'd shape it together. Me as empress, you as…"

"Your weapon."

"No, I don't mean it like that."

"But that's what I'd become, isn't it? Your immovable object. And what after you die? What am I to do then?"

"Keep ruling, of course, and…" her thoughts caught up with her. "Ah, I can see how that might lead to issues. It's fine to have a country ruled by gods so long as they have the courtesy to die now and then."

"It's not even that, I'm just not one for governance. Even after all this time, I have no idea how you people think or feel. There's so much I don't understand. Who am I to rule over what I don't understand?"

"Do you think I understand the pauper or the farmer? No. And yet I rule."

"Then perhaps that is part of the problem. Have you not considered that? You are elevated to such a point that you can't even fathom what your own countrymen must endure daily?"

"And whose fault is that?"

"I'm not assigning fault, just stating the obvious."

Cleopatra looked at her curtains wafting in the breeze. "I can see," she said, "A future where I am judged by my strengths before I can see a world where people govern themselves. If It weren't me sitting here, it would be someone else, either gentler or crueller, but an individual regardless."

"I hope you're wrong."

"Any other man who talked to me so bluntly, and I'd have them put to death. Why is it I almost adore it when you do it?"

"Because deep down, we both know you're just a person."

National Museum, Edinburgh — 20__ CE:

After days spent reading and sauntering and lounging and dosing, being supremely happy the whole time, South arrived at the designated meeting spot. He stood under the statue of an out-of-shape man in a bedsheet, sitting with a haggard face all but hidden by a wayward traffic cone, his right toes sparkling in the sun, like a shoeless vagrant with decaying socks. A revolving line of photographers and amateur models blocked the name of the statue.

The street was busy in a way that put South on edge. A heavy flow of one-way traffic limped upward toward the castle. The surrounding people were mostly tourists, a group South had grown to be increasingly weary of. As a recent subset of humanity, the tourist could stir any number of emotions ranging from respect to revulsion, contempt to concern. At the very least, the days of people only showing up to other countries to murder and enslave the locals and steal their land were far behind them. For the most part. Still, standing there, beneath a statue of the fifth best writer named David, South couldn't help but hear familiar, internal whispers of misanthropy as mobs of strangers inadvertently assaulted one another to get photos of themselves or messy panoramic shots of the street.

Among the tourists, hidden away under door frames or on the steps of dis-used buildings, was another group of people. Lonely people, largely men, with defeated and worn faces. Some played music, or had dog companions, others would flit from building to building asking limply for money they didn't expect to receive, and still more just stared off into the distance, fully mari-nated in their despair and isolation. South remembered his own days of lurk-ing under overpasses and sleeping on park benches and wondered if he could help them. As an old friend once told him, though, "To save the homeless you must first change the entire planet." So that was that.

One kind of person South couldn't quite figure out were the large congre-gations of adults parading through the street wearing cloaks. Some carried magic wands, others brandished broomsticks, but none of them looked like they belonged in Edinburgh, much less the twenty-first century. Had the Inquisition made a comeback? Nobody would expect that to happen, least of all South. Whoever they were, and whatever their nefarious purpose, their appearance was enough to take South's mind off what he was trying to forget was his first ever date. Plus, too, if it turned out they were the Inquisition, he knew exactly how to handle them.

"What are you staring at those children for?"

It was Alexandra, or so South thought. She was blistered and tired and didn't quite look as she had in South's imagination. The suit South imagined her in was replaced with a baggy army surplus jacket and a Zed Kenzo t-shirt. Had he remembered her wrong? Was it really her? A brief flash of worry as he took a moment to separate the reality of Alexandra with the concept that existed only in his mind. Breathe, he reminded himself.

"You see them too? Why are the hashshashin walking around Edinburgh?"

"They're wizards, Harold. Or at least they're supposed to be." She leaned in for a hug. It was tight, and brief. Small fireworks exploded somewhere in South's ribcage. He knew in that instant he wanted to hug her as often as possible. "Shall we get going?"

They got going.

The cavernous entrance to the museum reminded South of the various villain lairs seen on television in the preceding months. He had been watching spy films religiously as part of his studies in what women wanted from men. Dingy, dimly lit, decorated with antiques from around the world, the only thing missing was a hidden pit filled with piranhas. He hoped. As they walked to the stairs leading up to the main hall, South thought he recognised the face on the illuminated sarcophagi in the centre of the room. An old friend or someone who owed him money. He ran halfway up the stairs to the first floor before realising Alexandra had stopped some distance behind him. She hovered beside a plexiglass box full of coins and crinkled banknotes. South had the distinct impression he had just failed the first of many tests but tried to ignore his instinct.

"Aren't you coming up?" he asked.

"This place works on donations, you know."

He had several thoughts at once and settled on the last one. "Oh, yeah, right, I forgot," he said as he skipped back down the stairs and removed all the cash from his wallet, shoving the whole wad through a thin slot.

"I mean, they typically only ask for a fiver, but good for you."

Tensing his core to prevent a sigh escaping his mouth, South instead said, "It's all good." He was confident this was the kind of thing a debonair love interest would say, even as he looked longingly at the imprisoned wad of money he'd earmarked for later.

They walked up into the main floor, a dazzlingly bright open space with a collection of statues from all over the world. South could only recognise a few of them. In the old spy movies, this would be the bad guy's facade to the real world and—he stopped, finally realising six hours of television a night wasn't the best way to fight off anxiety. His doors of perception were tainted by fantasy. Regardless, the expansive, multi-floored museum was both marvellous and depressing. Marvellous for all the treasures it contained and depressing because it reminded South of all the things he missed out on. He had been preoccupied living in jungles, or under the ocean, or in pursuit of answers. Too busy being alive while history was occurring to pay much attention to anything that didn't involve him. At the time, there was no immediate benefit in learning such things.

So, while Alexandra would scan entire exhibits before inching ever closer to her personal favourite, South lingered over information plaques and photographs, almost tearing up with the influx of extra information. Entire epochs he knew nothing about presented in a detached, two-dimensional format. It was akin to handing someone an artisanal postcard and a message saying, "Oh, by the way, aliens invaded" and then expecting them to be able to process anything in a hurry.

They walked up through the animal wing first, looking at the stuffed and sometimes extinct creatures on display. Alexandra talking quickly about her time in Chile while South tried to not look too out of his depth with the info dump that was his surroundings. He hadn't even considered that animals could go extinct, for instance, but couldn't exactly say as much to anyone. In a private wake deep within his mind, he would mourn losses and celebrate victories as he discovered them, but he was aware that to Alexandra it looked as if he was barely interested in what she was saying. He tried to talk more because the alternative was not worth thinking about. Three months of crippling introspection meant he owed it to himself to at least try to engage with the woman. Even if that meant not dwelling on the sudden revelation that some bad things had happened to a Chinese dynasty he once dined with.

"Who's that?" he asked in a special exhibit on the fifth floor, pointing at a painting of a redheaded woman with an imposing forehead. She was clearly someone important, and yet South couldn't place her face or attire.

"Are you joking? I can't tell if you're joking."

South shook his head.

"That's Mary Stuart."

"Who?"

"Mary Queen of Scots. She was... well, she was a queen. Of the Scots."

A no idea shrug followed by a pathetic attempt to save face. "Oh, yeah, right, she just looks different in this picture."

"Remind me to never invite you to a trivia night." She took one last look at the painting, then looked at South. "You can read a dead language, right?"

All dead languages, he almost said, but: "A few."

"So, you can use words few living people understand, but you've spent half the time here looking like you just found out you were adopted. It's like you're just now finding out there's no more dodos and people walked on the moon. What gives?"

"I never had parents," South said too quickly.

"Oh, I'm sorry, I didn't mean—"

"It's fine. I haven't even thought about it, to be honest. It was just me and my, ah, sister back then."

"And you and her are still close?"

"I lost her a long time ago."

Alexandra hung her head, mouth half-cocked with the look of someone trying not to laugh out of embarrassment. "Well, I guess I suck at asking questions as much as you do learning regional history."

South flapped his hand, almost reaching out for her elbow, only to stop at the last second. "Don't worry about it. It was all a long time ago. We, I, I didn't get a formal education, so a lot of things were left out and there's only so much time to learn about the present, much less the past. Extinct species make me sad, and I was never was a fan of archaic hierarchies, so I didn't bother to learn about royalty. I focused on dead languages because," his mind raced ahead trying to find some noble excuse, a soup of uhs oozed out his throat as his words tried to catch up. "I wanted to give a voice to those who didn't have one. Not that any of it did any good."

Alexandra stepped closer. "I know what you mean, I guess. I got into anthropology to learn more about the people who weren't lionised by stuffy historians. Come on, we still haven't looked at the technology stuff, you'll get a kick out of that. We have these things you've probably never heard of."

Interest piqued. "Oh, yeah?"

"Yeah, we call them televisions, they're supposed to be quite good. Or the bane of modern living, depending on who you ask."

They meandered for an hour around the more hands-on side of the museum. Enjoying the kinetic energy machines and remote-controlled robots on display a little too much. It was only when they noticed children lined up behind them, they would move on to the next joystick, button, or interactive monitor. While they annoyed minors and parents, they talked more candidly. In admitting his lack of family, South had released an invisible pressure valve and created something akin to the refractory period. All at once it seemed as if they had known each other for more than a coffee date and a few rushed emails. Or at least, South saw it that way.

Like an overwrought television show about people trapped on a magical island, though, South had no idea how to end things. He knew it was coming. The museum's hours were clearly outlined at the entrance, and he knew it would be presumptuous to ask for much more time. Still, he couldn't just walk away from her after a prerequisite number of hours together were finished, nor could he try to coax her along to coffee shops, castles, or comedy clubs in a never-ending spiral to keep talking. No, a few hours were fine for now, he just—

"Oh, it's time I got going," Alexandra said as they hovered near a small coffee stall.

"Could we do this again sometime?"

"This exact thing?"

"No, I mean—"

"I know what you mean," she weighed up her words. "Listen..."

Even as inexperienced as he was with dating, South knew not to trust any sentence that began with that word. He braced himself, eyes misting over and legs all at once feeling an urge to sprint off into the sea toward Norway.

"This is hard for me," she continued. "You seem, well, I don't really know how you seem, but I get a good feeling from you. I just," she scratched her lips as if trying to dig out the right phrase, "I'm in recovery, which is what it is, but I've discovered the best way for me to live is by sticking to certain guidelines. So, if this is an attempt to see me naked, you need to know some things."

"I just like talking to you."

She smiled. "That's a start. I'm serious, though. I have a ninety-day rule for… for pretty much everything, actually. And, uh, you can't talk to me again for five days."

Five days for South was little more than a blink. "Perfect," he said, "That's plenty of time for me to learn the history of monarchs."

"Don't waste it on something like that. They're all French, anyway. Figure out a nice place to take me, preferably a place without alcohol or recreational drugs, and we'll see what happens. And, uh, thanks."

"Hm?"

"For not getting any weirder than you already are."

"Oh, sure, don't mention it. There're diminishing returns as far as that goes."

They walked away from the tantalisingly nearby coffee stall and returned to the entrance, where they lingered for several minutes. South was still unsure how to end the date, so was about to simply walk off to his home before Alexandra grabbed his hand.

"Where are you going?"

"Home?"

"You could do that. But I don't have your phone number and this date isn't technically over until we say goodbye, if you wanted to buy yourself something warm."

"Isn't that going against your time limit?"

"Technically no, and technically I make my own rules. It's not over until one of us says goodbye."

"What if I never say goodbye?"

"Never is a very long time, Alvar."

Indeed it is.

Alexandra's Bedroom, Edinburgh — 20__ CE:

The months had gone by quickly enough, not that South was rushing toward a finishing line. So much time was wasted in a single day. Eight hours at a call centre, each minute as vacuous as the next, filled with empty promises and meaningless goals. Then there was his burgeoning dependency on television, where a forty-five-minute show about hackers would transform into seven hours as a desiccated version of himself sat staring blankly at a flashing screen. The angst-riddled hours leading up to meeting   Alexandra were just as bad. But worst of all was the time he spent with her, not because he didn't enjoy it, but because it was never enough time, and no sooner would he say goodbye to her than he would realise with increasing dread there were around seventy hours of mind-numbing drudgery to go through before he would see her again. He finally understood how humans could sit down in their early twenties, blink, and become fifty-year-olds with nothing but debt and regrets to their name.

Their structured, limited time together would have driven a younger man insane, which was perhaps Alexandra's plan all along. For South, though, whose ideas of courtship were older than most countries, there was nothing wrong with taking things slow. He had all the time in the universe. That he openly referred to their infant relationship as a courtship was considered "cute" by Alexandra and "the sort of thing a fledgeling serial killer says before a spree," by her friends.

One thing he hadn't anticipated was the fact he was expected to meet some of those friends. South found it hard enough to single out and befriend people he wanted to know, so the sudden need to idly chat with an entourage of strangers he knew were collectively judging him was not something he enjoyed. Still, just knowing Alexandra thought enough of him to introduce her friends to him was something he considered a win.

There was Jill, a raunchy and loud woman who seemed to overcompensate for a defect nobody else knew she had. She was that cynical, judgemental sort of person who would relish the possibility of tearing a stranger apart with carefully selected, rehearsed words, but who also could never quite level that insight at her own problems. She got on well with South thanks to his inability to act like anything other than himself. Or at least the mortal version of himself.

Patrick was another close friend, although significantly closer in his estimation than Alexandra's. He was a man who would stumble over himself to correct a minor mistake, as if he were trying to score enough points to win a prize. If South said something incorrect, hooey, hokum, false, problematic, dated, oxymoronic, redundant, or otherwise weird, Patrick would make a comment that slithered just the right side of hostile. There were constant allusions to private jokes and to clinical depression, last-minute invitations to events but, oh wait, he only had two tickets. If one were to watch Patrick enter a bar, they would miss the collective eye rolls of those watching his pompous sauntering. Alexandra seemed to humour him mainly because the alternative would be messy in ways ranging from fake suicide attempts to drawn out court proceedings.

Xiaoyu was an effete photographer turned DJ turned painter turned copywriter turned social media manager for her dad's multinational box company. She was mostly harmless, in fact actually a bit of a sweetheart beneath her carefully constructed veneer. Her biggest issue was, despite her wealth and history of exhibitionist career choices, her confidence was so low that every sentence she spoke became a hushed question. The secret to winning her over was to give her a compliment that didn't revolve around her outward appearance. That was all it took.

Finally, there was Mags, a woman always around but who never seemed to talk. She would hover off in the periphery, only fully materialising an hour into the night before disappearing once more to the outer reaches of human sight. South couldn't rule out the possibility she was a ghost. The others, not really friends but not associates either, all merged into an amorphous, Cronenbergesque blob of monotonous voices, interchangeable names and jobs, and the unending, inane, highly specialised, career oriented anecdotes that suck the life force out of all listeners who don't know precisely what is being talked about.

Alexandra's friends thought South simultaneously came on too strong and sounded depressed in ways medication or CBT couldn't fix, talked like a Royal Shakespeare Company reject who spoke in obsolete jargon, and must have been a secret refugee from the eighties, because even the most vocal burnout of their generation didn't have the luxury of giving up on life completely. Most of this was said to his face, allegedly in jest. South learned soon enough that jokes were sincerely held beliefs phrased in such a way as to escape the threat of rebuke or reprisal. Suddenly, all the gay jokes he heard in the 60s and 70s made sense. Confessions masquerading as don't-hurt-me banter.

Through all this, South's incredibly advanced years proved to be a boon, because he didn't care what anyone under a million year old thought about him. Alexandra, Nell even, seemed to like him well enough, which was all he needed to know. He lost exactly zero minutes of sleep worrying about a fragmented group of friends, comforted knowing that, whatever else, he would outlive them.

With their probationary period grinding toward its end, South became convinced that something would end their romance prematurely. Some hidden final test designed to trap and ruin him all at once, which was a hard belief to counteract. If he were wrong about there being a secret test, no harm would be done. But since there was no real way to know if such a ploy even existed, he often found himself debating his own impulses, over-thinking trivial things and trapped in a circular argument. Preparing for imaginary traps is a madness all its own.

All the worry ended one snowy night a little over three months after their time at the museum. The two of them had schlepped to Alexandra's apartment, a fourth-floor shrine to the past overlooking Makar's Court. It was South's first time there. A cramped set of rooms in a building designed when people were half a foot shorter. Walls lined with leather-bound books, stone relics, hand-drawn posters from protests, ancient maps of the old world. The furniture was cat scratched although there was no longer a cat to accompany them. Her home smelled vaguely like the outdoors—spruce and wet leaves, a hint of lavender.

And Alexandra's lips found South's.

"Thank you."

"No, thank you. What are you thanking me for?"

"Your patience. Most guys run after the first month. Or as soon as they remember they have porn on their phones."

"Porn?"

"Shut up."

"I wasn't just waiting around to get into your home."

"I know. That's why you're here."

South scanned the room, trying to get a close look at her book collection. He wanted to see if his preconceived ideas matched the real world. Searching for proof the woman kissing him matched the fantasy he'd conjured months earlier. She took his hand and, before he could read a single author's name, they were in her bedroom. A slight wave of nauseousness fell over South as he calculated the centuries it had been since the last time. It didn't help the performance anxiety.

"Listen," he said, "not to ruin my chances, but it's been a while for me."

"Speak for yourself. I did it last week."

The flinch of a man who couldn't understand sarcasm.

"No," she continued, clasping his hips, "Me too. About a year. One year, two months, and seven days to be exact. How about you?"

"About two thousand years."

"Cute."

"You are. You're the best person I've ever met."

At that, Alexandra retreated slightly. It was not a reaction South expected. She drifted toward the edge of her bed and sat down with a sigh. She looked up at the ceiling, trying to find something abstract. "You keep saying weird stuff like that, and I hope it isn't true."

"But it is true. There's nobody else out there like you. You're perfect."

"If you honestly believe that you haven't met enough people." She shrank into herself. Her arms wrapped around her knees.

This would have been a good time for South to change tact, but how was he to know? Instead, he sat down beside her. He thought he was reassuring her, not digging his own grave. "Everyone else I've met is selfish or lazy or stupid, and they do not understand what is happening in the world. Or if they know, they don't care. But you're different. Special."

He tried to kiss her shoulder, but she recoiled and stood up.

"This is such a mood killer, Alvar," she paused for what seemed to last forever. "For all your quirks, you're a pretty good guy. But there's this pessimism to you I just can't scrub off. I can't... I can't stay around someone with such a defeatist mindset. It's not good for my health. Health I'm still working on improving."

"I'm only telling you the truth."

"It's a truth you've made for yourself. Let me ask you this: when was your last relationship?"

"Uh…"

"Let's be broader, then. I'm not even talking romantically. How about friends? When was the last time you made a friend? How come I have never met someone who knows you? Not even job buddies or guys at work you pretend to like."

"I've been busy."

"Right. And when was the last time you went out there and helped someone?"

"I translated those things for you."

"We both know that's different. That was the price of admission for the museum, let's not pretend it wasn't."

South found his hands pawing at the buttons of his shirt, his legs trembled, he could not remain still. "Have I done something wrong?"She took in a deep breath and returned to the bed. "It's not that, it's… Look, in recovery, they have this rule, a guideline really: don't think about relationships or make big decisions for the first year of sobriety. Because you're a baby at that point, and whatever choices you make are doomed to fail. Trust me. Even the best things in life can fall apart if you're in the wrong mindset. So, but, the reason they tell you this is that if you go for it anyway, your brain is so used to being numbed by your poison of choice that if you meet someone, you wind up diving in head first because you're replacing your drug with a new one. Except, the new drug is a person and the feelings they inspire."

"And what's any of that got to do with me?"

"Nothing and everything. You're just so insular, Alvar. You remind me of people I used to talk to at the clinic. Maybe you're not an addict–I hope I'd have picked up on that–but if you were honest with yourself, you'd know you're recovering from something. I don't want to presume to know if its psychological or physical, but whatever it is, you've been numbing yourself from it. Maybe talking to me was you trying to get over your issues, but you're so much closer to the start of the road than you realise. And so you've got this idealised version of me in your brain that isn't real, and it isn't good for either of us if you're pursuing that woman, because she doesn't exist, you know? I'm, I have wasted a lot of time on things that were doomed from the start, and right now that's us. You're smart, and funny, and you're romantic in this really refreshing, genuine way, but this view of the world you have is going to be our downfall eventually, and I just can't do that again."

South tried to unjumble what she was saying, and this was the best he could come up with. "So, you're saying if I get out there and better myself, we might have a shot? Because I can. I will."

Alexandra stood once more and led South to her front door. "I know," she said, "But you have to do it for yourself. I'm not a prize to be won, and you deserve to be the best version of yourself. For you. This isn't bye forever. We can keep in touch. I just think this has all been too much too soon for you. And me. This could all be projection, but I'm speaking as someone who has been there herself. Is probably still is there."

South paused in the doorway to admire Alexandra for what he assumed would be the last time. Her eyes bore no malice. Part of him already knew she was right. He'd been hiding in a cave for too long and wasn't used to the sun.

"I've still got your email," he said, trying to muster up a smile.

"Or, you know, maybe modernise a little and text me."

"Maybe."

They paused. Something inside South told him everything was going to be OK.

"Thank you," he said. "I think you're right. This was something I've needed to hear for a long time. I think I've spent too long in the darkness."

She kissed his cheek. "You'll be fine. The sun will rise. And hey, just about any other guy I can think of would be a whinging little goblin right about now, so you've got that going for you."

"Goodbye Alexandra."

"Not goodbye. Just goodnight."

Ancient History:

From the mountain that would one day be named Mount Nebo but at the time was called That Hill Over There, the two of them watched the last few remaining embers of their home shimmer on the ground below. Fresh, deep lines gashed the earth, revealing where the palace had slid into the dead sea. The remains of old towers continued their slow descent into the brine. Elsewhere, the debris of a hundred million years of history lay scattered amongst the rocks and shrubbery, already forgotten, lost to the sands and winds of the wilderness. Off in the distance, small groups of local tribes made preliminary searches of the wreckage, most refusing to even look at the sinking palace.

From their position on the hill, North and South looked on, indifferent, savouring the last few moments of calm before uncertainty claimed their minds once more. South looked out at the water, watching the bubbling water digest his home. North stood upright, head tilted forward, like a falcon watching mice as she spied on the scuttling humans below.

As the sun disappeared behind them, the dead sea took on a Tartarean glow. Somewhere beneath the surface, their home's power source was sputtering its last few bursts of energy. Shadows of the lesser beings were silhouetted at the water's edge, hypnotised by the sickly greens and violent reds emanating from the depths. North laughed.

"Let us go down there and kill those creatures," she said to South.

"Why?"

"That we might rule this sad planet."

"What's the point? What purpose would ruling this world serve? We need nothing, want nothing. It would mean nothing."

"We are gods, my brother. See their foolish, superstitious braying at the water and think how they would bow in awe of my majesty."

South kicked up a loose stone and watched it tumble down the hill toward the luminous water. "We are finally free from our shackles, North. Why force our will upon these things? Why not try to be better than what's come before?"

"Because I deserve it. I gave The Creator my entire life."

"But what of them?"

"What of them? When did you suddenly decide to go against the natural order of things? You didn't shed a tear when we annihilated continents or wiped out those giant lizards. Where has the South I knew gone?"

South stood motionless, felt the temperature change with the night's wind. He looked at the shadowy folk below and frowned. "It just feels like a waste of time. We could help them, learn from them, find our true purpose in this universe."

"There is no true purpose and all we have is forever. Why not enjoy our gifts?"

"Please, just leave them alone. Think about this."

North gave a tut and turned away from the water. "I will spare them today. For you, my oldest friend. But it will cost you our friendship. If you will not help me, I have no need for you. Once the sun rises, I will leave you alone. For all of time, South. Do you understand that? If you will not help me, you will become nothing. Is that truly what you desire?"

This gave South pause. He had never been alone, nor had he been threatened. "I don't want to fight any more."

"That's exactly what your problem is, South. Fighting is what life is. Leave me now. If I see you again, I will destroy you."

South stammered, unable to create a farewell worth saying. Turning away from his oldest friend, he walked down the hill and into the darkness. He continued for some time.

South
Nothingham Forest
The Universe
August 13th, 22 Billion AE

Hi,

Not so much an author's note this time. I just wanted to talk to you after thinking about that night.

Looking back on things, even I had defining moments. What better defines you as a person as how you react when things don't go your way? When North left me to my own devices, I made mopish, empty attempts at finding meaning. It was centuries before I did anything of value, consumed as I was with self-pity and doubt. For all my lofty plans of helping humanity, watching them from afar was about as much as I could bring myself to do. Those days remind me of old artist friends, who would drop out of college to pursue stardom, giving up on their dream after their first failure, and then spend their dwindling days gawking at other people on big screens or stages, playing the part of bitter critic. Although, I suppose there are worse ways to waste your life. They could have considered a career in HR, for example.

Back to the question at hand. How would you or anyone else define my actions after North turned her back to me? Pretty pathetic by anyone's standards. And so, in the end, I considered myself pathetic. All I did was hang out in caves and inadvertently inspire the occasional creation myth. Given enough time, anybody could do that.

The night you showed me the door, though? You were exactly right. I was walking a line between two worlds and for all my age and experience, I had no clue what it meant to be human. I tried to learn. Not for you, please understand, but perhaps *because* of you. As that door closed behind me I understood that, for as much as I wanted to be part of humanity, I was living in a grim fairy-tale version of the real world, a tunnel-vision induced fantasy world where only a handful of people existed, one I could leave with impunity. And while this way of living couldn't kill me, it was killing my spirit. If I have a spirit.

Nell was right, too. How dare I? How dare someone who has outlived the universe itself waste all that potential on a superficial, empty reality? I was in a prison of my own creation, locked behind walls of guilt and scorn, and that was selfish. Just as selfish as using my position to declare myself a living god would have been. Significantly less dangerous, sure, but just as egotistical.

Without you even knowing your impact, I tried to learn more. To engage. To talk to my fellow man. And do you know what? I learned a lot. You were right. Nell was right. Even that guy Jimmy, a man who once claimed we were living in a computer simulation, was right. Wasted potential is a crime, if not for yourself, then for those who don't have it.

For a time, that moving around worked wonders for me, and seemed to help a good many people too.

But nothing lasts forever, especially if you're not vigilant, and I should have known there was something waiting for me a little down the road. Some would have called it destiny; you would have launched into a diatribe about how destiny is a classist and restrictive form of control. I'll be diplomatic and call it the next couple of chapters of this book.

At any rate, Alex, how did what came next define me? Define you? What is the opposite of anonymity? We were about to find out.

South XOXO

Rome — 410 CE:

"Perhaps it would be best if we just let them in. They're not after people like us, and it's not like life can get any worse."

"Nor can it get any different. Besides, we've just as much chance getting murdered by our own countrymen before we reached the gates."

Three men scrounged through the dust and dirt surrounding the Colosseum. Moonlight reflected off its marble shell, creating an otherworldly glow amidst a world of darkness. They were hungry, the three men. Gremio and Cogidubnus hadn't eaten in almost a day. The third man, too poor for even a name, may well have never eaten at all. Sometimes they could dig up spare morsels from around the old building at night. Usually, it was their last attempt at finding food for the day, and they would invariably wind up falling asleep hungry. Despite their failures, Cogidubnus was quick to remind them of the time he found an entire vine of grapes tucked away behind a stall. If he did not remind them of that, he would remind them of the horrible alternative. Rumours of cannibal senators abounded, and several of their friends had gone missing since the siege began.

"All I know is that clown in Ravenna has left us here to starve," said Cogidubnus.

"But that's the story of human life, man: emperors play with their cocks while people starve. We fight wars that don't make me any less hungry. And all so they can own a new field they never bother to visit. Didn't help my grandfather out or his grandfather neither. It's a rigged game of dice. If I'm lying, may I find a loaf of bread," Gremio lifted an overturned bucket. No such luck. He turned to their nameless friend. "What's up with you? You have said little."

The third man kicked at a mound of straw. It had already been picked through during the day. He did not need to eat, but he felt for his friends; they were damned whether or not they opened the gates. Perhaps their search for food would have been time better spent searching for a way out. Into the hills. One thing he had come to know about life among the humans was you could take the least fortunate from one place and move them to another, and they'd be fine right up until a self-appointed noble took issue with them. It had worked for him at least, the life of a beggar, too low down the social ladder for anyone to notice. People busy surviving did not have the time to judge their neighbour, much less notice they never aged.

"We need to get out of here, soon," said the nameless man. "Things are getting bad and I don't want either of you to die."

"There're rumours they are hunting men like us down so the senators and their family can have something to eat," said Cogidubnus. "That should tell you who the real monsters are. I can't see that lot outside being any worse."

"Then you best hope starvation takes that rump of yours soon, my friend," said Gremio.

"I earned this heft fair and square."

The nameless man grasped his friends by their shoulders. "We should look for a way out of the city. We could head west. It's not like we have anything here."

"No, but leave Rome? I want to be here when it falls. I've never seen something end before."

"They'll kill you, too."

"I'm as good as dead already, we all are. You can run if you want but I want to see this great city tumble."

"Why?"

"Because my family has been here since the start, from all I can gather, and I'm still digging up scraps with you poor sods." Cogidubnus sat down. "It's not fair. I want to die knowing this empire followed after me."

Gremio sat beside him, "Think of all those stories of men like you or I founding great cities, becoming rulers, changing the world. That could be you. That could be us."

"Those days are gone. The future is already decided," Cogidubnus spat on the ground. "And either way, things would end. That's the sad truth: everything ends; nothing is permanent. What does it matter if it ends here tomorrow or out in the meadows in ten years?"

The third man fished through another pile of straw and grasped something. Then he turned to sit with his friends. He looked Cogidubnus in the eye. "It's true that things end, but then new things begin. It is also true they have robbed you of a future without your knowing it. But think to the end, my friend. If we flee this place, perhaps great things will come your way, or perhaps you'll die tomorrow. The only certainty in this place for you is your sad end. Nobody will mourn you and you won't be around, that much is certain. Don't you want to be surprised for once? If we're lucky, we can slip out before the sunrise and make our way to somewhere new. Barbarians don't concern themselves with people of our stature."

Cogidubnus thought on this. "I am hungry, I don't have the energy to escape."

The nameless man smiled, revealing the olives he had found. "It's not much, but is it enough?"

The olives pleased Gremio. Cogidubnus placed a dry olive in his mouth and said with muffled tone, "Yes, this will get me to the wall at least."

"I will carry you the rest of the way."

"Can I help you?"
"Yes, I was wondering if you needed any volunteers."

Various — 20__-20__ CE:

South quit his call centre job the morning after leaving Alexandra's apartment. The catharsis was almost euphoric, as anyone who has ever quit a particularly unpleasant job will tell you. Without a real plan, he was aware the job was an obligation he could remove, a contrivance he designed to impress someone who wanted nothing to do with him. Worse yet, it was a call centre job, morally only slightly above careers in marketing or lobbying. South, in all his time on earth, had endured many hardships, but the constant banality of sitting in front of a telephone to make someone else money was up there. It was not as difficult as living through war or genocide, or even abject poverty, but the slow, creeping death of absolute irrelevance was its own hell. He mourned the many thousands who didn't have the option to just walk away with their life intact.

In the afternoon he transferred a small fortune from the Claudio Sud International Memorial Investigative Association for Missing Interlocutors into his bank account. The organisation was set up decades earlier in case of emergencies. He had no real plan for the money—the whole concept of money as annoying as it had been thousands of years earlier—he only knew that he would need it. Need it for what? He had no idea, only that he was about to embark on a voyage of discovery. And then—

And then?

He wasn't sure. Perhaps his reinvigorated drive down the road of self-improvement would be enough to woo Alexandra all over again. She would see through that, surely. Tell Nell before she died he'd made up for the wasted years? Save the world? Start a travel blog? South tried not to think about the destination, promising to focus instead on the journey. Because when you are someone who will never die, there is never a permanent destination.

His new journey began in Dublin. After talking to a few homeless, and the families crammed into his own apartment building, South realised there was a housing problem. In past lives he had slept under bridges or inside abandoned train carriages, but assumed the problem was getting better for the general population. Not so. A rising class of landlords were buying up vacant properties, keeping them empty most of the time, or else raising the cost of rent, happy to turn entire streets into desolate wastelands if it helped their portfolio. People were systematically becoming surplus to housing requirements and forced out into cold streets because Landlord X wanted to use his slum as a short-term rental property or keep it empty until a mythical housing boom. Dublin just happened to be the first place South found with spaces open for eager volunteers. Plus, while he wouldn't admit as much for billions of years, it was an excuse to flee Scotland.

Once in Dublin he met with a self-styled Arthur McBride (real name never given), and a slew of other impassioned people who believed in abstract, deeply complicated concepts like "people shouldn't be sleeping in gutters when tens of thousands of homes are empty" and "a government which values profits over people is a failed government."

South stayed in the city for months, helping lay the groundwork for future efforts to help the community. The charity would simultaneously offer help for those who needed it and attempt to hold self-serving politicians accountable for their misdeeds. It was the former which proved easier. A corrupt politician is too busy counting their blood money to care about principles, and their clubhouse friends were molasses-slow to judge them.

Nothing about South's personal efforts were particularly spectacular. He canvased and called and volunteered his time, the sort of banal activities required for change. Others worked harder, lead better, knew more about what they were doing, and that was fine.

It was not like the homeless were homogenous, blank vassals, either, but an unseen group of people with a variety of issues, only exacerbated by cold nights outside. South knew this, having been one himself from time to time, but those in power had a small postcard picture of what a homeless person was, ignoring the rest of the image because it both suited them and they hadn't experienced enough of life to know any better. It was easy to paint people with the broad brush of drunken failures because it deflected the blame. Far harder to understand something outside your limited worldview.

All the various displays of meekness, selflessness, and determination showed on a minute-by-minute basis were humbling for South, who had long since forgotten about such people. He was far more familiar with the pious men and women of the world would could end it all tomorrow if they could only be bothered. He had known plenty of good people, to be sure, but they were too preoccupied with basic survival to have much time for others.

While leaving Saint Michan's Church one morning, South felt the urge to send a text to Alexandra.

Been helping out in Dublin. Really learning a lot.
Alvar.

The ease with which he hit send surprised him. Without dwelling on it, an impossibility only months earlier, he went on down the street toward Light House Cinema. An alien buzzing came from his pocket. A reply.

Great! Hope you're doing it for the right reasons.
Can't believe you sign your texts.

Not too long after that, he made his way to the United States. He volunteered at an urban farm in Milwaukee, where he learned about sustainable agriculture, and levels of homelessness and discrimination he thought were resigned to the history books. His general ignorance concerned and excited some more vocal volunteers. "I'll have you learning the truth like you never did," the Kenosha Kid told him one day while they were digging through manure. And the Kenosha Kid did just that.

Soon the two of them were diving from one city to the next, a pair of socially conscious banditos, to help with food shortages, lead-tainted water, red-lined communities, and whatever else seemed relevant to KK and their crew. For the second time in two centuries, South was crossing the States as an outlaw, a desperado, a liberator. Less blood the second time around.

South would sleep on unfinished floors in guest rooms while they recruited volunteers. Lost young men and women, angry, disillusioned, and numb, were eager to join whatever cause gave their lives meaning. When they discovered struggling community centres or promising but under-funded leaders, South would secretly contribute to their budgets.

At nights he would often think about Alexandra and then remember he wasn't supposed to be doing that, so instead thought of the hardships the average person was going through. They were living to work themselves to death to sustain the lifestyles of a sociopathic few at the top of the tower.

Socialism was a dirty word in America, but was something that existed there. It just so happened American Socialism only benefited those who already had all the money. He thought about the days he'd spent out in the old West and how much the country he'd once loved had become a parody of itself, existing more as a cautionary tale to any future countries that may come along. It was at once a bastion of prosperity and a third world hellhole, two countries existing as one on a race to mutual annihilation. A class disparity so severe the country was scared to mention the word. Class. Like a curse that could damn nine generations. Class, the only concept the entire American media could agree to never mention. Can't have three hundred million disgruntled patriots realise their problem is not with each other. Who would be around for the adverts?

In a motel just outside Barstow, South was thinking about the unrest of the great nation when his pocket buzzed again. Every time it happened, he had to remind himself it was a phone and not a sign of impending doom. His leg had gone unmolested since around the Chalcolithic age, so it was going to take time to adjust to unexpected vibrations.

```
Still in Dublin?
                Somewhere near the Mojave, I think. Alvar.
Not the response I was expecting.
Please stop signing your texts,
I feel like I'm talking to my grandpa.
Except he's more tech-savvy.
```

South smiled. She was still out there, thinking about him.

Except he still had work to do. For all his effort in helping the world, he recognised his efforts were Anglocentric. He knew this word because one of his potential volunteers said, "You don't care about non-English-speaking countries, you Anglocentric, xenophobic pig." The candidate then refused to volunteer for anything that required travel or lifting and made a list of wage demands a professional athlete would be embarrassed to submit. They were right about South's trajectory, though. He had been following in the footsteps of English colonists with little deviation.

In years long gone, South had walked the entire planet, and felt the urge to do the same again. The surge of empathy and the hits of pure dopamine that struck him every time he helped someone were sensations he didn't want to lose.

It was often the case, South observed, that people become addicted to things they choose to focus on. Fall in love with helping others, and that is all you will ever want to do. Decide you're a victim who deserves further punishment and you will seek said punishment until you find the grave. Pursue wealth and you will inevitably murder your own family if it yields a one percent boost to quarterly profits. "You are what you do, so be careful what you do," is a quote South invented all on his own and hoped to use in a speech one day.

But anyway, Cuba.

Cuba proved to be a hard place to enter from the United States. A photogenic, temperate country with a long and messy history, it attracted far more tourists than it could sustain. South spent many nights trying to sleep, pangs of guilt keeping him awake as he imagined the locals unable to eat or sleep because the local grocery store had been emptied by visiting amateur models and self-published Hemmingways. Affordable homes converted into trendy, tres chic couture apartments with reasonable weekly rates. It would have been very easy to fall into a pit of loathing, but South did not need to eat, and he brought with him just enough knowledge of sustainable farming practices to lend a hand.

From the southernmost part of the island, he looked toward South America and considered returning, but old wounds from mere decades earlier presented themselves like a paper cut in saltwater. Some things take time to heal, he told himself, staring off beyond an imperceptible horizon. The time can be several hundred years more than you realise. He sat in sand and old guilt and heard the familiar call of Pachamama, the Andes, the rainforest. He did not answer. Could not. How odd he'd been prepared to return to Chile for a stranger. Alexandra. Her name echoed tuning-fork style in the back of his mind. But she was already a fading ghost of his past and South America a roaring poltergeist.

So, he sailed to the Ivory Coast instead.

A wise man had once advised children to "look for the helpers," a helpful nugget of wisdom since perverted by inactive adults hoping to absolve their own apathy. It had become the "thoughts and prayers" of the secular crowd, along with half remembered lines from Martin Luther King Junior speeches and the idea that colour tinting your profile photo accomplished anything.

Still, it was advice South, emotionally a child himself, took to heart. He scoured the planet searching for helpers and asked them how he could help too. Some people did not want help, others saw him as a colonising force with an agenda, still more tried to abuse the goodwill for their own selfish ends. Frequently, though, people were grateful to receive what help they could. Others, upon seeing South sweating in a field or pounding the frame of a new house, would want to help too. Sometimes, you can dance alone in a field full of people and, if the mood is just right, people will run to join in on the festivities. They will do this without coercion or motive or payment because they have been given permission to do something they already wanted to do.

Teach a man to fish and before long a faceless, multinational consortium will ban private fishing, imprison the fisherman on bogus charges, and steal his rod. There were many things South could never fix. Conflict minerals, for instance, were the bane of innumerable people's existence, as were sweat-shops, tainted water systems, ocean plastic, terrorism, rising sea levels, eroding topsoil, regions fast becoming uninhabitable because of rising temperatures, a growing destabilisation and decentralisation of what few indigenous groups had survived imperialism, the worship of profits, crowdsourcing apps that ruined towns and all but enslaved desperate people under the guise of free-dom, nationalism, toxic individualism, a diminishing amount of everything, the growing threat of blood parasites, Leishmaniasis, and other diseases long since thought confined to isolated regions of the equator but now found as far north as Canada, the death of the bee, the death of effective, joke-based comedy, the commodification of everything, marketing companies exploiting race and gender issues for free publicity oblivious to the repercussions, disin-genuous false prophets bought and paid for by a death cult of ancient billion-aires, the slow death rattle of seasonal weather, and the normalisation of demented, megalomaniac scions of dead Nazis running anything more than a used car lot. To name but a few.

Of course, it was in South's power to fix a lot of these issues by shear virtue of being an unkillable man who couldn't be bought or threatened by mere humans. Some frustrating days he was tempted to do exactly that. But then he would think about how little his interventions had helped in the past and, to a lesser extent, how exposing himself as a walking manifestation of wrath would hinder his love life. Besides which, if he upped and decided he was the supreme moral authority on Earth, where would it end? Would he be ending world hunger and bringing about world peace one year, only to run out of things to do and demand a satisfactory ending for Quantum Leap the next? He hated the phrase slippery slope—a term used almost only by disingenuous, intellectually and morally bankrupt pseudo philosophers—but he could feel the loss of traction whenever he considered saving the world as a caped superhero. Creating a better future would require everyone's consent, a reconciliation of differences, a level playing field. The key word there being consent. You can't build utopia with a whip.

South did what he could, though, within the realms of polite human society. He worked laboriously for over three years without a break. One year was quite rough as the entire world seemed to go mad for a minute, some countries longer than others by a wide margin. He pressed on regardless. He helped, talked, listened, but most importantly of all, he encouraged others to do the same. Faster than he realised, there were little pockets of hope all over the world because people allowed themselves to think positively. Which seemed like a great idea at the time. If he had it all to do over again, he would have perhaps tried a lot harder to hide the paper trail leading back to one Alvar South, seven months late on rent with an untaxed fortune of over thirty million pounds sterling in what was supposed to be a basic student account.

There were times, far later in life, when South would think back on his travels, his work, the people around him. They felt so important back then, vivid even, but as the years passed, he would have to remind himself he'd tried to help. Strange how some moments seem so urgent while they are happening, only to slip into the refuse of the mind with all the other memories once the day has gone.

Mosfellsbær — 995 CE:

"I can't help but feel the old ways are truly done for," Hafrbjǫrn mused as an icy blast of wind cut through their furs. He sat beside Vǫlsungr, who hung his legs over the hole they were digging. Together they sat angled back on the mounds of earth they had already scooped up. Only a few hours of work remained ahead of them. Somewhere beneath them was treasure, or so Vǫlsungr claimed.

"One thing I have learned," Vǫlsungr said, squinting at the aquamarine water in the distance, "Is that the old ways are always done for and the new ways are doomed to one day become the old ways."

"Yes, yes, but I am not talking about the Romans or the Goths, I am talking about my ways. The ways of my father and his father before him."

"And what about before him?"

"All the way back, as far as history can remember."

"We both know that is not entirely true, Hafrbjǫrn. I am sure if you went back far enough, your father's father's father's oldest ancestor was part of some old ways you couldn't even comprehend. Before even the Æsir."

Hafrbjǫrn snorted. "There is no before them, my friend. Think before you speak."

"You don't think the Romans or the Greeks or the Egyptians said the same thing? And those are only groups you know of. So many more lost to the sands of time, yet all convinced of their own relevance right until the end.

"And how would you know that? You weren't there."

Vǫlsungr began to give his reply, but was fast to think better of it. The days of adoration were far behind him. Even the days of standing watch were drawing to an end. There were only a few constants he recognised in the world: expansion, proselyting, and corruption, followed by resistance, rebellion, and death. He knew, in some perverted way, North was behind the self-appointed ruling classes and their unending need to spread like the twisted screed of a false prophet. Through the years, he heard whispers of shadowy figures manipulating emperors and kings alike, puppet masters outside and above any forced hierarchy. He was far beyond caring about her as an entity, only concerning himself with preventing her poison from taking over the good folk of the world, whose numbers were dwindling by the day. He could not stand to lose them as he had the ruling elite, the pious, the scholar, and so many more.

"Vǫlsungr, remind me, why are we digging here?"

"I buried some silver here only a few years ago."

"Ah, I think you've confused yourself with Egill."

"No, I helped him bury it."

"But I heard he killed his compatriot."

"He tried. Let's get back to work."

They dug again. In their inactivity, their muscles had grown tight and the patches of sweat beneath their furs had grown cold, sticking to their clothing. It wasn't a pleasant feeling, but soon passed as their exertion thawed their limbs and reinvigorated their work. Before long, Vǫlsungr stopped to speak.

"I will leave this place soon, my friend. Once you have your silver, I don't expect we will see each other again."

Hafrbjǫrn continued to dig but slowed enough to consider his words. "Do as you will, but why? We have all the freedom in the world here! You and I could be kings."

"I've seen the damage kings can do. No, if I am to best serve this land, I must leave. There's a dark wind sweeping over the earth and if I don't stop it soon, all is lost."

"Then perhaps you are already too late."

Vǫlsungr stood upright. "It is never too late."

"These old times you were talking about, when they could see the end it was already over. If you're saying you can see a dark wind, and maybe you can, then the storm is already coming. Why fight the inevitable?"

"Because the inevitable is death."

"Yes, that's exactly what death is. And then if we live honourably, we shall feast with the kings and warriors of the old times. Death is not the end, it is the reward, Vǫlsungr, and I embrace it."

"That makes one of us."

Their shovels hit the iron edge of a small chest with a clank. Finally. They fell to their knees and dug up their prize and returned to the surface as fast as they could. Once there, they pried open the box and discovered purses filled with coins and silver. Vǫlsungr stood, indifferent, cold, perturbed by Hafrbjǫrn's avaricious handling of the treasure. A part of him knew what was about to happen.

"Well, since I did all the work, I think I should get the larger share," Hafrbjǫrn said, his hand sliding under his furs to grasp an iron handle.

"We agreed on splitting it in half."

"I could take it all, you know," Hafrbjǫrn whispered as he revealed his dagger.

"I wouldn't recommend doing this, Hafrbjǫrn. It would be extremely painful…"

Eye contact, a mixture of guilt, pride, and desperation. "I'll end it fast."

"My friend, please be rational. I haven't killed a man in many years."

"And that's not about to change." Hafrbjǫrn leapt to his feet and sunk his blade into Vǫlsungr's chest. Or at least he thought he did. When nothing registered in Vǫlsungr's eye, he pulled back his dagger and discovered the entire weapon had folded into itself. Staring at the broken blade, there was a moment of recognition in his eyes before the panic set in and he tried to beat on Vǫlsungr with the hilt.

"Please, stop," Vǫlsungr said, more disappointed than physically hurt.

"You won't get me, demon!"

Vǫlsungr gave a gentle shove, hoping to break free from Hafrbjǫrn's grasp. He had, of course, forgotten his own strength, and it was only after staring at the twisted, prone body of his old friend for half an hour he realised his old friend was dead. Vǫlsungr sat in silence for the rest of the day, hoping the miracles he had heard so much about were real and Hafrbjǫrn would regain both his life and his senses. What a waste.

"Goodbye, old fool," he whispered, finally kicking the wreckage of Hafrbjǫrn's body into the hole and returning all but one pouch of silver to its grave. The silver would serve as a reminder, everything else would be lost to time. Right until the moment Hafrbjǫrn attacked him, Vǫlsungr was happy to believe there were still good people around him. He refused to allow the sudden betrayal to condemn the common man, but it was enough to raise some questions. He was forced to admit he did not understand what was happening in the world.

North's plague was worse than he imagined. Looking out at the sea, he wondered if there was anyone left to save.

Hotel Pompadou, London — 20__ CE:

The Hotel Pompadou was the swankiest of places South had visited since Claudio Sud's sudden and violent disappearance from the Château Marmot seventy years earlier. Stylish in the way the nouveau riche and sudden lottery winners see style, not the exuberant excess of guillotined estates of yore. Faux marble pillars, real marble floors, gilded everything, vaguely minimalist counters, and décor. Chrome and monochrome alike everywhere. Propaganda from conflicting ideologies of bygone times downgraded to decorative wall art. People who looked like fledgling models but turned out to be bellhops, concierges, and shift managers. More glass than the Chicago skyline. Just below the ceiling, a tickertape LED banner ran the length or the foyer, blinking play-by-play updates on sports, shares, stocks, and squiggly symbols South couldn't discern. It was a hotel built and decorated by trendy architects who couldn't communicate with each other, like the old parable about the interior designers and the elephant.

South of all people was there because it turned out some charities spent upwards of all their annual budget congratulating themselves. Ask any of history's kindest people, and they will tell you it is very hard to feed starving children if you're not sleeping in a king sized bed with an ocean view, slippers hand sculpted by Trappist monks, robes sewn with love by a harem of mute nymphets, at least three exotic cars, and perfect fake teeth. Or at least that is what some organisers told themselves from the warmth and safety of their third summer house.

Why had they chosen South of all people? Because he was one of the few volunteers who both spoke English and had no internet presence. It is easier to invent someone's history when they have none. A weak attempt for the chairperson to demonstrate their virtue. South agreed to give the speech long before he was aware of the charity he was dealing with. His first suspicion that the organisation wasn't the most frugal was when he was flown by three consecutive private jets from the bottom edge of Mumbai to Gatwick. The second clue came in the airport when the head of marketing and his chauffeur escorted South to a purring Veneno. It was a cramped drive.

All this was to say nothing of the charity's many supporters and volunteers. The lower rungs of the organisation were upbeat people from various backgrounds, their bright eyes dimming to the indifference of modern living. They were delighted to be around other like-minded people, celebrating a cause they all cared about. Everyone was glad to be there. Except for the various department heads and the CEO, all decked out in absurd haute couture more Bosch than Warhol. That group of people, sat on a private table on the stage, didn't seem to want to be there at all. While the other guests milled around, bouncing from table to table, hugging and kissing each other like close relatives at a family reunion after a bit too much champagne, the people on the stage sat in smug silence, refusing to even acknowledge the people beneath them.

South's role was to be the preliminary guest whose sole job was to talk for five minutes about his work and then introduce the first spokesperson, a sports personality who gave a whopping 0.1% of his annual income to the organisation as a tax writeoff. The sports personality was one of seven new spokespeople, each paid around 30% of their annual income to take rushed photos and appear in promotional guilt trips with uplifting piano accompaniment.

A grinning woman, a Sunday morning newspaper editorial incarnate, took to the stage without applause or warning. "Without much further ado… about nothing," mouth agape with furtive smile, pleading eyes to an indifferent crowd, a lonely guffaw from some far corner, "Our first guest tonight has been all over the world helping a lot of charities, but over the past year he's been helping us. Perhaps some of you have, uh, have met him, ah, somewhere in your own, eh, travels? Um. He is this year's recipient of the diamond trophy for work ethic and but so without much ado about, ah, oh, no - please give a warm welcome to, to, to ah, Alvin South!"

Three claps. Total. South walked out from behind the stage and approached the podium. The audience were there for the drinks and camaraderie, still preoccupied with saying hello to each other and ensuring the Old Fashioned they ordered was poured the right way. Note: There is no right way to make an Old Fashioned, Daniel.

"Yes, hello, thanks for the warm welcome everyone, and thank you for the introduction. But you're wrong, working with organisations such as this is a coincidence. My goal has only ever been to help others. You know, everyone, this morning I flew here on several private jets and driven to this hotel in an expensive sports car. I assume it's expensive, anyway. Obviously, these guys here know more about luxury vehicles, so ask them. I just looked up the prices for this place, and the suite I'm staying in this whole week costs enough to put a village through school. If that seems like a lot of money to those of you who aren't on stage, that's because it is. What a shameful amount of waste, huh? Some of you, and by that, I mean the mosquitoes sitting behind me, should be ashamed of yourselves. But I don't think you have the capacity nor the propensity for shame. Anyway, you might know him as a young man who fought sexual misconduct allegations by driving three adolescents to suicide, others may have seen him play an average of fifteen minutes a week on television. That's 134 pounds a second. Allow me to—"

The mic cut off, loud music played, a small man dressed as a renaissance pianist approached the podium, unaffected by South's speech.

Later, when the higher-ranking members of the organisation left to take private helicopters back to their Devon cottages, the auditorium became more festive. Because of an oversight on the event planner's part, the room had been booked until noon the following day and one of the underpaid bar staff let slip the free bar was being paid from the CEO's third offshore account. So people drank. And laughed. And enjoyed the extravagance while they could, each knowing full well tomorrow promised nothing but a return to hungover drudgery.

South sat alone at the side of the stage. The hotel's sound system had been hooked up to a phone, and people were taking it in turns to play DJ. An eclectic mix of inoffensive pop and violent niche music. He enjoyed the spectacle, the ever-changing dancing, the confused singing, the celebration. The good thing about volunteer work is they can't garnish your wages and in South's case it wasn't as if the CEO could kill him. At some point, he knew he would have to go to his overpriced suite and prepare for the future, but he was pleased to enjoy a moment of blissful emptiness while volunteers all around him oscillated between popular dance moves.

Someone sat beside him. "Great speech," they said. He turned to look. She looked a lot like Alexandra, but with shorter hair, a few years worn with pride on her face, the light in her eyes now a controlled bonfire.

"You stopped texting me," she said, confirming South's notion she was indeed the woman he had fawned over.

"I know. You stopped too."

"Fair enough. You know how it is, you put something off for so long that by the time you sit down to do it everything feels weird."

"Like you've taken too long."

"Right. I almost didn't come tonight. Free bars are like bug zappers to my soul. And I wasn't sure I was coming for the right reasons. Did you know there's absolutely nothing about you online except your name in one newsletter? How did you avoid the all-seeing eye of social media?"

"Hid in Shelob's layer. And years of applied indifference."

Alexandra looked at her soda, tilting the glass as if enamored with the bubbles inside. "But, uh, but you've been doing all right?"

"I'm staying in the Roosevelt suite upstairs so I must be doing something right."

"Depends on the Roosevelt. It's weird…" she trailed off; conversation wholly different to the one in her imagination. "I started thinking about you again. I know we weren't really much of anything but a few dates, but it's a path I wish I was able to walk down."

"And you come all the way to this dump to tell me?"

"Not really, the research you helped with is in a museum down the road."

"Did they steal it?"

"Not this time. I gave my lifeblood willingly. Better than most can say."

They sat mute, eyes scanning their brains for things to say. Too many options. The music had veered without warning from a Gloria Gaynor ballad to an EDM mashup of The Ramones and LCD Soundsystem. Drunk dancers, strangers a few hours ago, spun around and writhed against each other. At the bar a team of seasoned cynics had found each other, the sort of people you find at nightclubs with arms folded and backs pressed against the wall, slamming shots of tequila and yelling half-remembered statistics at each other.

"So… Would you like to take a walk?" said South, surveying the alternatives.

"Like a real walk, or are we talking about the path metaphor still?"

"Both, I guess."

"I guess, he says. Way to build up my confidence."

They walked to a bridge and looked out at the city. South could remember a time when common people could see the Thames from the riverfront, before everything was sealed, sold, and neutered. Entire stretches of land once full of people now glamorised and exclusive and vacant. New, exciting complexes sat waiting for tenants who would never come. The pair walked with bodies drawing ever closer to each other, a single pulse firing through them both.

"What's next for you, Alvar?"

"I'm not sure. Thought I might come back to Edinburgh for a bit. To recoup."

"To recoup. Right? You didn't… You didn't spend a few years saving the world just to try to win me over, did you?"

"Maybe at the start. Then it turned out I enjoyed doing it."

"Good. I'd hate to help you get reacquainted with the city only to find out this has all been one long con."

"Do guys do that?"

"You'd be surprised what online dating has done to the male psyche."

"OK, so if I'm understanding this, you'd like to see if there's something between us, but only if I am not trying to see if there's something between us?"

"That's some catch, that Catch 22." They looked at the orange glow of the skyline. A distant fire siren cut through the chatter of city life. It felt like it was about to rain, the air growing heavy.

Alexandra continued. "What I mean is, I think we have some unfinished business. I still had a lot of work to do on myself back then, and I know you did too. I've thought a lot about you, about what would happen if we met again, and I miss you. But. I can't sacrifice the time I've spent rebuilding myself if you're just going to kick the foundation out from under me.

"I get it. And I know what you mean. I've missed you, too, even when I all but forgot about you."

The rain came all at once. They ran against near sideways blasts of water back to the hotel and discovered the party was still ongoing, reminiscent of the dance marathons of old without the cash prizes or summer dresses.

They spent the night in the Roosevelt suite. Fully dressed but pressed against each other, probing for a closeness they had both missed. Wrapped in each other's arms, they spent the rest of the night sharing tales of their time apart. It was an intimacy South didn't know, couldn't know, he'd been missing out on for his entire existence. Alexandra fell asleep mid-sentence and South lay there looking up into the darkness and smiling.

Author's Note:

More than a few times, I've checked in on mortals who took my interest. Only once every few decades. Not necessarily in person. The internet really helped me with this. I remember one of the kitchen workers I used to know had this great son. Just a fantastic little boy. He knew little facts about everything. How much Jupiter weighed, the average height of a gallimimus, over fifty theories about what happened to the Roanoke settlement (they turned into cat werewolves and moved to Louisiana). The boy was a pleasure to talk to. He didn't recognise me next time we met. Which was just as well. At that point he was in his early twenties and a lot of the brilliance he had as a boy was gone. No longer eager to share facts or dance or lift his shirt and rub his belly.

One reason he'd withdrawn was he was in love with his professor. They were having an affair. Love and guilt and a desire to be someone else were eating away at him. He was carving himself into what he believed the professor deserved in a lover. This doomed relationship consumed the glow he possessed as a child. It was sad to see.

Next time I check in on him, he must have been forty or fifty. We looked closer in age then, I guess, and so I pretended we'd gone to school together. He bought it. We talked for twenty minutes before I remembered the professor.

"Hey, whatever happened with you and the econ professor, anyway?"

He looked at me for a good thirty seconds, trying to remember. "Who?" he said finally.

And that was it. This person who had shaped so much of their early adulthood was as lost as the facts he used to recite. Funny that. One year you can barely wake up without thinking about someone, stomach flipping with the prospect of seeing them again, and then, not too much later, you can barely remember them. You might suddenly snap into a memory and think, "Oh, yeah, they were special, I wonder what they're up to," but mostly they've become a stranger.

I wonder how many people forgot about me or would act like, insist, they never knew me. I wonder if there are friendships I've forgotten, buried under a thousand worse memories. Sad, painful memories you both fixate on and try not to recall too vividly lest they destroy you again.

The boy wound up marrying a dinosaur expert, so I suppose it all worked out. I wish I could say the same about the rest of them.

No idea what made me think of that.

I am in possession of the few remaining sheets of paper in all existence, and I keep wasting them. Sorry. I know you expected more from me.

The "Americas" — 1178 AD Onward:

With the never-ending whir of battles and crusades, the rise and fall of empires, the permeating scent of North's influence across entire continents, South knew it was time to find a new home. He walked East from his underground home in Alamut and continued through deserts and mountains and jungles, all tainted with memories of old sins. He walked until the land became sand and slipped onward into the ocean. With no land left to walk, he swam ever eastward. South, unlike the so-called intelligentsia of the time, knew the world was rhombus shaped, and so wasn't scared of falling off the edge.

Paddling by islands, carried by currents, and beat down by the elements, South never broke his stare at the horizon. There was something way off in the distance he hoped North had forgotten about. In earlier times, after the major tectonic shifts but before the mass migration of humanity, there were lands almost untouched by their influence. He knew vaguely that large groups of people had escaped to those continents many years prior, and that was it. His hope was they were as unmolested by North's influence as possible.

Swimming ever further, he entertained visions of enlightened civilisations, unconcerned with wealth or faith or subjugation, like the three cities of Atlantis before they turned to ice. He knew it was a foolhardy fantasy–human nature was itself designed to fall for manipulation–and yet he continued to swim, regardless. The alternative was heading back to an incestuous murder waltz and mass executions disguised as martyrdom.

In the middle of a violent storm, sea furious and sky a blinding mist of heavy rain, South saw what he was looking for. Off behind the thick downpour was the unmistakable view of land. Rugged, uninviting coasts with an impenetrable row of fir and pine trees looming overhead. The monstrous waves carried him, tossed him violently into the craggy rocks of the beach.

He lay on the rocks as cold, stinging waves blasted him from all directions, his clothes long since eaten away by the sea. A baptism, a cleansing torrent of purifying water it lapped away his sins. He smelled the salt, the dew, the fog creeping inland, and savoured his rebirth. Then he slept for fifty days.

When he awoke, he found the ocean still, the sky a gentle blue, and the trees alive and inviting. He stood and walked into the forest, admiring the woods, listening for humans, for trouble. When he heard nothing but the birds and crickets, he continued to walk inland.

He walked through forests and plains, taking joy in each new, uncorrupted image. The wilderness, the virgin beauty of a land yet to be desecrated by empires. As he walked toward warmer climates, the land would present fresh visions to him. He peered down into vast canyons and walked barefoot over scorched deserts. Climbed over mountain ranges, stopping at snow-covered peaks to bask in the panoramas. There was a peace within him he had not felt in aeons.

Sometimes he would spy small groups of people communing in small settlements. This confirmed, he hoped, North's reach only extended so far. They didn't seem to be crusading or building palaces, at least. From dusk to dawn he would spy on those people, admiring them, but reluctant to get too close. They were uninfected by North's wrath, and South thought to keep it that way. There was no way to know what his appearance would yield. Far better to stay hidden, a neutral observer. Only bad things happened when he tried to interfere.

Down, down through wilderness he walked, across valleys and plains, over salt flats and rivers, into more forests and jungles, never with a notion of where he had been or where he was going. He walked an ever-changing patchwork of terrains and colours, through what felt like death itself, and onward until life returned all around him.

In time he found himself in a jungle filled with animals he had not seen in many thousands of years. Aberrations of nature he would have once expunged from existence moved freely all around him. The Creator's old orders now a hollow echo in the recesses of South's memory. He was free to admire the life surrounding him, even as spotted giant cats tried in vain to maul him and coiled snakes broke their teeth against his impregnable flesh. He slept naked under the canopies, waking more than once to find some wild beast gumming at his throat.

His years-long saunter was interrupted one day when he heard the roaring of a thousand voices crying out in unison. They were not the pained screams of the dying or the war cries of the victorious, rather almost a cheer. No. Actual cheers. The noise carried through the trees and sent the birds into panicked flight. South walked toward it. In time, the cheering now an almost constant recurrence, he could make out the top of a stone structure peering out over the jungle ahead of him. He walked with a slight skip, imagining what sort of festivities waited before him.

Many centuries later and people would complain of phones and tablets, and how people were too busy staring at them to notice where they were walked. Electronic devices were a new facet of an old problem as South demonstrated. His excited jog through the trees came to an abrupt stop when the ground beneath him gave way to a wide-open cenote he hadn't bothered to notice.

He plummeted into the water below, bouncing twice off the white rock walls on his way down. As he splashed into the murk, he could hear a different roar up above. Whatever the people were shouting at had ended.

South looked up at the circular view of the sky and floated on his back. There was something almost meditative about the bottom of the cenote. Before long, though, he could hear pebbles scuffling under the feet of a hundred approaching people. A loud, authoritative voice called something out from the edge of the ground above. South sank into the water, only the crest of his face visible to anyone who bothered to look. Not that anyone did.

Hidden outside of his line of vision, South could hear an elaborate song and dance number being performed, followed by a reverent silence. Before long, the limp body of a young, lean man was tossed headfirst into the cenote. The body hit the water with a muted plop and sunk. Another cheer erupted above, fading away as the other humans moved away, and silence descended again. When South was sure they were gone, he swam around trying to find the man who fell but found only algae-coated coins and other irrelevant treasures.

As night fell, South climbed up the side of the hole. He slipped and fell a dozen times before making it to the top. Pulling himself out at last, he waddled toward a nearby tree and contemplated his options before making slow, deliberate steps toward the rock structures. There he found a network of pyramids and other elaborate buildings illuminated by a giant full moon. He leaned against a tree and watched the alien terrain until the sun returned, then he sunk back into the trees and watched as the inhabitants of the land began their routine.

For months after that, he hid in the jungle and watched the civilisation, admiring the detachment from the warring crusaders and empires he had given up on.

As the years went on, South explored the continent more boldly. He would travel in whatever direction his mood took him in a search for other civilisations, finding many along the way. His life became a revolving hike across the Americas. South would keep watch over all he could, even naming some inhabitants. Elsewhere, he knew, there was a corrupting power, one his new wards only exhibited early signs of. The oppressive force of North was searching for them, for all of humankind, and it would not rest until it had destroyed them all.

At the time, he felt as if he could protect his chosen people for eternity.

"No creo que sepas lo que estás diciendo. Todo es galimatías."

Valladolid, Mexico — 20__ CE:

South returned to Edinburgh the following week, and for three months he and Alexandra hastily scrambled to reclaim lost time.

The city had changed and so had Alexandra. Her apartment in Makar's Court—the entire centre of town, in fact—had become unaffordable for people living in the city. Whole neighbourhoods had been bought up by oligarchs, property developers, and short-term holiday rental companies. Academia, too, had all but vanished from the area, forcing schools to shift focus to writing code and Alexandra into writing historic travel fiction for family-funded digital nomads.

Her friends had shifted around more time than a bad poker hand. Patrick, her clingy male friend, had taken South's departure as an opportunity to remind Alexandra of their special bond. She did not reciprocate, and Patrick was last seen running an Ayahuasca resort in Thailand under the name Obu Quinlank. Others had married, started families, became embroiled in sex scandals involving politicians and race car drivers, or otherwise disappeared. Mostly, people who disappear from each other's lives don't even realise they've done it until too late. Goodbyes are often the first thing people forget to say. Gone were the dates spent standing silently at Alexandra's side while she talked to a dozen friends, replaced instead by quiet nights at empty jazz bars or curled up in front of screens watching old shows about rich people being friends with other rich people.

Then came the trip.

Suggesting the title HOW TO LIVE LIKE AN AUTHENTIC JAGUAR IN MEXICO, Alexandra's editor wanted to send her to the Yucatan for a more authentic story. Who better to write about Mexico than a Scottish woman who had been to Chile once? She thought it would be nice to surprise South with a trip for two. How could she know, after all, that Alvar the well-travelled adventurer had unfathomable secrets? He received his gift with the faux excitement of someone receiving their thirteenth Christmas sweater from their kind grandmother. He knew, though, that to move forward, he had to let go of one last chunk of his incredibly long past. That, and he'd grown accustomed to snuggling into Alexandra at night.

They stayed in Valladolid. The coastal towns had been taken up by all-inclusive resorts and hostels, tavernas replaced by American eateries. People could spend a month in Cancun without mumbling a single por favor. A new motto for travellers in the twenty-first century: visit while you still can, because it will be underwater or a gift shop before long, but for heaven's sake don't talk to the locals.

Valladolid had already felt the tentative probes of inquisitive foreigners wanting to claim a part of the land for themselves, but still felt largely unmolested. The public cenotes, the sun-bleached colonial plaza, the idling colectivos tucked away near the ADO station. It was a beautiful town. One that reminded South of easier times.

For the first few days they strolled through the town looking at the small museums, the religious buildings, the tiny restaurants scattered down tight roads. Alexandra enjoyed discovering plaques that told stories from different perspective. Men called privateers in England were known as pirates, their faces placed mugshot-style above maps of colonial trade routes. Displays and exhibits in major museums were stolen property according to people who'd much rather have them back if it's all the same, muchas gracias. History has many faces, most of them hidden.

It was a town worth the visit. South enjoyed how unbothered the locals were and how most of his fellow tourists were more interested in exploring and talking than filming bad videos. But there was a knot in his stomach. He knew what was coming. The last time he had seen the ruins of Chichen Itza, Ek Balam, or Tulum they were full of people, just not sunburnt interlopers in sandals. He wondered how he would react to entering the living tombs of his past. Would he lash out as if there were thieves in the temple? Would he fall to his knees and mourn the forgotten dead?

Neither of those things.

On the fifth day they took a minibus to the ruins of Chichen Itza. Alexandra excited to check a World Wonder off her bucket list, South fearing his own unconscious reactions. They lined up with the early morning crowd, an hour before the Cancun busses would arrive in the parking lot, and walked, almost alone, through the trees onto the first opening. Still as majestic as South remembered it five hundred years before. But the people, the lost people, would never be there again. Instead, market stalls being set up by diligent workers, couples with their cameras out searching for strangers to take their photo, lone tourists who'd done their research clapping meekly at the ruins, and misty-eyed pilgrims at the end of their search fighting back happy tears as they engorged themselves on the view. "Should we?" said Alexandra. Without waiting for a response, she wrapped her hand around South and held her camera at an angle so that both they and El Castillo were in shot.

"I don't like my photo being taken," said South.

"Just this one time. I want people to know I'm happy. And the reason why."

A tender nod. "Go ahead."

They walked through the ruins for hours. Alexandra admiring the history, quoting half-remembered nuggets of information she learned in her university days. She was in her element, which had become a rare occurrence.

South watched her and smiled. All around him two realities, the past and the present, vying for his mind's attention. He focused instead on how Alexandra would try in vain to hide an excited little bounce every time they turned a corner or found stonework hidden among the vines. Seeing her so satisfied, so unrelentingly giddy to be there soothed the bitter memories of a stolen past.

As prophesied, the professional tour groups appeared like the invaders of old. All Birkenstocks and cargo shorts and five-figure camera rigs. With them, the fake jaguar roars of vendors and the chatter of strangers. Their moment of tranquillity had ended. South walked past the ball court and toward the sacred cenote with the anticipation and dread of someone attending a reunion. Strange that it would become the site of two of his rebirths. He stood as close to the precipice as was allowed and looked down. The bottom unchanged, a languid sapphire pool of secrets.

"Are you OK?" Alexandra asked him.

He looked at her. A newfound urge to confess his past. How could he not? He had never felt for anyone the way he felt for this woman, and yet he alone knew he would one day bury her. The need waned. Not the place to admit to immortality. Instead, he took her hands and looked into her eyes.

"I'm happy we came here."

They returned to the town via colectivo and looked for somewhere to eat. The only place open was an Italian restaurant on the Plaza de la Candelaria. A round table for two took up the middle of the room and gave an unobstructed view through the old wooden doors. They sat there feeling the breeze and eating pizza as the sky grew dark and a storm came in, its flashes lighting up the outside world. Outside were white chairs shaped like the Pisces sign, where lovers could sit facing each other, arms interlinked. There would be time for that later.

In time they made their way to their room. Damp from rain and sweat, exhausted by early morning cramped drives and the unrelenting heat, they were relieved to be near a shower and a bed. Their room was a long, narrow cavernous room, off on its own behind the rest of the hostel. There they kissed with a passion South had never experienced before.

"You've been very patient. Three years and change," Alexandra said, a hint of wine to her words. She undressed and stood by the foot of the bed.

"Yes," South said. A few hundred more than that, in fact.

They kissed again. Alexandra all but pulling his body into her own, their limbs entwined, breathing synchronised and faint. She stopped for a second and looked at him. His body was warm and inviting, but his eyes were looking into another world.

"Is everything good? You've been in two places all day."

South nodded and pulled back. The urge to confess returned. "I need to tell you something, Alexandra."

She flopped to the bed and looked down, dreading what was to come. "Well, what is it? Someone else? An STD? You don't really like me? That's it, isn't it? We should have tried the first time around. I knew I shouldn't have gone to that ceremony. I'm…"

South sat beside her and wrapped an arm around her waist, pulling her in close. "Alexandra, I'm roughly a hundred and sixty million years old and I will never die."

"Ah… Wha… Oh."

Bob's Fun Room, Los Angeles, 1949:

"Got a good feeling about the Rams this year, how about you Hank?" asked Roberto, a bartender with a jawline made for a romantic lead but whose mangled nose was designed for a punch-drunk boxer. Or that's what he a casting director told him.

"I'd take that bet," said Hank, the unkempt regular who clung to dark corners like Nosferatu on Demerol.

Claudio was slouching toward Mulholland Drive. He'd been drinking since noon but had yet to experience the numbness he was looking for.

Outside, the unrelenting California sun beat down on the road, light pouring through the open door and turning the exterior into an impenetrable white glow, the sort dying people claim they see before the CPR works.

Inside, Bob's Frolic Room did its best to appear dingy despite the squint-inducing light from outside. It smelled of damp, musty sweat stains, ammonia, spilt beer, and yesterday's cigarettes. Hank and Claudio were the only regulars inside, and they never talked to each other. At the bar, as far from Claudio's side as possible, an old man sat hunched over a pile of coins, counting how many more beers he could afford with the arithmetic skills of the professional drunk. A trio of young women sat waiting for one of the actors rumoured to be making an appearance later in the day. The entire bar a nest of rumours. Everything from Elizabeth Short's killer living in the basement to the backroom dalliances of confirmed bachelors were half-believed fictions. The whispers of the town's supposed underbelly drove people from all over the country to visit, and they would languish in dive bars and old hotels, trying to pretend they were part of the scene. Some imagined they were taking part in a Raymond Chandler novel, others creating stories of their own. Morbid tourism, even in those days, was an antiquated hobby.

"How about you, Claude? You feeling the Rams?" Roberto leaned in, pouring a generous serve into a fresh glass.

"I don't care about no Rams, but why are you dirtying a fresh glass?"

"The one you've been drinking from has reached retirement." He dumped the old glass behind the bar. "You doing all right?"

"Sure, bud. Leave the bottle, huh?"

Roberto took his hand from the bottle and walked off to make busywork near the hunchback. As the day went on, people would wander in and out, the curious, the destitute, and the drunk, all wandering without direction in search of the next stop. Claudio sat unmoving and untouched. He had nowhere to go.

He stumbled into Los Angeles at the end of the war and had continued to stumble ever since. Far from putting people off, his indifference was something of a rare quality in a city where ambition and dreams ruled supreme. A few minor acting roles, a writing credit, and Claudio was made. All because he was the only one in a full of hopefuls with no hope left. He felt guilty, how the less he cared, the more successful he was. It only fueled his self-hatred, his guilt, his newfound propensity to waste entire days pouring hooch down his throat.

"Urgle burgle," he said, gas escaping his stomach.

"I feel you, guy," Hank called out.

A chorus of reverent gasps from outside the bar. Wooden stools screamed as their owners swivelled their attention to the door. Excited chuntering at the tables, stressed vowels popping in the air as underaged women with good looks and big plans tried to keep their composure. "Lil" Nellie was coming in. She was that rare upcoming actress who looked better, taller, friendlier, almost regal, in person. The others Claudio had met seemed like miniature grotesque mannequins of themselves. But not Nell.

She entered with two of her minders. Lars O'Mackie, a former gumshoe turned hired muscle, and Nicky Morningstar, the occultist and alleged mobster. The studio had provided her with the two slabs of muscle. Secret geniuses both who within a decade would be lost to the sands of Joshua Tree for reasons unknown. They stood at her side like Gothic gargoyles watching over their minuscule treasure. Not so close her personal space was invaded, but not so far away they couldn't dismantle anyone drunk, dumb, or suicidal enough to get close to her.

Nell sat by Claudio, the most drunk, dumb, suicidal man on the West Coast. She waved over at Roberto like they were old friends. He nodded in return but kept his distance.

"You've been here all day?" she asked Claudio.

"Just one of those weeks, Nell."

"You've been saying that since we wrapped El Mentiroso. Don't you think it's time you told me what's bugging you?"

He looked at the two empty bottles of scotch sitting in front of him and wished he could get drunk. How he envied the young, star-struck newcomers at the far end of the bar and their ability to find freedom at the bottom of a glass. "Promise you won't laugh, Nell?"

"No. Since when do I make promises?"

Claudio nodded and retrieved a battered photo from his wallet. It had been protected with tape about thirty years too late. A familiar face stood in prominence with a cadre of recruited prospectors and former scalp hunters standing behind him. "This is from, what, 1853. I think."

Nell looked at the photo. "Now come on, you're a geezer, but you're not that old. This can't be real."

"I'm older than some of those dinosaurs in the tar pit out there. I helped build the pyramids and hung out with Mayan priests and pirates and knights, played cowboy with the not-so-fine gentlemen in the picture you're holding. Heck, I even hit the hay with an empress a while back."

"Jesus, Claudio, did you drink both bottles?"

"What if I did?"

"Fine. Let's say I believe you, what have you got to be miserable about?"

"Just, I don't know. What's the point, is all? I spent six years trying to end the war and couldn't do shit. I spent hundreds of years before that failing too. For all my power, I'm impotent. I can't stop the bad things from happening without killing you all."

"You were in the war?"

"Honey, I was in all sorts of wars. And I haven't accomplished a damn thing. You can't save everyone."

"No, I suppose you can't, Claudio, but there's nothing stopping you from saving the ones you can."

"That's just it, though. Why bother? I save you from one war, you're just going to die in the next. Or get old. Or hit by a bus. Or shot by one of your gorilla friends here. There's no escaping it, Nell. Unless you're me, then it's all too inescapable."

Nell stole a sip from Claudio's glass and looked at the silty mirror behind the bar for a few minutes, imagining her face as warped and ruined as it was in the reflection. She coughed. "So, let's say you're telling the truth here and this isn't some booze-soaked and overly elaborate practical joke. Let's assume that, and my answer would be this: so what? Is skulking around here or Shangri-La or Ken's going to help anyone? This little pity party of your is just making it worse for people."

"Maybe, but—"

"But nothing. If something has got you down, there are two things you can do: wallow in it or use it. The choice is yours."

For a moment it seemed like only Nell and Claudio were moving, the rest of the bar frozen in time. For a moment. Before too long, a wily reporter appeared from behind the snoozing Hank and rushed to take flashbulb photos of Nell and her soon-to-be-alleged beau. He was about to follow up one intrusion with another when Lars' squid like hand wrapped around the reporter's mouth and dragged him out of the back exit where he was introduced to such concepts as respect, personal boundaries, and the way small specks of gravel with dig into bloodied flesh if someone is dropped onto the floor enough times.

Claudio and Nell remained seated as if nothing had happened, both lost in their conversation. Nell stood up and smoothed out her dress. "Claudio, the choice is yours, so what's it going to be?"

"Are you leaving already?"

"We are, and that's not an answer."

He pushed his stool back and got to his feet. Fresh blood, or whatever ran through him, returned to his legs. Arguing with Nell was a fool's errand, and he'd been foolish enough. "Where to, boss?" he said, his attempts at being sardonic and decided failure.

"Thought we'd stop in next door and take in Beyond the Forest. Then we have a meeting with Howard."

"I'm not sure I trust your choice in pictures after the Capricorn fiasco. And I'm not sure Howard wants to talk to me right now."

"Nonsense. He wants me in some detective story, and I said I'd only do it if you got to play the private eye. We'll have a love scene and everything."

"I don't want to do a love scene with you."

"That's exactly why you're the only man in town for the job."

"But I'm not sure I want to be in films."

"Would you just stop whining for a minute, Claudio? It's a quick and easy gig and people will forget all about it by this time next year. For a man who's lived forever, you sure have little sense for adventure."

"Fine, I'll talk to Howard. I don't imagine being in a film is going to hurt any."

Television, 20__ CE:

"And finally, tonight, a strange story that involves a Hollywood actor who has been missing for over sixty years and a young charity worker's recent holiday snap that has some people on the internet asking if they're actually the same person. Becky."

"Val. That's right. It all started last month when an Alvar South was photographed by his girlfriend. Thanks to automated face-matching and curious followers, Alvar's face was found to be a perfect match for Claudio Sud. Some of our senior viewers may remember Claudio from the Golden Age of Cinema and his sudden and mysterious disappearance in the early fifties. But this is where it gets weird, Val, as you can see from these other photos Alvar also looks like this soldier from the Battle of the Somme, a militiaman from the frontier days, and numerous miners, oil riggers, and kitchen workers. This week alone he's been matched with over two dozen people thanks to archival photos."

"And, Becky, it is also true it appears his likeness has shown up in everything from stone carvings to Jack the Ripper sketches?"

"That's right, Val. While obviously not as accurate as the photographs, a man matching his description has shown up in several historical portraits with more being found every day. We're not sure what to conclude from all of this, but many are beginning to speculate just how and why this man's face is so prevalent throughout history."

"Oh, aye, he were Richter back then. He came t'work in t'mines with me dad back in... oh, about fifty-five. Showed up with nowt but his kegs. I were a bairn back then, like, but I remember him."

"And did he seem off to you at the time? Anything to suggest he was an immortal?"

"Nah, I can't think of owt."

"Thank you. Back to you, Shirley."

"The Willis Faroe Bank has announced they will be conducting a full investigation into the withdrawals made from the Claudio Sud Memorial Fund. While they acknowledge that nothing illegal happened per se, a spokesperson today has stressed that their bank only functions with other people's money and they need the accrued interest more than the fund's owner."

"Now you've been around for a lot of years. If I've got the science right, you've been alive the entire six thousand years this planet has existed. Don't you think, sir, that the real problem, sir, is the so-called liberal intelligentsia and their reductive, excuse me, post-modern Marxist approach to totalitarianism?" the television host read from his cue cards, the cheque from oil barons already cleared in his account.

"Not particularly," said South via satellite.

"Let me finish, please, sir. I wasn't done talking. The real problem, as I am sure a man of your age is aware, isn't quote unquote rich people or shortages. No. It's this entitled, scruffy millennial belief that everyone deserves everything for free. We have movies coming out these days where they've clearly inserted hack actors to appease their whining baby audiences. We have…" this went on for some time. For brevity's sake he talked about the following, using seven hundred words where none would do: feminism, social justice warriors, people who are simultaneously incompetent idiots and in control of the world, how minority protesters are the real Nazis and how feeding and clothing the poor went against the teachings of The Bible. All peppered with the odd "No, sir, please let me finish" directed at silence.

"Are you done?" South asked finally.

"Yes, now are you going to answer the question?"

"I don't remember the question. It feels like you've just brought me onto television to talk about the same things you talk about every day."

"Sir, these are important topics, sir."

"It just seems like you're choosing to get upset about things that have no impact on your personal well-being when there's so many bigger issues out there right now. The world is burning, and you're worried about hypothetically getting arrested for talking to people you're never going to go out of your way to meet? Who is paying you to say this ridiculous stuff?"

"I haven't finished, sir, please don't interrupt me again or we'll end this interview."

"I'm sorry. Go ahead."

"... That's better. You were saying?"

"Well, it just seems if you were a little less intellectually bankrupt, you'd be able to notice that most of your big problems are the result of the capitalist structure you're refusing to critique—"

"Shut up."

"I mean, it's not clandestine gangs of teenagers ruining movies, it's billion-dollar production companies run by people you probably hang out with. They're the ones courting advertising money and pussyfooting around inclusivity in such a way that they make a slither of a percentage more money. It's…"

"Please shut up."

"The public aren't creating censorship, it's amoral networks and publishers and websites scared of losing revenue and doing whatever they can to make as much money as possible. So, they milk whatever is successful until the next thing comes along. That could be you and your attempts at sophistry, or it could be yet another remake of some boring film except this time around the boring lead is a boring woman instead of a boring man. It's all the same. It's all part of the combine, man, so don't pretend you're not a part of the same system that churns out historical erotic literature every day. They don't care about anything but…"

"No, you shut up. Shut up right now."

"It seems to me that most of your complaints about the world should be directed at the upper echelons of power and not defenceless teenagers and poor people. Although, I guess if you had that kind of integrity you'd be out of a job, huh?"

"I've asked you repeatedly and very politely to let me finish. You've done nothing but interrupt me. I don't need this commie rhetoric on my show. Capitalism might not be perfect, but it's the best thing we have."

"I've heard that said about a hundred different systems. If you don't remove outdated systems, you can only progress so far. It's like being sixteen and saying, 'hey, I read Atlas Shrugged, I don't need to develop as a human being anymore.' Although, actually, yeah, seems that's exactly what you did."

"Sir, I—"

"Not wanting to progress as a society because you're fine with the current status quo is unambitious, cowardly, and frankly detrimental to society. I thought you were a forward-thinking intellectual?"

"You are very rude, sir. I am cancelling this debate and I am the winner. Mark it up, Tony!"

In the studio a giant scoreboard was lowered from the rafters. Debates Won with FACTS emblazoned in flashing neon lights proclaimed the host's 2,000,053rd debate win streak. Years later, the same television host would be forced to stand by his paid for opinions after his own daughter's partner was gunned down by police. The family seeing with sudden clarity the host was in all ways a fraud and mercenary with no moral compass of their own triggered an irreparable domino effect. Divorce, unemployment, alienation, public ridicule, a redemption arc begun too late to change anything. In his sunset years, the host died a slow death. Alone, unwanted, a relic of a bygone era making a gradual descent into purgatory while living in a black mould encrusted, flooded Lower-Manhattan apartment he couldn't sell because it was partially submerged.

"Course, I'm immortal too, but nobody ever believes me when I tell them."

"Yes, but this man has a plethora of documented evidence that seems to back up his claims."

"He didn't even claim it, though. It just got announced on the TV one day. But if you want evidence, I'm immortal, have a look at this."

Screams from the live audience as the established politician unholstered a chrome .450 and levelled it against their dome.

"Now, shit, look, you don't have to do anything drastic. We believe you, OK? Don't we, everyone? Let's hear it for this immortal."

Stunted applause from an audience trying to writhe unseen to the nearest exit.

"No! That's just lip service. I've had enough of that for a lifetime. I'm going to prove I'm immortal and I challenge that chundering dunderhead to do the same."

"Please don't, we're live."

A sonic blast as the egotistical and newly deceased politician eliminated their own map and fell to the floor. Arterial spray and brain matter already dripping from the steel girders above. The audience and crew watched the twitching corpse with anticipation, hoping for a miracle. They screamed almost in unison when their denial ran out and the producer cut to a commercial for pro-LGBT t-shirts made by children in a country with a death penalty for homosexuality.

"Now I know some of you have a lot of questions. An immortal? In England, of all places? Surely, you are saying, this means there is no God after all? Ha! I say, ha! Actually, the opposite is true. I talked to God for an hour more than usual last night and He said that it just shows how scared Satan is these days. We have almost won against the Dark One, my children. Almost won! And that is why he is resorting to wicked new tricks. He is a coward in the night with one last hand of chess to be played. But we know he's bluffing, yes Lord. And we have God on our side. That is why we're asking all y'all kind folk to double, no, quadruple your tithing this week. And all future weeks. Our holy congregation has almost bested Satan, it is true. Your continued support will allow me to personally confront him on my own private island. Now, we don't have this private island yet, and that is why we're asking for more than just tithes. Please call the number below to help us purchase a holy yacht and a blessed private island and hire a divine and godly architect. Do not delay. Judgement day is close at hand."

"Big news about immortals these days, but what does that mean for producer power couple Rich and Jenny Bloom and their new film The Man Who Could Have Died Any Time but Didn't? Will this hurt their chances come award season? Find out next. But first, a look at fresh rumours about Mick Havaway and Allison Stone's new baby? Is Mick the real father? Is Allison the real mother? This Staten Island psychic says no."

"Whose business is it is he is immortal? Don't we have bigger issues at hand?"

"But don't you think he has a responsibility to—"

"No."

"You don't think he owes—"

"Listen. You work for one of the largest multinational media conglomerates in the world, yeah? Are you personally responsible for all the weird stuff you company gets up to? How many mass shooters have you inspired? How many genocides have you downplayed because they weren't happening in popular countries? How many of your bosses—that one over there, even —are known rapists who never went to jail? What's your responsibility?"

"Well, that's completely different."

"It's the exact same thing. Leave the man alone."

"All right. Some conflicting opinions down here on the street, but this is one story that won't go away—"

"—Yeah, because you won't let it go away."

"But we'll be right here as more information comes out. Back to you, Constance."

"Thank you, Virgil. And up next, she's a reclusive author who doesn't like making public appearances or being photographed. Find out what she said when we found her home address and investigated her living space. That's after these messages."

"Hey, it's me, Rocco Molero. You might remember me from hit action movie Iron Cop 6: Oh, Unholy Fight. I'm here today to talk about this new testosterone booster available only on my website. You may have heard about this immortal punk on television recently, but did you know he uses this same ancient Chinese supplement found exclusively in Alpha Supremo? That's right. I guess you could say me and this guy aren't too different after all, thanks to these sacred oriental herbs and spices and antioxidants that boost male virility and lengthen life expectancy. Who wants to live forever? I do. And that's why I used Alpha Supremo five times a day. Use promo code ROCCOSSECRET to save five percent off your first annual order."

South's Living Room, etcetera, 20__ CE:

His foot was somewhere on the other side of the television screen, now a shattered black pane giving out brief flashes of purples and greens as it died. It seemed like a great idea in the instant he did it, to kick in his only television, but doubt set in a half second too late for him to do anything other than look at his ankle sinking through the shattered glass and cracked plastic. It was only after the momentary release of breaking something he remembered all the criticality acclaimed miniseries he had yet to finish. Replacing the set wouldn't be difficult, but that wasn't the point. The fact was, any number of television stores would have loved the opportunity to imply their deals cause immortality.

Which was one reason he had just kicked apart his television. The first few weeks post-revelation were exhilarating enough. Attention for the first time in ages. A platform. People pretended to care what he had to say if it allowed them to either feign offence or confirm pre-existing beliefs. He could kid himself he was important, a delusion even South wasn't immune to. The novelty wore off within a month. Like a sitcom which should have ended after four seasons, things soon became predictable and boring. People weren't interested in his immortality the way scholars are interested in old books and new facts. They wanted something from him, either to commodify his very essence or confirm pre-existing opinions. Some people wanted film rights to his story, a story they would subsequently ignore and repurpose for their own ends. Others saw him as a way to create revenue, settle arguments, or to use as propaganda. Nobody really cared about him or his experiences.

He'd expected huge queues of strangers looking for the secrets of time and space. But outside of the gaze of the internet, 24-hour news, and rabid consumerism, nobody seemed to care he was an ageless being. It was as if the public collectively took one look at him, realised that for all his permanence even he had been reduced to working in restaurants and call centres, and had a good long think about their own existence. Perhaps, they thought, growing old and dying wasn't so bad after all. At least their lifelong drudgery had a finish line.

The speed at which his face was matched with so many past identities was not something he could have anticipated. One moment he was boarding a plane in Merida, making the slow return home with a confused-but-supportive girlfriend, the next he was disembarking at Gatwick, greeted by the smirks of strangers. He was the punchline of a joke he hadn't heard. By the time they'd gone through immigration, Alexandra's phone was unusable, and South knew his days of anonymity were gone for at least ten generations.

Alexandra was the first to realise what it all meant for South. For them both. With a misty-eyed certainty, she walked him out to the taxi stand and apologised for what was about to happen.

And sure enough, the following days had teetered somewhere between invasive and banal, like a proctology exam. With his secret out, it was harder for him to volunteer, or to do anything he enjoyed, without some predatory stranger looking to add their own subtext. Anything for a quick buck or a hundred thousand likes or upvotes or shares. He could feel the modest life he'd carved for himself slipping away, replaced with meaningless attention. All sense of self, of identity, began to slip away, and he began to think maybe he did owe the entire world something by virtue of being so old. And that was about the time he decided to kick the television in. That and they'd just announced a Buckaroo Banzai remake with a cast of precocious preteens.

Removing his foot from the jagged remains of his television took time and precision. He was wearing some new pants. Not an impressive revelation by any means, but Alexandra had bought him the pants for an "important meeting," so he felt protective over them. He didn't want to tear the fabric, despite his own impulses being the only reason it was a concern to begin with. He also didn't want to have to explain why he destroyed an innocent television set when there was a power button right there on his remote and an entire world outside.

With enough finagling, he freed himself and hid the remains of the dead set under a blanket. The slight knotting on the inseam was only noticeable if you were looking for it. He left his new apartment and wound his way down into an underground parking lot. Alexandra was waiting in her car. Any excursion, big or small, had all at once become as clandestine as a paramilitary training exercise.

"Oh, what did you do to your pants?" said Alexandra before his entire body was inside the car.

"Caught them on something. Sorry."

"I don't mind. It's just we're going somewhere with a dress code."

"Don't worry about it."

She looked at him with an amicable amount of distrust. "Please don't try to do that thing again."

"I have no idea what you're talking about."

"Yes, you do. The thing. You know: 'Oooh, everyone, look at me, I'm immortal and important so you better give me a bottle of wine on the house and upgrade my hotel room, so it has an ocean view.' That thing."

"Oh, that thing."

"Yes. That thing. It's embarrassing for everyone involved. Especially you."

"How is it embarrassing for me?"

"Aren't you too old to be acting like an entitled minor celebrity?"

"But I am an entitled minor celebrity. Besides, you love it."

"Ok, fine," she drove to the exit ramp, "I admit it can be funny in small doses. But not today, please. Please."

They drove toward a large hotel in the middle of town, the type of place visiting dignitaries would stay back when international relations were still a thing. To the right of the car was an entire day-trip worth of adventures: parks, museums, galleries, church towers, old streets, a castle, five coffee shops making familiar claims about former customers. To the left: phone stores, one after the other, frantic and underpaid consumers, everything-must-go closing sales, the homeless. South thought of all the effort put into pretending what was happening on the left didn't exist.

"Are we going to that hotel?" South asked as they parked beneath the hotel.

"Worried you'll bump into a ghost you know?"

"Ghosts don't exist any more."

Alexandra was stumped.

"They stopped existing in 1705. Everyone knows that. Why are we here?" asked South.

"I wanted you to meet someone. An old friend. Kind of a big deal in government PR or something, but nobody's perfect. No ghosts, huh?"

"Why?"

"You're the one who was alive in 1705, you tell me."

"Because… No, why do you want me to meet this person?"

"Because I want a threesome, Alvar."

South's limbs set, rigor mortis style, as those syllables bounced down his ear canal. "Uh… I don't know if I. I mean. I guess. If it's something you want to do, I'm sure we can—"

"Relax, hot stuff, I'm messing with you. I'm scared the whole world knowing you're immortal is going to get out of hand, so I thought I'd get some other opinions. You just want to get back to hiding around your living room, and that's fine, but we need help to make that happen."

"I'm sure people will forget about it soon enough. Just like in 1705."

"Sure, but just on the off chance this is the one time they can maintain attention on one thing for more than three days."

He took her hand and entered the elevator. "Let's go see this friend then."

"Oh, and hey, good to know you'd be up for a threesome."

"I never…"

"Hush."

Baby blues and whites, as delicate as a chalk outline, made up the treacly colour scheme of the hotel's restaurant. They walked by small groups of former débutantes who sat dissecting poached eggs as if living on another sphere of time. Scurrying waitstaff tried their best to get the guests to leave, suggesting the kitchen was shifting menus or by ferreting away utensils from under the inattentive noses of the diners. The room was like a museum, both in it preserved the simple and sophisticated palette of a bygone age and that it smelled of dust and stuffed animals. Specifically, it smelled of the civil war room tucked away above the rotunda in Boston's MFA. Even after the diners stopped eating, there seemed to be a constant chinking of cutlery and fine China.

In the reserved section near the kitchen stood a man who did not seem to want to be there. Or anywhere. He wore a loose suit like disgruntled customer service representatives wear smiles. Stood with a slouch, one knee jutting out. An old war wound. His eyes were consciously trying not to look at the asymmetrical layout of the knives and forks. His fingers played an invisible toy piano. Clare de Lune.

"Dean!" said Alexandra. They hugged just as soon as they could. "Alvar, this is Dean Mund. Dean Mund, meet the immortal Alvar South."

Dean limped toward him and extended a hand. "Pleased to meet you, Alvar. I've heard a lot about you."

South looked at Alexandra.

"On the internet, I mean," Dean continued. "I did some research. Maybe read a few too many articles. Do you prefer Alvar or Claudio or Richter or Nigel or Edwin of Todd or Jeb or—"

"South is fine. That much is a real name."

Dean nodded. "Good, we can work with the truth. That's good. Shall we?" He made his way to the nearest table and sat down, stretching his weaker leg out fully.

"Work with what?" South said. "And why are you so interested?"

Dean scratched his face. "I wouldn't say interested. Scared. Scared is what I am."

"Of me?"

"No, if you were going to kill us all, you'd have done it years ago. And who could blame you, honestly? No, my fear isn't so much about you, but what you could represent to the government. No, that's not quite accurate," he clenched and unclenched his hands. "All governments. That's what I mean to say. There are whispers here and abroad already, and I'm not sure what they're up to. It could be a lot of things."

"Like what?"

"Eh, they could scapegoat you for stuff, wash their hands of old blood. Or they could use you to justify wars or racism or sexism or–just pick an ism. It just takes the right spin and people could use you to prop up all sorts of dark shit."

Alexandra rolled her eyes. "Of course, someone's going to try and exploit you. You're a real boy now, Alvar."

"That's not the worst of it, Alex," Dean said with a familiarity South ignored. "I'm concerned they might try to use your being around to maintain the status quo. You know, the one that's slowly killing us all."

"But I did nothing."

"That's precisely what they're going to say, South. If a legitimate ancient being couldn't stop slavery or the uneven distribution of wealth, why should governments of fallible mortals be expected to do any better?"

"Brioche?" a waiter plopped a heavy plate of breads onto the table while a second swung a carafe of coffee around.

Once the staff were gone, Alexandra leaned forward with bread in hand. "Your actual concern is my guy being used as an out for soulless politicians and corporate types. I knew you hadn't sold out completely, Deano."

Dean tilted his head and grinned. "Even self-hating publicists have scruples. Sometimes."

South could sense incoming in-jokes and political statements and didn't want to listen to either before their food arrived. He swallowed his sourdough and rested an elbow on the table. "What are you proposing?"

Dean sipped his coffee. "I think this may be our one chance to play them at their own game. Unify the masses. If we, you, uh, we can get ahead of it, you might set the narrative a little. Because, really, the world is all but over and this could be it for us if we keep arguing about increasingly minor differences of opinion. While the… They, the rich, those in power, the controlled media, they're going to be coming for you soon enough, just wait and see if you don't believe me. And maybe you can't die, but I can. Alexandra can. All those villages and towns you helped around the world, they're going to either burn or drown within a hundred years. So that's my confession: I'm being a little selfish in approaching you. But I have your interests at heart too, South. You and Alex should get to enjoy your time together, not find yourselves broken on the wheel."

It was at that exact moment South first acknowledged Alexandra would one day die. He mourned this realisation. Alexandra's hand reached out and found his wrist.

"And how much is this going to cost?" South asked.

Dean shook his head. "I wouldn't worry about it. Pro bono doesn't extend to this kind of work, I don't think, but I'm not interested in money. The rest you can get for free. It's amazing how much free publicity you can get once eyes are already on you. All I personally ask for in return for helping is you don't let these people off the hook. When they come for you, I want them held accountable."

There was a moment of silence. Five moments of silence. Dean had a look on his face as if he were resisting the urge to ask something. "Can I…" he began, before mumbling into a piece of bread.

South looked at him. "I have a rule, Dean, it's a new one. I didn't need it last year. I know people are interested in the past, but I will only answer one question per person."

"I haven't used mine yet," Alexandra said with a smirk, walking the line between sincerity and irony.

"There's just one caveat," South added, "No religious questions. Trust me, you don't want to know. But if you want to ask something, and it looks like you do, feel free."

Dean sunk into his chair and looked to the ceiling. His hands danced across the table as he tried to visualise his question. There were so many possibilities but too so many assumptions. South could talk for days about his old friend Diogenes, but people thought he had the gossip on Plato or Pythagoras. He'd lived in lost civilisations and travelled continents and lived under water, but nobody ever asked about those. And why should they, when they could ask about Marilyn Monroe or Dracula? Hand dance over, Dean sat upright, folded his arms, and nodded.

"OK, I think I have it. Think." Dean paused, ensuring he had the wording just so. "What's a commonly held fact about history you know to be a complete fabrication?"

South smiled. "Ha, that one's easy."

Author's note:

I don't remember what I told Dean when he asked. It could have been a lot of things. Even facts have a way of drifting in and out of your consciousness. Really, though, history itself is the biggest fabrication of all. Even my eyewitness accounts had bias, so what chance does the rest of the history of the planet have? Think of all the leaders and artists and healers and thinkers who were forgotten before you were born. You can't. Because they were already forgotten by the time you came around. Sure, some people may have a vague knowledge of them, a blurb in place of their biography, but mostly, they're lost forever. Just like the rest of you at this point. I've made it a point to forget about certain people while I'm lost up here because they didn't deserve the courtesy of existing anymore. I have that power now, don't you know?

There's a through line in history that goes like this: Someone makes a stand, others get inspired, motivated, start asking the wrong questions, and then that person is murdered for their troubles. Even the history books do a poor job covering this up. Advisors of the King bravely meet with the scoundrel to negotiate a fairer society and then change their mind and kill them. Roguish leader inspires a region and then, just as things are looking good, they're stabbed courageously in the back by an assassin. Outspoken, loving, charismatic freethinker unites the masses against a common oppressor and then gets mounted on some wood. And so on. It's happened countless times. More than I remember. The status quo goes on even as the spilled blood cools.

Worse than that, though, were all the many millions of great minds who died in anonymity. Maybe they were too busy being worked to death, or maybe they weren't objectively attractive enough for anyone to pay them any mind, but there were so many people out there with nothing but potential who were bashed against the rocks and cast into the sea.

I remember one guy was around back when kings and queens were still figuring out their stories. Divine rights and all that. He would claim that, no, he was the divine king of the region, and he'd refuse to pay taxes or yield to others. He didn't last long. Apparently it was first come, first served as far as claiming to be chosen by god was concerned. Odd how that worked. Odd how they'd get holy visits, calling for wars and taxes that only really benefited their immediate family. You'd never get someone saying, "Oh, I talked to my higher being last night, and they said we should give all our money to someone else." No, it always seemed to go one way.

That guy had the right idea, though. Imagine if we all played by the same made up rules. Oh well.

This is what I'm talking about, though, because even though I *do* remember some of these people, this mini memoir of mine can only cover so much ground and I don't want to dilute my memories of you with a thousand unrelated things. See? Even after saying what I just said, I'm damning these people. And those are just the ones I can recall. What about everyone else?

I suppose even when you're as ancient as I am, you miss out on a lot of things. I wonder how many great people were out there doomed to obscurity thanks to chance or censorship or murder. Probably not worth thinking about, huh?

I Am an Immortal Entity AMA:

Hello, I'm South. Yes, that's my real name, and yes, the entomology behind it is confusing. I was recently revealed to be an immortal being thanks to unregulated deep data breaches and Orwellian social media practices. I am the only living thing to have seen the dinosaurs (and I'm not talking about the underrated television show), I have hung out with people like a young Aleister Crowley, Howard Hughes, and Kublai Khan, and I briefly worked at an Edinburgh-based call centre, so there's a good chance I tried to sell your grandparents useless insurance. Since then, I have shifted my focus to volunteer with some amazing charity organisations and at least one which wastes 90% of its donations on useless extravagance. It's been a mixed bag of a life.

I didn't want to do this, but was told it would be a great opportunity to share the following links [links no longer work because of the universe being destroyed] and to help me get used to the fact I'm going to be known as "The guy who is, like, really old."

Anyway, ask me anything!

<u>Edit 1:</u> Just to get this out of the way, I am not answering questions religious in nature. I did this one time not knowing better, and it ended poorly. They're still finding bits of the guy in the Thames. Trust me when I say you don't want to hear the specifics. Regardless of what you think you believe. Faith is called faith for a reason.

<u>Edit 2:</u> Okay, so another thing is, I will not be posting the nude photos of old celebrities and monarchs I foolishly alluded to owning in one reply. Do you really want to see the fleshy bits of someone who has been dead for seventy years? Don't answer that.

<u>Edit 3:</u> That's it for the day. I could answer these forever (literally), but I have other things to do. Thanks to most of you for dropping by to talk. The rest of you should find a better hobby.

When were you born?

Mid-Jurassic. I think? There were Allosaurus around, I know that much.

What can you tell me about Jerusalem 2000 years ago?

Ha. Nice try.

Big history buff here. What was your favourite time period and where?

You've never heard of it. Kidding. Probably around 900AD. I was moving around a lot at the time, and things seemed pretty pleasant compared to a lot of the past.

Sponge Daddy.

Uh. Thanks.

Do you watch a lot of television? What's your favorite series?

I have spells where I watch a lot. It's a great way to pass the time when time is all you have (books are great too). I don't understand why people who'll be dead in fifty years spend so much time watching it, but there you go. Anyway, I'll watch anything with Bea Arthur or Madeline Kahn in it. I may have some catching up to do.

As our only immortal, are you going to give us your gift of eternal life?

It's not really a gift. But no, for two reasons.

First, I don't think it's possible. I'm impenetrable, so I can't give blood or what have you, and even if I could, what would that do?

Second, let's say some boffin does come up with an immortality pill. We all know it would take seconds before some group of rich dicks turned it into a commodity and either restricted it to a rich-dick-only pill, or else use it to create an immortal army of slaves. Probably both. Don't act like they wouldn't.

So, yes, it would be great to help people out if I could, but it's impossible and even if it wasn't, it would just lead to further corruption from elitist numpties.

How about music? Do you listen to a lot of music?

I tell ya, you kids these days with your instruments and your fully formed spoken lyrics, you don't know how good you have it. But I pick up about an album a year. I'm in no rush and want to save as many good moments for later as possible. I'm going to need something to do when you've wasted all the planet's resources and killed each other.

What is living forever like? Does it get sad?

Have you ever been in bed and had some little jingle play in your head? Like the boot up song for the first PlayStation, or an advert from the 80s, or a musical number from an old cartoon? Aren't those moments so bittersweet? You have this nugget of a memory, and maybe even get a little sentimental thinking about it, but you'll never be able to go back to the moment it came from, you know? You can recreate the experience, I'm sure, but that event itself is gone forever. The people, the feeling, the smells, the noise, everything around that bit of music is gone. There's no Sound City. That's what it's like. I'll never hear native Latin or hang out with Black Bart or glimpse the polished alabaster shell of the pyramids again. All of that is gone. And it stays gone. And all the things I never got around to doing? Those are gone too. Like tears in the rain, as a robot once said.

Which historical figure surprised you by how much of a dick they were? Were any famous bastards surprisingly nice?

It's strange, because I think a lot of famous bastards sort of had to be a little nice to get to where they were. But I haven't met that many historical figures. I mean, Tacitus was a whiny windbag. Schopenhauer was a fun drinking buddy and a terrible everything else. For the most part, though, I think it's safe to say that even the nicest historical figure would be what the kids call "problematic" and I call "Kind of a piece of shit."

Was there anything you regret not being able to stop from happening?

Yes. Lots of things. There are also things I stopped that you're never going to head about. So perhaps it's a wash. Probably not.

When you were Claudio Sud, what was it like backstage? Did you know Black Dahlia?

Elizabeth was a sweetheart, and it's sad to know she's remembered more as a corpse than the young woman she was. Backstage was as corrupt as you're probably imagining. Not much has changed, except now it seems they're more inclusive in terms of which attractive young people with rich parents they allow into their ranks.

Settle an argument: Is humanity getting better or worse?

How do I settle that one? It really depends on which aspect of humanity you're talking about. But no, it feels like it's getting better in a lot of ways if I ignore my own pessimism. One thing you all don't seem to realise is this: you're mostly good people who just want to be left alone.

But there's also all kinds of people in power who seem intent on destroying the world for profit. Perhaps not even intentionally, more a by-product of their way of living. And I guess it's a race to see who wins. Either way, I'll be around long after you're dead. I'd just prefer trees and clean water than scorched earth.

Crunchy or Creamy?

I don't care.

Are you worried about people blaming you for everything now the secret is out?

Depends on how slow the news is in the next few weeks.

How do you stop yourself from getting bored?

Who says I do? The trick it to just live forever. After the first fifty million years, a month will feel like nothing.

I wouldn't have given you an extra £20 if I knew you were a god!

That's not a question and I don't think I'm a god, but you can have it back whenever you want.

Got some good advice?

I don't know. Most of your worries are self-inflicted. Not in a victim-blaming kind of way. Just that things are always worse in your own head. Maybe. Sometimes. Like I said, I don't know.

Any predictions for the future?

Someone with their own interests at heart with ruin something good for good people and act like they did nothing wrong.

Why didn't you stop my grandparents from getting killed?

I'm sorry they are gone, but I likely wasn't in their neighbourhood when they died. I'm a really old guy, not an omnipresent superhero. I have to catch the bus like everyone else.

Earth, 20__ AD:

Tall poppy syndrome dictates that if anything gains traction online, it will inevitably be attacked by miserable people with nothing better to do. This rule never applied to self-appointed elite, however, who could, and did, punch small children and murder family pets and have a set of mawkish ghouls defend their actions on national television, or else pretend it never happened. And so, as with anything in a world with an unending news cycle and hundreds of millions of unfulfilled and anonymous internet denizens, South's foray into the public eye took a swan dive about three minutes after he signed away the film rights of his life story.

For a moment there, he thought he had accidentally brought about world peace. In an instant, the whole cyber spectrum was united against him. The peace did not last long. Even unified by hate, no group of internet strangers could quite agree why they had all decided to protest South's existence. Some said that he was evil because he'd allowed slavery and war to happen without interceding. Others said all that was fine, actually, but the fact he wouldn't announce his race to the world suggested he was an agent of a shadowy and unspecified cabal of bankers, released upon the world to somehow disrupt cryptocurrency. One group would break through the furore to accuse South of inventing Patriarchy, only for another group to all but agree, but how that only meant they deserved government mandated girlfriends. Religious groups all simultaneously tried to claim South as proof of their own divine beliefs or else an unholy abomination who proved them right all the same. Strangest of all was the group of angry young men who took South's immortality as proof their favourite film franchise was ruined by women and surely a man being immortal meant that all main characters should be men and maybe less of the token minority characters too, please.

It was a mess.

The core of their complaints, and one Dean predicted, was this: Why hadn't South, in all his indestructible-if-increasingly-doughy splendour, bothered to stop all the bad things ever from occurring? There were some disagreements about what constituted as the bad things (even clear-cut atrocities had supporters), but everyone agreed South alone could have done more. So why hadn't he? Was it his fault the world was such a mess? Could he fix everyone's problems, even right at that moment, but just didn't want to? Had South ruined everyone's hopes and dreams? It certainly wasn't an imbalanced and cruel class system, so why did South do it? Or was it all an accident because he was just another lazy and entitled man? These were the things the public wanted to know, and South, in all honesty, couldn't blame them for wondering such things loudly and incessantly at every available opportunity. They were coming at it from the wrong perspective, or course, but being wrong had never stopped a human before. If anything, it encouraged them.

Before long, people were picketing outside his home, calling up charitable organisations he'd worked with, finding what little scraps they could online to harass and denounce him. The films of Claudio Sud were reprinted at huge cost just to be burnt. A man named Alvin Serf was chased out of his Essex home by an unruly mob of disenfranchised youths and beaten on a nearby green. The attackers only stopped when Alvin's blood and pleas for mercy suggested he was perhaps not an unkillable ancient being, but in fact a twenty-year-old one of them had gone to school with.

Many of the more irate members of the masses seemed to be carried along by a current of discontent. They had no real arguments for pursuing South, nor did they seem to care if he was ever brought to justice. Sure enough, many would latch on to the next obscene event with frothing fury just as soon as they knew chasing South hadn't filled that void where their soul should be. It was all just a performative act of multimedia pantomime for them, a declaration of their own intrinsic goodness without having to sacrifice or suffer, or even leave the bedroom.

After a while, out in the real world, things calmed down. But for a sullen troop of photographers who stalked his time outdoors, and the infrequent heckle of "immortal wanker, gan tae fuck, ya wee bawbag" it seemed to South people had moved on already. Perhaps someone on television had kicked a dog or a new remake was out in cinemas. There were larger concerns people were only just starting to focus on, too. Diminishing food supplies, stagnant wages, rising water levels, increasing amounts of heat waves, civil unrest, and a new miniseries about an alcoholic detective and a reformed serial killer who solve crimes except this time there's no sexual tension at all. These things needed attention in ways South didn't. It wasn't like he was going anywhere, and neither was the entirety of human history. Away from dim screens, South was again free to walk from place to place. He attended onboarding interviews with charities all over the continent, happy to get back to what he enjoyed most. And during the interviews themselves everything seemed fine. It was only when he received rushed messages from coordinators things seemed off. From soup kitchens to global task forces, he heard only excuses. People he used to work with, Kenosha Kid for instance, wouldn't answer email, or else would reply with a curt "we can't talk, blocking you." In some cases, it seemed that branding and marketing opportunities outweighed actual help. In others, his rejection occurred just moments before the charity would announce huge new donations made by anonymous benefactors.

The storm was not over. He understood.

He returned home after one such interview to find a collection of four imported black cars parked on the double yellow lines in front of his door. Large men in black suits stood watch over the vehicles, more concerned with each other's presence than the cars themselves. As South approached his door, one guard made a step toward him. The others would follow suit, so the first guard would step back, causing the others to step back. They eyeballed each other Sergio Leone style, shimmying around each other in a stunted version of the hokey cokey. Stepping forwards and backwards, a do-si-do with a group of tall, muscular, stiff-faced killers. South walked by them to his door. They barely paid attention to him, instead circling each other like territorial, neutered dogs.

"He's here," they said in four different languages, speaking into their hidden microphones.

South entered his home.

In his living room, four replacement television sets were pressed up against the door, making it difficult to enter. Squeezing through the frame as best he could, he saw the room had been rearranged. Four chairs set up X-shaped. Behind each chair, two large people stood with their arms crossed and eyes covered by sunglasses. In each chair sat a diplomatic-looking person, all four wearing expensive suits, watches, and a sickening amount of cologne. Each group was incapable of taking their eyes off the other three. Their eyes flickered side-to-side as if unwittingly watching a fast-forwarded game of tennis.

"Uh, hello," said South, realising he had nowhere left to sit. He consciously avoided standing in the middle of the chairs. Nothing good ever came from the middle of a circle.

"Please forgive our intrusion," said the bearded diplomat, "I am Hassan and--"

"Call me Stroud," said the diplomat with giant porcelain teeth. Stroud leaned forward to extend a hand but was pulled back into his seat by one of his minders, who gave a reproachful shake of their head. "It's awfully swell to finally meet you, buddy, it sure would mean a lot to us if--"

"Stroud, please, we agreed we'd do the introductions first," said the bald diplomat. "I am Yevgeny, it is the most great pleasure to make your acquaintance."

The final diplomat nodded at Yevgeny, appreciating his few words, before looking at South. "I am Ming. It seems we're all here for--"

"We're all here for the same reason, buddy," said Stroud. "Thought we should tell you to your face there's a hearing planned at the UN soon and, gosh, it would be just super if you could come as my guest. My friend. It would mean so much to me and my country."

South had given up on looking for a chair and balanced himself on two of the television screens.

"You're an insolent swine, Stroud," Hassan said with an unwavering voice. "We agreed we'd get an equal amount of time to talk and you're just--"

"He is complete nincompoop with his interruptions," Yevgeny interrupted. "I am authorised here today to invite you to the hearing as an honoured guest of my most noble country."

"And my magnanimous kingdom also offers their most heartfelt invitation to attend the hearing as a cherished brother of ours."

Ming waited a moment, starring at Stroud. "I am afraid these three offers are extended under false pretences, Mister South. However, my country has delivered a sincere and beneficial request for your partnership at the UN building. Only we can guarantee your safety."

"Whoa, there, hold your horses just a second, miss," said Stroud, struggling against the confines of his seat. "We agreed when we got here there would be no idle threats."

"I must agree with the bombast," said Yevgeny, "If we are to resort to threats then my country wins hands down."

"I think you're all forgetting what my country has got away with for decades," said Hassan.

Yevgeny waved his hand dismissively. "Please, we were making threats when your country was still a baby."

His minders pressed him down into his seat, but Stroud gesticulated wildly. "If ANY act of AGGRESSION is to BEFALL anyone here today, it's going to be by my hands."

Ming laughed. "As you see, mister South, they are all champing at the bit to make threats. Do you see how quick they were to reveal themselves? But you can trust me, or perhaps I should visit Alexandra and see what she thinks of all this."

South stood up. The visit had slipped far beyond just being a surprise annoyance. "I can tell you right now if you don't leave her out of whatever you're doing, I will--"

"Yes," said Hassan, "I have a network of snipers who are watching your agents and the young Alexandra, Ming. Believe me, they will stop any attempts you might take on that sweet angel's life. Don't worry, South, my friend, no one will hurt you or yours while you are a friend of mine."

"Snipers, huh, bucko?" Stroud said. "I guess I should reveal that we also have trained snipers trained on your snipers and Ming's snipers. So, if either of you get any ideas about making any kind of threats or acts of aggression, you'll be hearing from my snipers."

"Ha, that's rich," said Yevgeny. "My snipers have been watching all three of your guys' snipers. And Alexandra. And South. And me and all of you. As you can see, if anything happens to anybody at any point anywhere, they're under strict instructions to shoot everyone." He winked at South. "Except you, obviously."

Ming laughed. "Oh, yeah? You pack of fools; I knew all about your snipers all along, and they just think they're tracking my snipers. That's why my real snipers are tracking all the other snipers and watching this house. One if even hidden in the floorboards, just waiting for a chance to put an end to all this. Now, do any of you want to make any more threats to try to get this man to the UN? We all heard him already say he was coming with me as my guest."

"You get ahead of yourself, my impudent friend," Hassan began, "It is my turn to reveal that in fact we have snipers--"

By this time South had left the squabbling behind and walked up to his bedroom. For the first time, he could empathise with children of dysfunctional families. As he pulled open his bedroom door, he found another four people sitting on his bed playing cards. They looked up at him with sheepish smiles.

"Sorry, they've been arguing down there since just after you left this morning," said a man holding bleeding edge recording equipment.

"No, it's fine, I understand. I could barely handle five minutes." The reality of the situation began to creep in. "And who are they, exactly?"   "International delegates. I've heard there's more on the way. We just work for them, though."

"Are they trying to impress me?"

The man shook his head. "I think it's some sort of human rights tribunal or something."

A woman holding three aces and a flashbang grenade turned to face South. "They're going to woo you in private and condemn you in public."

The man nodded. "Business as usual."

"Right, well," South said with a melodramatic yawn, "In that case, I should probably have a lie down before it gets any worse." He gestured at the door and the four strangers collected their cards and equipment before pushing their way out the room. The man stopped behind the other three.

"If you want anything," he said, "We'll be right outside. I'm Hugo."

"I'm good, thanks, Hugo," South said as he stretched out on his bed.

He lay there for a moment, not sure how to process what was happening to him. The arguing continued downstairs as if he hadn't left, perhaps louder for his benefit. He closed his eyes, took out his phone, and called Alexandra.

"Not a good time, South. There's like fifteen people following me around," she said, out of breath and a little rattled.

"Yes, I've got visitors too. Could I come over? I think we need to talk."

"Ha. Do you have more secrets? Can you fly? If I find out you've been able to fly this whole time, I swear to all you hold dear--"

"No, I haven't been able to fly for ages. I just want to talk is all."

"Yeah, I don't think I'm going outside again any time soon."

"Great, see you soon. Oh, and Alex?"

"Hmm?"

"Stay away from your windows and keep an ear out for people under the floorboards."

Somewhere in The Amazon — 1532 CE:

South ran. Through the Badlands, the swamps, jungles, and forests, over lake and hill alike, across coastlines, plains, and deserts, he ran with complete abandon. An unending sprint for years across the Americas with a ceaseless knot of dread resting in his vacant gut. No lightning bolt could slow him down, no roiling river could stop him. He was sent to chase down doom itself before its wiry fingers dug up the very souls of the people he watched over.

They were coming. North's men. Men from other continents, corrupted by her influence. He had seen them on only a few beaches at first, but they spread like the virus they were. Arriving on boats in growing numbers, they destroyed everything they saw. For a time, South hoped they were clueless travellers, but they fast revealed themselves as mercenaries and opportunists, seekers of glory and gold, thieves in the night. As the years rattled on, huge chunks of land fell to their claims of destiny, bodies of the innocent piled up like discarded food. They would talk of kings and queens, divinity, preordained rights from a holy being, as they claimed what couldn't be owned. They cited ancient writing the locals could not read, books perverted by greed and wrath, to justify their grotesque impunity. Worse even yet, they brought with them death magicks that claimed the bodies of a million or more of South's neighbours without a single blade being raised. So much had been lost.

And so South Ran. From the Moche settlements, through Nazca lines, and up into the mountains. He carried nothing but a warning.

It would be impossible for even an immortal to stop them all, much less stop their supernatural weapons. South needed to deliver his message to all who would hear it. If not to prepare them for war, then to encourage them to hide. He hoped that a unified set of nations might prove strong enough to defend the lands he had grown to love.

Few would listen. Many of the leaders would refuse to even see him, branding him a jester from the trees, a chaotic imp, an hallucination. His years of hidden, fleeting, impartial observation betrayed him. When he arrived full sprint to the edge of their lands, screaming in several tongues about plague bearers and invaders, Villagers would shriek, and rulers would hide. In retrospect, this method was not the wisest way to enter a village.

As he made his way up the jungle path to the city of Patiti, he wondered if all was lost. The disease of North's men was crawling behind him, invisible and as cruel and evil as their forebears, intent on claiming the new world for its master. A wish granted by a dreadful djinn. Hope was all that pushed South forward. He brought with him memories of fallen continents and could not allow the same plague to destroy his home.

With the stone gates of Patiti cresting the tip of the mountain, South pushed on. He paused. A piercing howl rattled his ears, his eyes bulged, and alien sensation commandeered his senses. Someone was close by. His strength began to ebb. The howl drew closer, an invisible bell's chime rung in his ears. Trying to fight against the invading sensations, he spun and screamed, and in return he found himself writhing on the floor. A giant clash of flapping and rustling branches came from all around as every animal fled in terror. South gripped a fleshy vine and tried to pull himself to his feet. His strength had escaped with the birds. Vision, perfect since creation, all but lost in an instant, revealing only drab brown and green smudges. Everything stung and nothing felt real. A fever dream. Or nightmare.

"I knew you'd reveal yourself eventually," said a voice from behind him. It was a language never spoken by humans. North was behind him. She moved; a dead branch cracked underfoot. Close, dangerously close.

"What have you done to me?" He wanted at once to spit bile, to wake up, to sleep, but his consciousness was trapped in a hall of mirrors.

"I've done nothing to you, old friend. This is just your reckoning."

He clawed at where he thought she was, his limp hands flopping to the floor with every pawed movement. "Please," he said, "Do what you want with me, but these people. Leave these people alone.   You've already got the rest of the world. Isn't that enough?"

She laughed. "What are you talking about? I told you what would happen if we met again. Did you take me for a liar?"

South heard a rush of wind, a solid blow to his temple. He spun back down into the ground but clambered to his feet. His body devoid of anything but a pulsing darkness. Tried to swing a fist and tumbled back to the floor. North grabbed him by the hair and lifted him above her head.

For a moment, he wondered if he had just woken from a bad dream. He was flying, a sensation he had long since forgotten. But this was no dream. North had thrown him downhill away from Patiti. He travelled some distance before his body found the ground again, landing hard, limbs tearing at the ground as he slid ever downward. He pulled himself up with what strength he could find. And ran.

North chased him like a playful cat, leading him up into the mountains over three days and nights. Sometimes she would toss him forward, beat him, to remind him she meant to end him. They wound their way up past the woodline and onto a snowy peak. South turned at last to stand his ground. But it was no good. North had primordial magic in her veins whereas South had only regret.

She beat him down once more. North sat beside him with as much sympathy as she could muster. "Just stop," she said.

But he did not. He leapt. Not at her, but at the edge of the cliff. Before she could grab him, he was careening down to the ground below, bashing against the rocks, severing trees with his body, hurtling to safety. He landed with a sputter on a rock slab. The sounds of the great river stirring beneath him. Blind. The cold humming in his body slithered away. If he could just sleep, he could regain his power. Just sleep. His aching body yearned for rest. He lay motionless and broken in all ways but physical.

A loud crash announced North's arrival nearby. He couldn't bring himself to move. She stepped closer to him. There was pity in her voice where there had once only been contempt. "You can't stop progress, South. Neither can I. When I next see you, all those you care for will be dead. It doesn't matter if it is by my hand or not. How does that feel? To know what none of this matters. You have saved nothing and no one. You have barely stalled the inevitable. And now it's time for you to go." She stood over South, a prone and pathetic shadow of his former self.

South looked up at her, his vision returning. He sputtered and reached up for her hand. She did not offer it. "Just do it already," he said at last.

She booted him over the edge of the rock. He fell into the midst of an unending torrent, and the river claimed him for its own.

Over unknown days, the river dragged him through the continent, his limp body dragged pliantly along the rocks of the great riverbed for hundreds of miles. At last he was spat out into the ocean itself and South sunk downward. All hope was gone. There would be no saving the world.

The United Nations HQ, New York City - 20__AD:

It was John Stewart Mill in his forgotten classic Utilitarianism who opined, quote, "The good of the many outweighs the good of the few, unless the few in question make over 1,000,000 USD per annum, in which case all bets are off" unquote. This idiom was very much in play when belligerent clans of high-ranking government officials and oligarchs met in the grand cloak and dagger room on the third floor. Behind the fake panel. Near the vending machine.

A recording of this clandestine conversation was given to South a year later by someone who wished to remain anonymous. That person was Hugo Khrushchev, a man who, despite his best efforts, died countless years ago and thus rendered anonymity as useless as the lensless glasses he would wear in public. Here is a transcript:

(Heavy scraping of chairs against a marble floor)

A: You're late

B: I had to talk to a media consortium. Sorry.

A: Was the meeting satisfactory, at least?

B: As ever. They'll push the narrative we want. But this undead guy, should we be worried?

A: I don't think he counts as undead.

B: Well, whatever he is, then.

A: I don't think so. Give the people a spectacle and let him talk freely. Chances are the masses will move on to something else by January. They always do.

(Squeaking. Perhaps from a spinning chair.)

C: But there's something else to consider.

A: How long have you been here?

B: *(Overlapping)* How did you get here?

C: It doesn't matter. What is important is that His Holiness would like to pass on his reminder than an immortal running around could be bad news for religion. All religion. Especially if we

don't do our best to neutralise him. We must ensure we don't bring
up certain parts of our history. A few billion people all losing their
faith at the same time could be bad for *everyone's* earning
potential in the fourth quarter. But we must be cunning. A few
countries have already tried and failed to gain his friendship.

A: We are the invisible hand and such plebeian ideas as countries is
beneath us. Our reach is infinite, our intellect supreme.

B: Jesus Christ, man, I hate it when you try to sound all portentous.
No offence, cardinal.

C: None taken.

B: But what if we just condemn him publicly as an abomination? The
faithful would cling to that readily.

A: We could destroy his credibility a hundred different ways.

C: Yes. But if we don't spin this just so, we are looking at the royalest
of fuck-ups. Gargantuan proportions. Think about how
close that little black book came to scuppering us all a few years
back. But this guy makes war crimes and sex slavery look like
baby's first play time. He poses a genuine threat to all of us.

D: And us.

(Soft sound of a false wall panel opening up)

A, B, C: You!

D: Yes. Our friends in the energy industry want to ensure we can
buy this guy. And we know how much they like buying
people. We need to make it look like this guy knows fossil fuels are
superior and climate change is a hoax. And if we could, maybe get
him to praise our new brand of reusable straws.

B: It's a bit late in the day to be worried about climate change. You've
seen the news.

D: Sure. But we're worried if enough people figure out what we've
been up to it could be *(Either cartoonish throat slitting sound effect
or choking on food)* for all of us.

A: Oh, don't be silly. They're too busy fighting each other. The whole
idea of a mass rebellion is a joke.

D: Even jokes have punchlines. But here's the crux of our concerns: there's still money to be made from oil, and we're worried we'll leave some of it behind when we move down into the bunkers.

C: Here's what I don't get: What are you guys going to do with all that money when you're in the bunkers? Doesn't it become worthless then?

D: The same thing you're doing with all the tithes and commandeered art, I imagine. But let's not worry about that. Just because they think they're in charge doesn't mean they're smart.

B: Well maybe, and I'm speaking completely hypothetical here, but maybe a little revolution wouldn't be the end of the world. As it were. It could help us, that's for sure. Who wants to rule a dead planet?

A: If you ask me—

(The door creaks open)

E: Oh! Sorry to bother you! I thought this floor was closed for the night.

C: What is it!?

E: It's just… Do you have any trash in here? I'm running a sweep before we get   ready to   vacuum.

A: …

B: …

C: Just get the fuck out of here.

E: No need to be rude, your holiness. I'm just doing my job.

(Twenty seconds of silence)

D: Actually, yeah, you can have this cup of coffee. It got cold a while ago.

E: I didn't ask for your life story.

(Rustling of garbage bags)

(Door slams shut)

D: You were saying?

A: If we're smart and play this just right we could come out as the true winners either way. Not the people who think they're in charge, not the masses. Us. What is it the French say? No Men, No Masters?

B: Something like that.

C: So it's decided. We will work toward—

(Door creaks open)

(Something is plugged in)

(Vacuum is switched on)

Author's Note:

How have you been liking the flashback chapters? I think they're pretty cool and stylish, and I bet a lot of very smart reviewer types would agree if they hadn't been eradicated on a subatomic level a few billion years ago. It really shows the difference between the person I was when I was with you and who I was back then. And now that the flashback timeline is becoming more linear, the intuitive and classy reader can pick up on the fact that it's all leading up to something. Powerful writing. I'm winning prizes this year at the award show I'm judging.

Right here is supposed to be a chapter called something like Two Hundred Years Under the Sea, and it was going to detail exactly that. After North threw me in the ocean, I lost all hope. I swam around, checked on some sunken cities and lost boats, tried to see what was in the Mariana Trench. It was great practise for exploring sunken cities in the twenty-second century, but I didn't know that then.

I wrote all that, thinking I was on to something, but reading it back it was just three thousand words of me floating around in the darkness feeling sorry for myself.

It was a lousy time, all things considered. I felt like a failure, and I knew people were dying above the surface. Not just dying, either, being wiped off the face of the planet by invading forces. And I couldn't bring myself to float back up. It was too all-consuming, oppressive. The guilt, the shame, the powerlessness. It was far easier to just sink down into the darkness, pres-

sure trying to crush me, and wallow in my failures.

It's a shame there's not an applicable metaphor
hidden in there somewhere.

Compared to this prison in the heavens, though,
I almost miss it. At least then I could overcome
self-pity and doubt and swimming back up to the
surface, reinvigorated, determined, strong. Not so
much these days. There aren't even days these...
days.

Anyway, back to England.

South's Crypt — 20__ CE:

"Wait, so when I was eighteen you would have been…"

"Eternity years old."

"And when I was ten?"

"Eternity years old."

"I think I'm going to need a moment. For a few reasons." Her knees trembling, ready to run, her eyes scanning the room for ghouls, she tried to keep her distance from the walls and cobwebs. She was standing almost reverently above the mummified remains of a forgotten poet.

"You're only just now thinking about the age gap? I mean, if you really want to get technical, I'm not sure I count as the same species."

"Oh god, not helping."

They had descended into the forgotten catacombs of a cathedral, torn down back when Henry VIII was going through one of his bad break ups. All that remained above ground were an assortment of weather-worn rock piles and a hidden entrance to the tombs. To the hikers who pass by, it was little more than a desolate photo opportunity, a field with a stolen history. The owners of the land were reclusive, having gone into hiding generations earlier after one Dairo Soof disappeared. Except for South, the only people interested in the area were the most desperate of land developers, and they were out there waiting for a consumer boom that would never come. The last of those had been and gone.

The upper levels of the crypts were damp and mossy and smelled vaguely of old clothes left in a washing machine for six hundred years. It had taken three hours to coax Alexandra down past the first level. For South, he was visiting the remains of an old church, but for Alexandra she was climbing into a place that wasn't supposed to exist. An unlit, subterranean crypt that wasn't supposed to exist.

Down in the third level of the Catacombs, illuminated by old sconces, South had set up a small office for when he was between identities. A hiding place where IDs and plans could be forged, and priceless mementos hidden. Once he had offices hidden in tombs and caves all over the world, but most had been compromised or else built over. The one benefit of a hidden stash in a country for England was the people were so used to ruins they would barely acknowledge them. He hid his most treasured goods in the tomb. Or at least what he hadn't left trapped under a Des Moines casino.

The four sconces illuminating the level sputtered as their flames snapped at the wafting detritus. One burnt brightly over South's old stone coffin. He had been laid to rest there many years earlier and was apt to sleep in it from time to time for sentimentality's sake. By his grave, his chest of treasures sat open. He was fishing through his possessions for Alexandra to see. A lonely child showing a new friend his best toys.

Once Alexandra had adjusted to the light, the location, the smell, she knelt beside the chest and looked inside.

"And all this was part of a cathedral? How come nobody remembers this place?"

"That's human history for you. Do you have any idea how many wooden cities you've never heard of? How many civilisations sank into the sea? And don't get me started on the lost libraries."

"I don't want to know about any of that. It's too sad to think about."

"I could revitalise your academic career, you know. You're the only person who hasn't asked me a single question about history."

"I want the whole story or nothing at all."

Looking like a cash-strapped punter at a public market, she picked up and put down several antiques. She cringed at the crumpled black and white nudes, twirled a sacrificial dagger in her fingers. Silver and jade and gold twinkled under the light of the fire. So many stories.

She continued. "Part of me thinks it's like reading a recap of a television show you've never watched. You can pretend you understand what happened, maybe even blag your way through a conversation, but it's nothing without context. And if I think about it, I just get depressed."

"Because I'm so old?"

"Oh, I'll never forgive you for being so ancient. But no, I just don't enjoy thinking about everything we've lost. The cities we'll never know, the music I'll never hear, the stories we've lost to cotton fields and slave boats and war-zones and disease. There's just so much behind us we can barely visualise, let alone understand, and the only thing sadder than not knowing enough is knowing too much. Which is why I understand finally why you spent all those years feeling sorry for yourself. You have all that stuff in your head and nobody on earth who could ever hope to understand."

He crouched beside her and investigated the chest. "You never ask about anything, though. I've done some bad things. Terrible things."

Alexandra stood up and rested her hands on his shoulders. "Yes, I'm sure you have. And that's terrifying in its own way. But you stopped, right? By choice. That's why I'm still here. It is so much easier to just keep doing things the way they've been done. A bad person, a truly bad person, isn't going to work in a chip shop or a call centre as some weird form of penitence. You've made a choice to be as good a person as you can, and that's something few people do. And us mortals have barely an iota of the power you do."

"But I—"

"Can we not? The whole forgotten crypt vibe is bad enough, I don't need an emo boyfriend fouling up the mood on top of it. I'll leave it at this: If you lock someone in their past, you take away their future. Ask anyone who's ever gone sober or sought redemption. So I can look at this pistol or this dagger, and I can guess what you've done, but that's not you anymore. If it was, neither of us would be down here."

"Thank you."

"You're welcome."

South stood, turning to face Alexandra. His lips were trying to form a sentence but sputtered. The words alien. "Is this a weird time to tell you I love you?"

"We're underground in a lost catacomb surrounded by mummies and spiders, and we're standing next to a chest full of murder weapons and nude photos."

"Right, stupid. I'll tell you later. I guess I've already said it…"

"Don't be silly, that's every girl's dream right there, South. And I do. Too. I think."

Silence. A waft of air drew the flames toward the door. Another patch of dust lost to the fire. The wind howled through the tombs like a banshee and reverberated through slits in the rock. It sounded like the unremembered dead were calling out. Alexandra shuddered, then noticed something in the chest.

"Hold up," she said, "Why do you have a bag of silver?"

"It's mine. But before it was mine, it belonged to Egill Skallagrímsson."

"You met Egill Skallagrímsson?"

"Yeah, we were friends for a bit when I was, well, I guess you could say backpacking."

"And he gave you all this silver?"

"No. I helped him bury it and then he kicked me down a hill."

"What a dick."

"Yeah, he had his moments. But I got it in the end and he's dead, so I'd count that as a win."

"Imagine if he was still out there trying to get his silver back. I couldn't imagine two immortals walking around."

South let out a soft sigh and turned his attention to the ceiling. After losing himself to thought for a moment, he got to his knees and retrieved a telescope. Alexandra looked at it. The possibilities of who it once belonged to were limitless. She smiled, excited.

"Oooh, don't tell me! Collingwood? Nelson? Um... Columbus? Drake!? No. Wait, James Cook? Anne Bonny? Um. Ooh! Marco Polo? Is that Marco Polo's telescope?"

"Please, I won this in a game of cards against Olivier Levasseur."

Alexandra scrunched up her face. "Who?"

"He was a pirate. He said there was more to it than it seemed. I found some coordinates on the side, but I never followed-- What?"

Alexandra chuckled. "Are we really doing this?"

"What?"

"You're telling me you got a clue to some buried treasure after gambling with pirates."

"Gambling? I ran my own ship."

Alexandra leaned against South's grave. "Well, I can't not hear all about this, can I?"

The Caribbean Sea — 1720 CE:

When South got around to resurfacing, an oar greeted him with a whack to the back of the head. He sputtered, turned over, and remembered how much he enjoyed oxygen.

"He's alive!" a wizened voice called out from up above.

Blinded by the intense and alien sun, South couldn't see his surroundings. Frantic voices carried over the waves. Water lapped the side of something. Wood creaked. A lone gull shrieked somewhere above him. As his vision returned, he could make out the rocking, dark form of a ship's side, figures peering from over the edge down at him, the cloudless sky above. How he had missed the endless nothing, an invitation to contemplate infinity.

"Let's just shoot him!" came the garbled cries of someone with a shattered larynx.

"Yeah!" their shipmates jeered, slapping the side of the boat in unison.

South spent this time bobbing up and down. He knew he should have spent a few more years bobbing along at the bottom of the ocean. But no, he had to pick that precise moment to float up next to the narrenschiff. Grinning at his own misfortune, his teeth glimmered like cinematic diamonds, unnatural in their whiteness.

With his vision adjusted, he could see the sailors. A crowd of scruffy miscreants stained with everything from gunpowder to spilt rum. Probably some blood, too. They looked down at him with leering, unearthly faces. Some wore tattered clothes borrowed from dead men and stolen cargo, others dressed as well as they could under the circumstances. Their skin was subdermally baked and pock marked. They were a new breed of men entirely. Not quite the sneering conquistadors, nor the tribes he remembered.

Bang.

A lead ball ricocheted off South's head and skimmed the water. He thrashed in shock. The men aboard the ship laughed.

Right, lads, I think that's enough. Get him out of the drink already."

With whaling hooks, oars, and makeshift netting, the crew lifted the supine South and deposited him onto the forecastle of the deck. He landed with a watery splat. The rough surface beneath him was hard, two things he had forgotten about in his life aquatic. His body pulsed and prickled as it adjusted to the floor. It made him think of the live births he had witnessed, of drunk men renegotiating control of their own bodies, of madness. No longer was he weightless.

"And I thought I was pistol proof," someone standing over him yelled. South struggled to understand the words, a new take on an old language. "Somebody, quick, fetch this poor sod some clothes and food. How are you feeling, fella? Where did you come from?"

South looked up, but his voice only creaked, his words gone. The man standing over him wore fine silk clothes. Beneath a rich bouquet of perfumed water, the unmistakable stench of a man of the ocean. Sweat and rotting teeth and pustulating sores. His eyes, though, were kinder than what South would have expected, and that alone put him at ease.

After thirty seconds, the man nodded. "Ah, you're a mute, are you? Can you hear me at least?"

South nodded.

"Then you can follow orders, which is good enough for now. But where is your ship? We've seen no wreckage or driftaways?"

South pointed to the bottom of the ocean. The man gave an appreciative "ah" and looked out at the sea. He then offered his hand and tugged South back to his feet for the first time in two hundred years. South's knees buckled and contorted in inhuman ways as he tried to remember how to walk. The crew, but for the man in silk, turned away. There were already murmurs they had rescued Death himself.

Soon clothes and a bowl of broth were found and South set upon both with eagerness. The crew watched agog as he slurped at the bowl and hiked up the loose pantaloons, concluding en masse a man so pathetic could not be Death. But perhaps a friend of Death. Their own captain was said to have shaken hands with Death years earlier. Their leader stood over the hunched South, helping him to his feet once more when the bowl was licked dry. South's strength was returning at a preternatural speed. His voice still trapped behind some thoracic cage, a prison in his chest.

"Well, lad, you're welcome to join our crew. Or we can set you aland when we next take to harbour. We only ask you to work when you're able. Do you read, friend?"

South shrugged. Despite his hyperpolyglottal gifts, it had been some time since he had read anything of note. The leader of the crew did not know this and assumed the shrug was that of an embarrassed idiot. He placed his rough, bejewelled hand on South's back and guided him down some steps.

"We'll get to that later. We have a charter, don't we lads? The papers of a free man!"

The crew cheered.

"Rest up tonight, my boy. You'll need strength in the morning. You're a pirate now. Welcome to the Good Fortune!"

South sailed with the Good Fortune for the rest of the year, his voice never once returning. While an abjectly poor conversationalist, he was fast to prove himself a capable deckhand, adapting with ease and working with the perseverance of a hundred carthorses. The other sailors called him Loud Sally, a nickname too nuanced and intellectual to explain here. He made fast friends with those around him. The musicians took an instant liking to his inability to sing along. Captain Bartholomew, too, found in him someone he could confide in, as did the sailors Noah Blake, James Skyrme, Gasping Jensen, Montingy la Palisse, Sailor Prentice, and William W. Williams. Dead men, it was said, could tell no tales, but nor could men without even the most rudimentary of speaking abilities.

Life wasn't all about singing and dancing and listening to confessions. Every few weeks, they would come across a ship and they would plunder it. The crews of those boats were treated as fairly as they deserved, with the fate of their captain's left in the hands of their crew. Some cruel captains lost their lives, others were set free, penniless but at least alive.

At first, South found it difficult to reacquaint himself with the violence required of his new career. It was something he had sworn off while walking through the first crusade. But he saw in the eyes of the privateers and navy men pursuing them the same glow that consumed the invaders of the Americas. His anger, thought lost to the bottom of the ocean, unfurled once more. Those poor unfortunate souls to cross his path no longer men, in his eyes, but the minions of his betrayer.

As an unblinking and unkillable fighter, his shipmates feared his relentless sword strokes. The only man who matched him in combat was Captain Bart himself. At least that's what South had them believe.

For all the roughness that came with his new position as a sailor, South admired their code of ethics. Captured men from other boats were just as surprised. There was a loose hierarchy, but everyone received a fair share, and those who didn't work didn't get paid. Their plundering and celebrations ashore were wild, animalistic even, but there was a necessity for consent. For respect. Respect for each other, for unarmed strangers and working folk. Punishments, too, were fair compared to the actions of other captains, of those kings and queens he had heard so much about. It made for a strange juxtaposition the more South learned of the world, how cutthroats and brigands could somehow be more empathetic and civilised than the guardians of empires.

Taken as he was by nihilism and a spiritual malaise for which he had no name, South saw himself as a bastion of the natural order. At war with an encroaching evil which hid behind flags and holy books.

The Good Fortune and its sister boats ran roughshod across the ocean. In time, South was given captaincy of his own ship. He dubbed it The Astomi. He kept his crew small, but there were always those who wanted to join him. People spoke of him as if he were the Platonic ideal of captaincy. And for a time perhaps he was. But his career as a captain ended almost in an instant.

They had caught up with a frigate flying no colours and earned a quick surrender. The crew of the frigate were not fighters. Most fell to their knees as South and his men boarded. Some pleaded to join them. Others dived overboard and swam to their deaths. South surveyed the miserable men, seeing nothing but sloth in their eyes. Alone, he walked down into the cargo hold.

Not cargo down there, though. No. People. People lined up and pressed together across the hold. Chained together by thick steel. Manacled men, women, and children all forced into horizontal positions, emaciated, broken, bodies warped by inactivity. Those with open eyes lay frightened or dead, limbs twisted either way. Stomachs protruding with hunger. Of those who were dead, many were already beginning to rot, festering beside the living. The putrescent stench of death and captivity clung like mist. The prisoners could barely bring themselves to call out.

A helplessness returned to South. North was still out there; her corruption had ushered forth a new era of inhumanity. He had failed again. Shaking with guilt, hatred, and pity, he sat about unshackling those he could. The people looked at him with defeated eyes. Even freed of their shackles they did not move. Could not. What would be the point? They were still condemned.

South walked backward up to the deck and fell to his knees. The sins of North and his own failures plagued his mind. She had to be found and stopped. Or humans would continue to suffer. To make each other suffer. Forever.

His eyes turned to the captured crew of the frigate. They sat huddled in the middle of the deck. Their indifference to the people in the hold stirred something in South. His strength returned. He selected half his crew and using his voice for the first time, he said, "Go below deck and see to it we help those people." It took a moment for his men to recognise he was speaking, his voice jarring and medieval in tone. Then they jogged down the stairs.

The rest of his crew stood staring. "And what of these poor sods?" said his quartermaster.

South looked again at his captives. They betrayed no emotion, no shame, no guilt. "Keelhaul the lot of them. And make it slow," South said, returning to help those below.

He ignored the pleas of the captives. They had forfeited their lives when they joined North's death cult.

Hôtel d'Temple, Paris — 20__ CE:

Across the river, the miniature outline of Notre Dame lay covered in scaffolding. From their hotel room, they could make out the figurine-sized people scrambling to restore it to its former glory. It wasn't the first time Paris had suffered and it pained South to know for certain it wouldn't be the last. He had almost brought back the stone angel's head at Alexandra's insistence. But bringing it back wouldn't return the cathedral to its past beauty any more than returning de Payen's spurs would bring back the Templar. Those things were gone. Ship of Theseus be damned.

Paris was one of the few extant cities to remind South of his age. He had seen it in its infancy, walked the streets in three separate millennia, watched as ruin and pestilence and war made attempts on its life. It went on in defiance of its past. So much had remained, yet so much had vanished.

It was a vague rule of his, but South did his best to avoid such cities. Visiting Rome, Paris, Alexandria, Damascus, Varanasi, or any other ancient town was a depressing experience. It was how he imagined a dying man might feel while looking at photos of friends and family long since departed. But then, too, there were the cities lost or forgotten, some known only to South, and in his loneliest moments their memory would fill him with existential impotence. It was like how the last native speaker of a language would feel, waiting for a conversation that would never come, a simple "hello, how do you do?" no longer a guarantee.

"What are you thinking about?" asked Alexandra, pressing her hands against the pane and looking out at the city.

"Time."

"You've got eternity to think about that. How about we do something fun instead?"

"But we're supposed to meet Dean. You know, I haven't seen him outside of a hotel yet."

"That's because he's the ancient god of hospitality."

"You have a knack for meeting gods, then."

"Ooh, so you've upgraded yourself to deity now?"

South winced.

Alexandra continued. "He won't be here for a few hours yet. Let's take a walk around the city."

So they did.

They walked first to the scaffolding, but when they reached it they could not bring themselves to look at the shell of the cathedral. It was missing more than just the tangible aspects of itself and the closer the pair got to it the more they could feel the spectral loss. Around them, on the bridge and on the square, other tourists stood in place, transfixed. They were mourning a missed opportunity to see the city as it had been. As it never would be again.

"This must have been something else two hundred years ago," Alexandra said, taking one rueful look at the cathedral as they crossed a bridge toward the English book store.

"Yes," said South. He was all at once overtaken by his own memories. Too many to keep track of. Wrestling the panic of an unfocused mind, he stopped at a bench outside the book store and held Alexandra's hand. "I have too much inside me, Alex."

He slumped onto the bench, resting his head in his hands.

"Too much?"

"History. Images. Memories."

She sat beside him and together they sat looking down at the cobbled stone. His breathing grew irregular and shallow, his mind aswarm with a million memories.

In a limp whisper, Alexandra leaned forward. "What can I do?"

A pause. South regathered himself. "Why don't you show me what Paris is to you?"

"OK," she stood up, affecting the poise of an over-enthusiastic tour guide. "See this bookstore here? They let volunteers sleep inside. But only if they work a certain amount of time there. And they've got this cat that's really aloof even by Parisian standards. And I don't think half the volunteers know what soap is, because when I was trying to be a writer one summer…"

She showed him Paris that evening. Her Paris. A Paris South had never seen. She spoke of the summer she had spent there, hiding outside restaurants, too nervous to order in French but adamant she wouldn't use English. How she'd been inspired to learn Ça ira after too many revolutionary walking tours, and how she tried to sing it with a ukulele at her student union right before ukulele songs became too gauche to perform in earnest. She spoke of the warm evenings spent retracing the steps of other outsiders, Baldwin, Davis, Burroughs, et al. And how those thinkers had each in their own way shaped her own view of the world. Together they stood outside cafés and bars as the sky grew dark and Alexandra spoke about how she used to try to instigate philosophical debates with people she barely knew, her attempt at emulating the Sartre-de Beauvoir-Camus conversations of old. Of how she had once followed a man she believed to be Anthony Bourdain from Les Deux Magots to Bataclan only to realise, sore feet and all, she'd been following a random stranger. She spoke of how much you could miss people you never met, of how she always thought she'd get that chance to meet her favourite artists, and how one by one they were all dying before she could. The two of them crept through parks and Alexandra recalled a wine-infused night spent hunting pigeons in an attempt to outdo Hemmingway. She remembered vague childhood images of windows welcoming other countries, especially allies, and how much more connected the world had felt in her youth. How the Eiffel Tower once had no fencing underneath. How they'd visited a patisserie on spring break only for her parents to vow never to return because her father couldn't remember the word for cheese. She remembered the dusk in which she'd somehow found Saint Chapelle by accident during a depressive slump, and the timing was such that the cherry blossom glow of the windows was enough to save her from what would have been her first suicide attempt. And oh, and oh, how she loved her memories of the city.

Through the evening, with glistening, wide eyes and an unbreakable smile, Alexandra shared this Paris. South walked beside her with a love and a joy he never imagined he could feel. He admired how her past was interwoven with the tapestry of countless other people. He envied her view of the world in ways he could not verbalise. His shaking had stopped many memories earlier, and for that moment at least South felt connected with the human experience. They were, after all, a network of small connections.

Returning to the lobby, the pair were greeted by several teams of incognito security professionals. It wouldn't have been obvious they were security professionals if there weren't so many of them. So many, in fact, that the fire marshal was at the front desk trying to explain to the concierge they were over capacity. Meanwhile, small teams of nondescript men in nondescript suits were flashing immunity badges at the concierge and insisting in a cacophony of languages they weren't going to leave the lobby because of very important diplomatic work they weren't allowed to talk about.

"There's a ballroom literally through these doors right here," the fire marshal tried to explain.

"Tell that to them," one group said, pointing at another team. Then they argued in a neo-linguistic patois, borrowing words from every country on the planet as they yelled at each other, themselves, the fire marshal, the concierge, the hotel itself, a random family in Packers jerseys who just wanted their keys, please, if it's not too much trouble.

The arguments stopped once South and Alexandra walked through the foyer to the elevator. At that precise moment, every single person in the lobby who most definitely wasn't working for one secret police force or another spoke into their wrists and gingerly milled out of the hotel completely, congregating beside a limo to make phone calls. The fire marshal threw his hands up and turned to the concierge, who could barely muster a slight shoulder raise before returning to their computer.

"Hey, guys!" a voice yelled out just as the elevator arrived. It was Dean Mund. He stepped out from behind a pillar.

"What was that all about?" said Alexandra.

"Just some spies. Nothing to worry about. Apparently, some journalist paid off room service and got caught trying to enter your room, so everyone rushed out of their rooms to ensure their listening equipment wasn't compromised. But upstairs was too cramped, so they brought the conversation down here. They only just figured out you left the hotel."

"And how do you know all that?"

"They sure do talk too much," Mund replied. "I even heard some launch codes. Anyway, place should be deserted for a bit. Tea?"

The second-floor restaurant was busy. For every customer there were thirteen people dressed as waiters skittering from table to table. For an expensive hotel, it was refreshing to see them hire so many inexperienced, unattractive people over the age of thirty. It made finding a table difficult, however, as some of the waiters had outright given up on doing their jobs and were sat huddled around much of the window seating. The trio found a quiet booth behind a piano.

After spending five minutes trying to explain their order of three cups of tea to one waiter, they were left alone. Dean clucked, "Still don't know why they dropped you off in Paris for a night."

"They are romantics," said Alexandra, half serious.

The waiter arrived, spilling the tray at the edge of the table. While he cleaned up the mess, South scooted inward so the three of them sat squished together. "They flew us in a private jet to Beauvais and had a limo drive us to this hotel. We have to get up early to be taken to Schiphol for our flight to Geneva. I don't understand it."

Dean blinked, figuring out the logistics in his mind. "That's uh, some interesting cost cutting from the international elite right there."

A second waiter arrived with a second tray of four coffees. The first waiter pulled him to one side, and they argued. The trio tried to tune out their talking.

"I'm beginning to think they don't know how to spend money," said South.

Alexandra agreed. "Sometimes I forget that they work in a different scale than the rest of us. It's like they've forgotten how people, regular people, live." She switched to her faux-aristocrat voice, a banal impression that scared South in ways he couldn't understand. "Upset we're cutting school budgets? Just hire a private tutor. Not making enough money? Sell some of your stock in your father's company."

"Yes," Dean nodded. "They don't worry about toxic water supplies because they think all drinking water is bottled."

A third waiter arrived with mimosas and five croque monsieurs. The first two waiters grabbed him and sat him down at a nearby table.

South eyed them for a moment and pushed away his glass of water. "So, uh, if they're so detached from the real world, why am I talking to them? Seems like a waste of time."

"Uhm," Dean scratched his face with one hand and his one hand with the other. "Because you're not really talking to them, but through them. Best-case scenario is you open up some eyes, wake people up from their self-induced comas, make real, positive change happen. Failing that, you might just help monetise basic human decency."

"Monetise?"

"Oh, sure. These governments and the major companies who I'm sure will be watching won't do anything unless they can somehow make money from it. It's why you've got people polluting the oceans in the morning and selling metal straws to clean the same oceans in the evening. But, basically, change only happens on two conditions: there's more money to be made elsewhere, or the ruling class are scared of the guillotine."

Alexandra gave a disappointed sigh. "Just enough to save their heads."

"Same as it ever was," said Dean. "But it's an incremental push forward toward, what is it, liberte, egalite, and, uh--"

"Fratricide," said South. "But now what do you suggest I do when I get there, Dean?"

"Just don't let the bastards dictate the conversation. All they want to do is absolve their financiers and wash their hands of a billion murdered souls. So, hold them accountable. I'll be there for when it becomes a spectacle."

"I'll bring the popcorn," said Alexandra.

A fourth waiter arrived with three cups of tea. He'd poured the milk in first.

Road from the Gila River — 1850 CE:

Dust kicked up by the front riders created a wall of white grit, causing the men behind them to move onward with a perpetual squint. Behind the dust and the horses and the arid land, a black mass sat on the crested horizon. One hundred and forty-two men rode onward in the wilderness. At the back, protecting the carts and the mules, two riders sat with fingers stroking the triggers of their rifles. Their orders were vague and their destination unknown.

Those two riders had crossed many miles in silence. Malachi Roberts did not speak until spoken to and his compatriot, Hector King, was not much for talking. Hector rode like a man trapped in a haunted house, the land too familiar for an alleged Yankee. He was in good company: none of the men were who they pretended to be.

Hector spat what little fluid remained from his mouth and looked over at Malachi. "Anyone tell you why we are doing this?"

"Shit, brother, did you not hear?"

"All I heard was how much they were paying me."

"There was some sort of massacre is all I can tell."

Hector's heart dropped. "Who?"

"Some mercenaries. Scalpers. Bad men. They held up a ferry, and the Yuma got them."

Hector nodded. The cruelty of men was a muddled thing. "Was there a woman with them?"

"I don't reckon a woman would fare too well with these folks if you catch my meaning."

"This woman would have handled herself."

"Good for her. At either rate, I didn't hear anything about no woman. I'm just here for the wage. You'd have to ask the captain out front. Is that why you're here? Looking for this woman? It's always a woman.   Women or gold or the drink, how any man's story starts."

"Sometimes all three. She owes me more than you could know."

"I bet." Malachi looked up at the clear sky and wiped his brow.

Hector opened his eyes wider and rubbed at the grit and the sweat. He murmured softly, his voice lost under the galloping hooves beneath him, then turned to Malachi once more. "This expedition of ours means war."

"How can you be so sure?"

"Because it's what men do."

"True enough. First sign of real trouble and I'm out of here."

"Just be sure to get your wages first. I remember… stories of privateers who were promised a generous wage for their time on deck only to be crimped before they could collect their coin."

"Duly noted. You think the folk back home would trick us like that?"

"It's what men do."

"You're not too fond of your fellow man."

"Not overtly, no, but it's not their fault."

"Whose, then?"

"That's a story longer than this ride of ours."

They cantered onward. The vast herd of animals and riders alike had moved eastward toward an unseen destination. Hector would look for signs of the woman and go his own way when the opportunity presented itself. The less time spent in the accursed plains, the better.

"It is peculiar," said Hector, "That these dead men made it all the way here before dying. Strange they could continue for so long."

"You said it yourself: it's what man does. But sooner or later, your deeds will catch up with you and you will be judged accordingly. You can't outrun your past. It either catches up to you or you die. The ending's the same either way."

Hector nodded, that was the hope. "But what if you live forever?"

Malachi was taken aback by this question. He squinted at Hector as if he were riding with the man of La Mancha. "You mean like Cartaphilus?"

Hector laughed. "Now how's a man in our position get to learn a name like that?"

"Same way a man in our position gets to know what I'm talking about."

"Then yes, like Cartaphilus. What if you can't die and you keep outrunning your past?"

Malachi pondered the question for some time. "Time has a long reach. The more past you have the more better to catch you with. It's like those mountains yonder: put a pebble behind a boulder and I don't guess much will happen, but enough pebbles and enough time you've got yourself a landslide, or else the mountain itself turns to dust. It's inescapable. Death and your own past race to see who can catch you first."

Geneva, Switzerland — 20__ CE:

The airport vending machine was charging too much for snacks, and South didn't like the look of the chauffeur with his name on a whiteboard. Or the chauffeur with his name on a piece of cardboard. Or the nine chauffeurs with LED signs with his name on them. Maybe it was the early start or the feeling they had been followed from the moment they left the hotel in Paris, but he was reluctant to get into any cars. Alexandra doubly so.

The two of them ducked down behind a group of arriving passengers and crept through the long arrival gate, down into the train station below. A train was waiting as they arrived, so they quickly entered and sat in a second-class carriage. After two private jet flights and three prolonged limo rides, it was nice to once again be sitting among people who didn't care one jot about them.

The train took them to the middle of town, their feet took them to the waterfront. The sky was clear, revealing the jutting, snow-capped peaks of the mountain range far beyond the lake. Water glistened, all but transparent in its cleanliness. Stubby trees and healthy land extended out to the horizon, green and plentiful. A water fountain blew a spout into the air like a whale trying to impress its captain. There had been no fountain the last time South traipsed through the land. He remembered how overcast it was back then, how people thought the world was ending. Instead, just a year without a summer. How things had changed, now summer made up most of the year.

They walked together hand in hand through the streets of the city, climbing up to the church on the hill and its ancestors in its basement. From there, they spiralled downward, trying their best to get lost. It seemed they couldn't go more than three minutes in any direction without finding a plaque dedicated to an influential author or scientist of old. They hiked away from the town to a hill where a Frankenstein was originally conceived as a buddy cop detective series. They visited the graves of Borges, Piaget, and Calvin for reasons South pretended he understood. South never understood some people's need to visit the tombs of dead celebrities.

It seemed the neutrality of the country extended to the people, as nobody was interested in the pair. A welcome reprisal from their recent routine. And for most of their jumbled tour of the town, they had only each other and the beauty of the city for company. But as the sky grew wane, transforming into a delft blue, they could spot people in among the pedestrians and the tourists. Humourless people in suits staring at them, whispering into invisible phones or else making it obvious what they were up to. Men and woman hired into governments by metrics and online testing and relatives, yet incapable of following the most basic of instructions, namely: be inconspicuous. Their day trip had ended, and they walked with a slight skip to their lake front hotel.

South, who had necked with the last Pharaoh, set foot in Camelot, and attended galas celebrating the Spruce Goose, thought he knew opulence. He did not. The lobby of the hotel could have been carved out of dinosaur bones and decorated with meteors for all he knew. More a continuous and mechanical collection of expensive goods than a lobby, the two of them entered a ticking, finely tuned, immaculate room. They approached the front desk. Alexandra groaned to herself, tired of hotels and sick with guilt over her proximity to such wealth.

"Ah, non, monsieur, not in here please, you are to wait in the waiting lobby until your room is ready," the concierge said.

They followed an aye-aye length set of fingers to an oaken door, guarded by two giant men in bespoke suits. The waiting lobby was on the other side, a smaller version of the one they had just left, reserved just for them. It was decorated with pristine antique furniture, wartime loot from the last seven centuries, paintings from a bygone era long thought lost.

"Have they never heard of Ikea?" South asked.

"Shit, I think Sotheby's would be a downgrade for these guys."

The room had no other guests, and they weren't sure which chairs were to sit in and which were priceless decorations. South lowered himself on one bench but stood upright the moment it began to creek under the weight of his posterior. After some deliberation, they stood, and walked from one part of the room to the next with that slow and deliberate movement of someone who doesn't want to look like they're rushing through a museum. A brief vision of their day in Edinburgh. *This must be how mortality feels,* South thought, *experiences interlinked with no reason.*

After thirty minutes, the door opened. A small, sallow man with bucked teeth and a baggy seventy-thousand-euro suit entered. It was exactly the same as a cheap suit, but more people had died in making it. He smiled as much of a smile as he could muster. "Ah, splendid, you brought a friend," he said. His voice that of the colonisers of old. South knew the type.

"And you are?"

"Why, one is named Reginald Periwinkle Blythe-Dervish the third, and it is a most wonderful honour to make your acquaintance." He extended his damp paw, it trembled in the light.

South looked at the hand and then at Reginald. "Are you staying at the hotel?"

"Oh, here? No, one finds such establishments incredibly… how would *you* put it, tacky? It belongs to friends of the family, however, and as such one is sure they appreciate your staying here within this fine establishment." His hand still fluttered before South.

"Can I help you with anything, Reggie?"

"Oh, my dear boy, of course. It would be most helpful to one's estate if you could find it within yourself to repudiate the following things." His hand disappeared into his pocket and returned with a waxed sheet of card. Three demands were listed on one side, written in almost indecipherable calligraphy. "And then there is the simple matter of immortality. You *must* explain to me how one can live forever."

South took the card and looked down at the list. The offenses were ones the Dervish family had long since been accused of. Even so, it had taken over a hundred years for their past misdeeds to garner even a smidgen of public attention. South shook his head. "No."

Alexandra looked down at the card, let out a series of mildly blasphemous phrases, and walked to the far corner of the room, as if even associating with the writing was harmful.

"One is terribly sorry, but—"

"And cut the façade, you're fooling no one, Reggie."

The man's face tightened, brown furrowed. "Very well. We're not used to being told no. Maybe there's another way…" he looked at Alexandra. "Accidents do happen all the time."

With a speed and ferocity that scared even him, South's hand shot out and grasped the man's oily neck. "I'm not doing it. And as of this moment, if my darling over there so much as sneezes, I'm going to track you down. I will take my time, and believe me, I have enough of it."

He let go of the lord who buckled slightly, having never been told "no," much less physically threatened. "Funny," he said, "How you're so ancient and yet such a failure. My success is immeasurable, and you will be hearing from my lawyers."

South stepped closer to the man, who tried to remain still. "You've been given everything from birth, and you've lost half of it. I know your kind. You mistake being born for hard work. You're the guy who gets your newspapers to smear working people while staying quiet on what your daddy's friends get up to, aren't you? I know your secrets. Dervish, right?"

"Yes, on my father's side, but—"

"I could talk about that great grandfather of yours, if you want. Not to repudiate what's on that paper, but to confirm."

"No, that would be--"

"But let's forget all that, Reggie. You think you're a success, and right now maybe you have things going for you, but you're living in a book that isn't finished yet. How do you think you'll be remembered?"

Reginald had no answer.

"I was here when your family were publicly murdering people, and I'll be here when your bloodline runs out, Reggie. Think on that. Respice finem… Amici. That's how you like to talk, right? Quoting dead languages to flaunt that expensive education and feel special?"

Reginald regained his forged confidence as he stepped backward to the door. The ill-founded courage of the rich and the simple returning as the door creaked open. "Yes, very clever, little man, I'll have a good think about that in my yacht this evening."

South chuckled. "Qui totum vult totum perdit." He winked as Reginald clambered out of the room.

"What a dick," said Alexandra.

"Yeah, I should have just said that."

They hovered around that room for three more hours without further incident. Alexandra had grown fond of a painting depicting an old man in Elizabethan garb standing over the pyramids. There was a scuffle outside the door and one of the guards poked their head in. "Ah! Ich habe Dean Mund geschlossen…" he trailed off.

Dean entered. He looked tired, as if he had just spent too much money to fly from Paris to Bern and then driven to Geneva to find his friends. "Hey guys, having fun?"

"What are you doing?" Alexandra asked.

"The fix is in, guys, the fix is in. I'm being moved to Angola in the morning. Just thought I'd come tell you goodbye for now."

The pair didn't know how to react.

"It's fine," Dean continued, "given the circumstances, it could be a lot worse. But I just wanted to tell you there's more going on than you know."

"Yes, I just met Reggie Dervish," said South.

"Well, shit, that's not good. Look, I'm going to drive back to Bern and get packed, but I just wanted to tell you in person that people who we aren't supposed to know about are scared. They want to keep you bored, and they're used to acting with impunity. Please, just be careful. Right, well, it's been a pleasure."

And with that, Dean left.

Later, when their penthouse suite was ready, South and Alexandra sat on the third-floor balcony and watched the city and the lake glow in the evening light. Their home for the week felt too close to 1789 Versailles for either of them to feel too comfortable inside.

South looked over at Alexandra. "What do you—"

"Can we not?"

He rolled back into his seat and leaned back.

She sighed. "For this evening at least, can we just sit here and watch the sun go down? I'm not sure what tomorrow will bring. This could be our last night of freedom together."

"And you want to spend it looking at the sky?"

"Well I'm a few years sober and we can't go outside without a bunch of suits stalking us, so yes, I would like to spend it looking at the sky."

South nodded. "Could we watch some television later?"

"You know, I saw a grand piano and a stuffed rhinoceros in there but no television."

London, England — 1889 CE:

A limp pair of legs swung mere inches from the floor. Hands with broken fingers and missing nails chained to a rafter. Wrists red, skin scraped red by bondage. Mouth gagged and bloodied. Eyes swollen and watery. His bare chest an impressionistic canvas of slits and bruises. A primal whimpering trapped in stammering lungs; diaphragm contorted by heavy blows. The room consumed by the stench of burnt flesh, copper, human waste. The man's head hung low, engulfed in his own shadow. He was trying to find the energy to sob, but even that had been taken from him. At once numbed and aching, his body called out for death.

Sat down at the far side of the cell was Georg Downs. He looked at his work and felt nothing. He placed his hand above a nearby candle and the man watched as Georg sat unflinching for five minutes. The man knew of Mister Downs but had hoped never to meet him. An inquisitor for hire, paid handsomely on occasion by her majesty's constabulary to extricate answers from nefarious men, Georg was less a man than Retribution itself.

Georg took a scalpel from the table and warmed it above the flame. The man recognised the blade as the one he'd used on... no. He shuddered. Georg smiled a laborious smile as the tip of the blade glowed.

"Tell me once more," said Georg, rising to his feet.

The man could not form an answer. He stammered through his blood-soaked gag with sounds closer to Morse code than the spoken word. Georg removed the rag and tossed it to the stone floor.

"Tell me once more, my friend, and all of this will be over for you."

"I..." the man's words caught in his engorged throat. "I did it. I killed them women." His strength, what little remained, escaped him, and his body fell supine once more.

Georg stepped back and nodded to himself. He knew as much. Through the caged door of the cell, a constable watched on in disbelief both at the acts of cruelty and the confession. The constable turned and ran out of the jail in search of a superior.

Once they were alone, Georg's left hand was upon the man's throat in an instant. He slid the still-glowing scalpel behind his prey's ear. It hissed as it seared a patch of flesh. "Good," Georg began, "That's a start. But you know why I'm really here. I know about your organisation. You better tell me everything you know about your cult of death."

"Wh-what?"

"Did you do them girls back in Austin, Texas, too? Or was that another member of your order?"

"I have n-never left this country!" The blade cooled and almost stuck to the man's skin, leaving a raised triangle of bubbling pustules.

"When they get back down here, you're going to be put somewhere horrible for the rest of your life. I could end it all right now for you. Make it quick. No shame or dishonour dying here. All you have to do is tell me about your death cult. Tell me about your master North and her plans."

The hanging man's eyes probed the room, unable to focus. In time, his exhausted stare met Georg's. He coughed up a thick sting of dark blood. It swung pendulously over his chest, smearing phlegm as broken ribs rattled in his chest. "You keep saying these words," he gasps, "And I don't know what you mean. I don't know what to tell you, but I will tell you what I can." He sucked in air as if his last breath and rolled his broken head. "All I did was kill some women what deserved it."

A surge of energy. The man began to tremble and shake. "You have my confession!" he screamed. "You have my confession! What do you want from me?"

Georg was unmoved by the performance. He slid the tip of his scalpel across the man's cheek. A red line appeared, promising to bulge outward and reveal the musculature buried underneath. "Tell me about North!" he raised it voice. It had been a while. He threw a fist into the man's solar plexus and the man swung there, gasping for air.

A stampede of worn boots made its way down the stairs and a dozen men were in the cell doing their best to hold Georg back. He raged against them but knew the moment was lost. Even if he killed them all, there would be no confession. He broke free of the constables and sat back in his chairs. The constables left single file. In their stead, an aristocratic woman, a giant, a child, and Detective Blight entered the room.

"Are we done here?" said Detective Blight, admiring Georg's work. He stood beside the shaking body and shook his head. "You won't be killing any more people, will you, Lord Dervish?"

The hanging and broken man couldn't form words between his whimpers and pained hisses, and instead said "y-y-y-ssshhh-ssshhhh-uuh-wuh-ohh." He trailed off, losing consciousness again. The woman and the giant attended to him.

Georg looked once more at his scalpel and considered killing Lord Dervish anyway. Detective Blight's rough hand grasped his forearm, as if anticipating the plan. The detective lowered his head to Georg's ear and whispered. "Can't let you have this one, lad. He's friends with the queen. The lady here has something better for you, though. We'll get you the woman you're looking for."

Georg nodded. He watched as the aristocrat cut down Lord Dervish. The giant hoisted the shattered man up over his shoulders and carried him out of the cell and up the stairs. The young boy skipped behind the giant. Before the aristocrat made her exit, she stopped at the door.

"I shall return later, detective," she said, "I must get this poor man home first. But I will stick to our arrangement." She looked Georg up and down, the disdain not even hidden, and all but evaporated.

When they were sat comfortably and unwatched in Blight's office, Georg spoke. "What was all that?"

"You know how it is. Those types live by another set of rules. Lord Dervish, though, has been stopped for good. He'll spend the remainder of his days in agony and anonymity in some asylum or another. That's unfortunately as far as justice goes for men like him. The public will never know the case was solved."

"Good for them. But my case wasn't solved. He was about to tell me, Blight."

Blight leaned back in his oaken chair and lit a pipe. "Oh, don't you worry about that, Georg, we have news on that. We just have to wait for that… woman to return. Best to just wait here for her."

"And when will she be back?"

"No telling with that sort. Brandy?"

They sat and waited. Blight asked Georg of his past, of his search for North, and Georg answered as best he could without incriminating himself. He spoke of the years infiltrating mercenaries, gang, and despot militias in the search for clues. Of the battlefields he'd scoured and the suffering he'd witnessed. He couldn't explain to Blight how he knew it was all connected, but he tried anyway. North as the leader of a secret society intent on poisoning and destroying the human race. Blight wasn't convinced. They talked of this until they all but fell asleep.

The aristocrat returned just before dawn, the giant and the young boy in tow. The boy carried a heavy leather tome with gilded pages. He tossed it hard onto Blight's desk. The detective sat upright with a jump. Georg, who had slept through Waterloo, took longer to wake up.

"Desmond, Georg, please forgive my impertinent tardiness. This book belonged to the New Hellfire Boys, and they were far more reluctant to surrender it than I anticipated."

The giant let out a low "ha" and nodded at fond memories.

Detective Blight poured through the manuscript. Swirling red ink, blotted handwriting, Latin, languages unused by any known human, demonic diagrams. "Lady Morecombe, I don't understand what this is."

"No, but then this isn't for you, is it?" she gestured at Georg. Beneath her crisp accent was her real voice trying to escape. "This is a ledger of sorts. All manner of crimes committed of the past hundred years; every syndicate known to man. It's all in there. Mister Downs, my sources suggest there's a growing problem in central Africa. You might start there. At the very least, I would urge you to stay out of England for a while. We have a reputation to maintain, and your gorilla antics make it hard for people to take us seriously."

"He was a murderer."

"Yes, but a useful one. Without your interference, we could have… At any rate, what you're looking for isn't here, but our work is, so the sooner you leave the better."

The boy spoke up, "We could use him, Lady."

"He has his ways, I agree," said the giant.

"I too wouldn't mind keeping him around," said Detective Blight.

"He wouldn't pass initiation, and you all know it. A useful tool is still a tool. And you wouldn't want to join our ragtag crew of irregulars anyway, would you, Georg? Because then they'd learn your secret."

Georg thinned his eyes. "I have my own work to do."

"Quite right, boys, would you wait outside?" Lady Morecombe said. They obliged. She picked up the book and scanned it for a map of a city in the Congo "Here, see, this hellish playground disguised as a republic? I would start there, Mister Downs. You can get your revenge and we can get back to the good fight. Hard for us to concentrate with an aberration like you around."

"I'll miss you too, Priscilla," said Georg. Lady Morecombe made to speak again, but Georg continued. "I'll leave you to your parlour tricks and robbery, missus. You can keep pretending to be something you're not uninterrupted. But if I find out this book is a forgery, or you've sold me a tale, I will be back for you."

"Your threats mean nothing to me, Georg the Undying. We're both pretenders here. Just remember there are fates worse than death." And with that, Lady Morecombe vanished into the streets.

"I think she's taken a fancy to you," said Detective Blight.

"Then it's a shame I will never return to these godforsaken lands."

Blight stood and approached Georg. "In that case," he extended his hand, "Thank you for all your work. We made a good pair for a moment there. You got some real monsters off the street, and that's no small feat. No small feat at all. You are a man of great importance."

South
Just outside where a group of planets used to be
The Universe
No Clue

Alexandra:

You used to ask me what immortality was like, and I tried to explain it through many metaphors and similes. None of them really conveyed what I wanted, especially since you mercifully executed metaphors some time ago. I've had a few billion years up here to myself, and I've been replaying those conversations just as much as anything. It's got to where I often wonder if I'm remembering the event itself or what I wished had happened. Reality is a tricky thing, as it turns out. It's a customisable and subjective ball of clay where even facts can be altered. It was true for history books and all the truer when you're alone with all of existence in your head. Still, it's not like there's a fact-checker floating around wanting to correct the things I've done. The things I only think I've done. Delusions.

But, yes, anyway, immortality:

Do you remember when you were depressed but also on some strict deadline for one of your travel books? Or even the times you just wanted to go out and do something? And you'd have this lengthy itinerary in your head about how the day was going to go, and all the things you'd do, but by the time you willed yourself out of bed and got dressed half the day was already gone. You, the prisoner of your own head in those bad days, your body rebelling against your desires. You, just sitting there and staring at a menagerie of screens all while your inner voice was screaming out "What are you doing? We have stuff to do" the entire time. Hours wasted flicking through meaningless things while you grew to resent yourself more and more, which only fed into the disease. Entire days, weeks even, lost to inaction, even with the best of intentions behind you.

Yeah, it's a lot like that. But forever. Always wanting to do more, but never being able to do anything, locked up in a dungeon of your own making. At least *you* kept trying, though. Even in the worst moments, you found the strength to keep going. Those rough days made me love you all the more, I think. I know.

At any rate, mi amor, we found ourselves in the midst of a lengthy questioning from the UN. Or I did. You were all but sequestered in the hotel. We knew something we couldn't see was at play. Even now, I'm not sure just how many different groups of people were conspiring against each other. It would have been easy to lose myself under the expectations, the subterfuge, the invisible agenda. I could have just walked away. The world was always more humanity's problem than mine, as evidenced by the fact I'm still here. You didn't let that happen.

You, glorious, sweet you, had some different ideas. Said I had an obligation to myself as much as the people around me. And maybe, in the end, none of it really mattered on a universal scale. But as you always said (and by always, I mean once at a picnic), if you can't try to be the best version of yourself, why bother getting out of bed?

Beds, coincidentally, are something I miss a lot more than I thought I would. I have a list of all the things I miss, and they broke into the top fifty, snuggled between museums and the tide. I was shocked.

You, of course, my impermanent you, remain at the top of the list.

As little good as that does now.

Trademarked Sporting Arena Near The UN, Geneva - 20__ CE:

When you are about a hundred million years old, days bleed in together. Even with the best of intentions, time has its own plans. For South this was no truer than it was the morning of the first meeting. The moment he was standing on a small staged in a packed stadium felt, to him, exactly like the moment in which he was eating cold toast and being told good luck by a tired Alexandra.

He looked out at the audience. Thousands. Thousands? There weren't a thousand countries, were there? That was later. Geographical norms were a hard thing to keep track of, much like remembering what the internet thinks is funny (weird Japanese GIFs, ironic racism, bona fide racism) or how much nudity is considered socially acceptable (lots, a little, a bit, lots again if it's a slow news week). He noticed Them, They, the people who ruled more than just countries. Men and women the result of both incestuous union and centuries of wealth consolidation. People like Reggie Dervish standing up in the balconies looking down on the theatre with his equally ghoulish oligarch friends, the kind of men who would be running used car lots and paying for unfulfilling sex were it not for their parents' parents' parents. Country representatives looking back at their corporate sponsors like nervous children at an audition their mother dragged them to. Five hundred journalists all owned and operated by eight drinking buddies, not a notepad or laptop between them, the story already written. Those eight drinking buddies sitting in a private suite above the floor, old, haggard, soulless husks with more power than the gods they pretended to believe in. It was clear South was not at a regular hearing. He was back at the Colosseum, the sacrificial altar, John Merrick's medical presentation.

From a podium at the side of the stage, a speaker coughed into their microphone. Earpieces the room over emitted low white noise as translators in a separate room got ready to talk. "The first thing I would like to do is welcome you to this hearing, uh, Mister South. It was very generous of you to offer to attend such a meeting. I understand that some have chosen to approach you recently, but please know this was not at the UN's request and the issue is being looked into."

South realised for the first time he was sitting alone on the stage. A spectacle. "Thanks," he said.

"We have gathered today both to ascertain the world's accurate history and whether you are a threat to modern living. I see that you have mainly worked menial jobs this century, and I take that to be a positive sign. But I, and I think I speak for everyone here when I say this, am concerned about one thing. You are an immortal, indestructible being of a prehistoric age. Compared to us, you are like Ares of old. So, I ask you: why haven't you chosen to rule over us as a god emperor yet?"

"Yet?"

"I mean, no, forget the yet."

"I suppose the answer would be: and then what? Have you any idea how boring that would be? And there'd be repercussions I'd have to live with. You live very brief lives, so it's easy to overlook the ramifications of your actions. I don't. I suppose that's why. I couldn't imagine doing it for the rest of forever. And, uh, yeah, I think that's also why people in this room, for instance, are so adamant on sticking to their script even at the cost of their grandchildren's lives, you know? You'll be dead soon enough so you cling to the things you think might make you immortal, not worried about the consequences. It's why those we've chosen to remember have either been revealed as horrible frauds or else become lionised propaganda figures. It's—"

The speaker's hand went up and South's mic cut out. Whispers in a multitude of languages as the UN representatives and the journalists talked to their masters. Dean had been far too optimistic in his version of events.

"Thank you," a different speaker said. "Would you be willing to start at the beginning of it all? How you were born? Important life events we could learn from? Was there an ancient civilisation of people like you? Do you have any technology?"

"NO! LEAD IN TO THAT YOU DIMWIT" someone yelled from up in the rafters. South stood and took a step back. He scanned the room a third time.

"I can't do this," he said to no one in particular.

"Is there something wrong?"

"Yes, this is a sham. I agreed to talk to the UN and to the people outside, not corrupt journalists, not your financiers, and certainly not the people sitting up in private suites. If we're going to do this, I want this to be broadcast on live television on every available channel. I don't want reporters owned by the state in the audience, and I don't want people who've never worked an honest day in their life fielding the questions."

"That's a lot of people you're kicking out."

The crowd laughed.

"Another thing," South stood over the mic revealing his true stature for the first time since ancient Egypt. "Just so we are clear, I have remembered every face in this room. I've already had this chat with my friend Reggie, so for the benefit of the rest of you, if so much as an embarrassing accident befalls anyone while I'm here, if anyone else is shipped off overseas, if anyone protesting outside suffers because of your actions, I will pursue every single one of you. You're all accountable for what happens in these coming years, and I'm a reckoning you can't run from."

"Is that a threat?"

"Yes. And there's nothing you can do about it." He shrank back down and smiled. "Be nice and I will be too."

More murmurs, a few yells. As sufferers of inflated ego and arrested development, the crowd were not used to being told no, unless, that is, unless they were paying for the experience. South remained motionless. Rustling sounds as sheets of people were thrown about in distant corners of the auditoriums. A few cries of "he can't do that" and "does he know who I am?" in whiny voices. But they weren't in a restaurant and South wasn't a waiter. He smiled.

"Hey, guys, thinking of this as a learning experience. You've made it this far without someone standing up to you. It'll be good practice for when the people finally have enough," he said.

Someone cut his mic again. Slow dromedary gaits from a slew of billion-aires as they filed out the upper regions of the room.

A new speaker took to a podium.

"Mister South, we will see you in the morning, thank you for your time."

South bowed and left the stage. He felt like doing a lot of things, but mainly he wanted to skip along the lake to the hotel. In the old days, it would have taken him an entire year to annoy so many dignitaries at once.

The SS Lapland, Somewhere in the Atlantic – 1919 CE:

"I heard this ship was haunted," the acne-riddled DeLindt boy said to the other children. They were sat semi-circle looking at him, each whispering in their own brand of broken English. "There were people on board who were supposed to drown on the Titanic, and Death cursed this ship for saving their lives. When Death comes for you, you best come the first time, or unspeakable horrors follow you and your rescuers. My poppa told me it almost got blown up in the war and everything. Ghosts are trying to sink this ship and they won't stop until they do."

"Let me see if I catch the cut of your drift: it's haunted by ghosts who want to blow their own vessel up for some reason?" said the preppy Trevarrow girl. She was the only child in the group with the confidence to speak up when DeLindt started with his stories. The others huddled together, both believing and not. It was an eclectic bunch of children who bonded down in the bowels of the ship because there was not much else to do. They were equal parts bored and frightened of things beyond their realm of understanding, each unified by their contempt for the world as a whole and their dread of an uncertain future.

The whole world was haunted, was what Gideon Grieves wanted to say to the little ones. They had entered his hiding place, and he had hidden behind a cart of soiled linens. The whole world a ghost story. He had seen first-hand how the ghosts of old empires were still ravaging the planet. In his journeys since Whitechapel he had seen it all: the so-called Free State of the Congo; the slaughter of civilians, Hereros and Namaqua, Armenian and Greek; The White Terror; The Great War. More still, he heard about in passing, knowing the truth was more inhumane and crueller than the story he was given. He had fallen in anguish beside piled bodies of soldier and citizen alike across the continents, never grasping quite what it was all for. He imagined the mountains of the innocent dead had a few questions of their own, too. The curse of North and her cult of death ran strong through the veins of progress.

They were living in an era of untold advancement, of automation, where bright futures seemed ever present on the horizon. Writers and politicians alike spoke of utopia, dreams never believed possible. The crueller facets of man's history were allegedly behind them, replaced by hope and opportunity for all. For all, they said. Yet despite this talk, Gideon could see the world had not changed all that much. The wording was smarter; the cruelty concealed behind plucky slogans. Old methods were gone not for their inherent cruelty but because there were more efficient methods with which to rule the world.

He wanted to look at the children. Ask them why they and their parents were running from one place to another. What they expected to be different. They could not hope to escape suffering because life itself was suffering. And so, it would remain until Gideon could finally save them all.

His research had revealed the death cult were once again convening in the Americas. Their operations ran through borders and languages. He had connected a huge network of industrialists, politicians, and landed gentry across the world and it was clear they were the true rulers. For all the United States' talk of Justice and representation, they had replaced a king with a dozen puppet masters, just like the rest of the world. An invisible hand moving the shape of history to suit its needs. It was the only explanation. Why else would supposed Free countries turn a blind eye to the massacres and colonialism of others? Because North was manipulating them all, of course.

"I think I heard a ghost," said the Evett child, running a mucus covered sleeve across their nose before pointing to the laundry hamper.

"Poppycock," said the DeLindt boy.

"No, I heard it too, a growl or something. It's coming from behind those dirty clothes!" said another child.

The group all stood and stared at Gideon's hiding place, each hoping another would find the courage to peek behind it. Gideon did not have the patience for indecisive children and stood up from the shadows. The children screamed. The younger ones ran off screaming toward their quarters. Only four brave souls remained: Trevarrow, Evett, DeLindt, and a fourth child who wasn't on the manifest. They stood poised, ready to fight an unwinnable battle. Gideon smirked in appreciation.

"Are you spying on us?" said DeLindt.

"Are you a stowaway?" said Trevarrow.

"A ghost?" Evett.

"Yes," said Gideon.

"Well, which one is it? Speak up, sir," DeLindt said, puffing his chest out and taking on the posture of someone whose only knowledge of fist fighting came from drawings.

"All of them. Do you children want to hear a real ghost story? I have one for all of you." Gideon leapt onto the dirty linens and sat with his legs swinging. The children sat and faced him, deciding in unison the strange man was more pathetic than scary. Of the children who fled, several made their slow reappearance, brought on by curiosity or guilt. Soon Gideon had a full audience.

"There was a ghost who haunted a whole… castle. They haunted it since the dawn of time. It wanted only one thing: for man to kill man. And—"

"What about girls?" Trevarrow.

"Them too. It wanted everyone to kill everyone else because death was the only thing it enjoyed. It wanted the whole castle to itself. The ghost would wait until the humans were sleeping and then whisper lies to them, turning brother against brother, sister against sister, neighbours into enemies. And people would hear the ghost's words and kill their new enemies. And the ghost would smile."

"Why?" Evett.

"Well, you see, uh, because," Gideon paused. That was a question he hadn't asked himself in ages. "Shut up, kid, that's why. The ghost wanted the entire castle to herself and…"

"How grotty! A girl ghost?" said DeLindt.

"Ghosts can be girls too!" said Trevarrow.

"Nuh-uh," a small child pipped, "My daddy says only soldiers get to be ghosts."

"That is absolutely preposterous," said Trevarrow. "Besides all of which, girls most certainly can be soldiers if they put their minds into it."

Gideon coughed, trying to win back their attention. "Well, in a way this ghost was a soldier. The first solider. Like the God of soldiers. And she—"

"Like Athena?" asked Evett.

"No, Athena is way overrated these days. Back then people didn't… I mean, yes, sure, she was like Athena. Anyway--"

"Shiva was the goddess of war too, right?" someone asked.

DeLindt shook his head. "No, Shiva is a boy and is probably still around."

"Well then, Freya."

Gideon groaned. "Right, yes, but we've, we've gotten a bit off topic, haven't we?"

"There's a haunted castle," Evett offered with a conspiratorial wink.

"Yes, a big castle. And this ancient evil ghost is going to destroy it all if she doesn't get her way. And only another ghost can put an end to it, but it's hard for the other ghost because he's not a part of that world. And there's, um, these murderers outside the castle, too, and--"

"Maybe she's just lonely," said Trevarrow.

"What?"

"Yeah," Evett agreed, "If you were the only ghost in the castle, you'd probably want to make friends or something. She might just want to be heard."

DeLindt gave the considered nod of a seasoned scholar. "Hm, yes, quite. If I were a ghost, I imagine I'd be quite cross there were no other ghosts in the castle and the only ghost outside wanted to kill me. I suppose given the circumstances; I might get quite naughty myself."

"Yes, that poor ghost girl just wants a friend," Trevarrow added. "When you think about it that way, this story is very sad. So sad she has to resort to murder."

"And that is assuming she even is making people kill each other, perhaps she's actually trying to save them," said DeLindt, who by that stage of the story was an authority on ghosts. "Maybe she was just trying to get rid of the baddies."

"I prefer cowboy stories," said one of the younger children with a yawn. "I'm going to be a cowboy when I get to America."

"No, you can't. There are no cowboys anymore. Not real ones. Not the ones you're thinking of."

"There are too, and they all have pretty horses."

"No, they all got killed in a war and so did the tribe people. All that's left is people in suits and dresses."

"That doesn't sound very fun."

"It wouldn't be. But there's gangsters now. I'm going to be a gangster. You get to play with machine guns!"

"Well, if you can do that, I can be a cowboy."

Gideon rubbed his temples and looked down at the children. "I will tell you a good cowboy story next. But back to this ghost. She wasn't alone, and she wasn't trying to help people. That would be ridiculous."

"How do you know?" asked Evett. "You're not a real ghost."

"And how are you so confident I'm not a ghost?"

DeLindt stood up and kicked Gideon's leg. He turned to face his fellow children and nodded. "You can't kick ghosts. How about you tell us the cowboy story, because this ghost one is completely off the rails at this point."

Children just didn't understand the truth, Gideon thought. But he nodded. He would tell them the cowboy story.

"It all started when there was the gold rush. I was up in Oregon at the time and--"

Trevarrow's hand rose.

"What is it now!?"

"No, you weren't."

"Now, uh, South, would you mind beginning today by telling us which race you identify as?"

"Uh, what?"

They were in a smaller auditorium now that the bankers and moguls and journalists were gone. Many of the representatives sat on repurposed school chairs instead of at their desks. South sat alone on a stage designed for twelve people. He chose the third seat on the left, so the representatives all sat with a slight tilt to their bodies. The older members of the audience would have to stand up and stretch every third minute to prevent their backs from locking into that position, causing them to look like Bruce Lee mid heel kick, if Bruce Lee had a BMI of 33% and wore stretched out formal wear that seemed to cling on for dear life.

"Your race. What is your race?" The representative salivated right behind the microphone.

"What does that matter?"

"Well, you see, it's just important we know what race you are since you're the oldest person on earth and—"

"Oh, I see where this is going. I'm not a person and I'm not a race."

"But everyone is a race. Race is very important."

"I've gone hundreds of thousands of years without being a race, and it's worked wonders for me. But let me ask you something, what race were the Neanderthals? Or the homo habilus? And why the hell is this, out of all possibilities, your first question?"

Another representative grabbed the microphone. "We just thought it would be important to determine your race for reasons and stuff."

South threw his legs onto the table before him. It was going to be one of those conversations.   "I'm pre-racial, guys. I was there before your ancestors got pale and created artificial divides."

"Interesting you should say that. Are you saying you chose not to stop those divides from occurring?"

"How would I do that? How would I stop your ancestors?"

The representatives talked among themselves. They had a hard time deciding what they would do in the same situation, but each of them was convinced they could have handled it well. "We'd have just told people to stop being racist."

"And how has that been working out for you?"

A few of the representatives coughed. Their chairman who had a mic of their own tapped the black bulb and spoke into it. "This conversation about race is making me uncomfortable, Mister South. Perhaps we could move onto greener acres? Now, tell us why you didn't stop slavery when you had the chance."

South slumped further into his chair for a moment before regaining himself. He sat as an irate coach in a losing game of basketball, legs wide, back hunched, his hands wrapped against the base of his microphone. "Which time?… But no, I tried. Not that you'd believe me on that. The problem with huge issues like that is one person, immortal or not, can't bring about a systemic change without destroying the system itself. The scope if too large, the repercussions too many to think about. None of you would be here today if I did that."

One representative spoke up. "We'd have stopped it."

South smiled. "So how come there's more slavery now than there ever has been? Why aren't you doing anything about that? Or the genocides going on in a few corners of the world? Or the billionaire sex rings we all know about but seem helpless to stop? Why aren't you doing anything about them, if you're so righteous and angry and just and capable?"

"Those are, uh, matters we are looking into."

"You're representing the entire world and you haven't stopped shit. I'm just one depressed immortal. Why aren't you stopping the atrocities happening right now? Why is so much of your work so hollow and performative? You seem to think you have all the answers, but what the fuck have you actually done to end any of these tragedies? At least I'm out there helping where I can. You just sit around assigning blame and accomplishing nothing."

The chairman tapped their engorged stem again. "Sir, we're not on trial here. We just want to establish if you're responsible for the predicament the world is in right now."

"Wait, so this is a trial?"

"No. Not entirely. I'm sure you can appreciate having an ancient being in our midst raises some questions and we want to see what impact this will have on the world as a whole."

"And your first move is to ask me what race I am?"

"What would you rather we ask?"

South spat out a disappointed laugh. "I don't know, maybe how we can collectively improve the world for the people out there? I know you're all sleeping very comfortably at night pretending to do things, but I don't know, I thought this could perhaps at least encourage us to try to bring about change."

The representatives looked at their shoes. "We're not worried about that right now. We're concerned you might lead people to nihilism and despair. You undermine a lot of belief systems by existing, and if you could just clarify some things for us, that would be super."

"Clarify what?"

The chairman's tongue darted from cheek to cheek like a ping-pong ball. "Tell us about God."

"No."

"Oh please. Go on."

"What good would that do? It would change zero minds and only make things worse."

"If we could just learn where we came from…"

"That's what faith is for. No. I'm not concerned about the past, I'm concerned about right now. The world is dying, and people are suffering. What do your belief systems tell you to do about that? Or don't you care? I want to help people. I'm not interested in alleviating your guilt or massaging your tortured belief systems. It's the people I care about. That's why I'm here. That's why I've done all of what I have. For the people."

"And what would you have us do?"

"Anything would be a start."

"We're not too good with that."

"Then let me. Give me a chance to make a statement to the people, and we'll see what action looks like."

The representatives conferred among themselves. Without warning, they rose to their feet and walked out of the auditorium, leaving South alone on the stage. He sat there with the shivers of someone trying to recreate what they'd just experienced. This was not the meeting of great minds he'd envisioned, more a Saturday morning chat at the library with a new support group. He closed his eyes and inhaled. There was so much to learn from history, but the most important lesson of all was: there is no future in the past.

The representatives shepherded themselves back to their seats, and the chairman stood before them. "You can give your statement tomorrow. But today we want you to answer some questions."

South gave a begrudged sigh. "I reserve the right to ignore all stupid questions."

The chairman smiled. "Great! Everybody line up, please."

The room was at once abuzz with excited chatter. As much as anything, they'd wait for this moment. Some delegates had binders full of questions and stood, transfixed, by their chairs trying to decide which question to ask. Others whispers to their nearest friends and giggled like nervous school children at a special assembly. A line formed at the base of the stage and a microphone was set up. It was the fastest the UN had ever worked. The first representative stepped forward. "Hi, so, like, what was ancient Rome like?"

"Smelly."

A few murmurs in the audience, most pleased with this revelation. The representative smiled and skipped back to their chair, the information clearly confirming a long-held belief. Another man in a suit took their place and nervously puckered their lips against the microphone.

"What's your biggest regret in life, South?"

Cerro Azul, Chile - 1932 CE:

South marched through terrain he no longer recognised, cities lost or rebuilt or brand new. Borders ever changing. Kingdoms lost to the sad annals of history, closer to footnotes than tomes. But for the outlines and scars of a forgotten life, there was nothing he remembered. The land remained the same but the rest nothing but whispers.

Dense, swirling smoke plumes of the volcano engulfed the sky before him as he walked toward his destiny. His body vibrated. A presence nearby stirred the ancient receptors in his brain. The missing part of him was waiting interminably beneath the thick, black clouds. He walked upward toward the destination, both knowing and not knowing what he would find.   It   had taken thirteen years since leaving the boat to track the trail of carnage North left in her wake. Her bloodied breadcrumbs crossed the northern continent, with South arriving too late to prevent a dozen or more tragedies. He saw it all as he followed: unsolved crimes, axe men, murder, assassination, revolution, syndicates, a general medley of suffering big and small. South had only to follow the ample toll of the dead to realise she was leading him back to where they last fought. His bones rattled to her siren song. It echoed through the blood-soaked homes and bullet riddled streets like the clang of a malicious tuning fork.

He forced his way up the side of the volcano, clawing his way up loose earth and coarse rock. She sat there on the precipice, dangling her legs over the edge. The heat and the stench of sulphur was enough to drive off and kill a mortal. He looked at her, and if she were not so close to hell itself, he would have thought it was a different woman. Her eyes were hollow, cheeks desiccated, frame skeletal, a living cadaver of her former self. She had wrapped herself in furs and her hair was matted with gristle and soot. South remembered how she would dress in the palace all those aeons earlier. North looked up at him, her neck weak and eyes dim.

"I've been waiting for you," she said.

South thought back on all her crimes and did his best to remind her of them as he skirted the edge of the volcano to reach her. He spoke in a language only they knew. "I will finally stop all this madness. I've seen what you've done, North. The wars, slavery, how you poisoned leaders, corrupted kings, told armies to murder their own people, to colonise and corrupt. It ends, North. I am not what I was when we last fought. Did you mean for me to find you? I was at Whitechapel. People have told me all about Villisca and New Orleans and Lava Lake, and so many places. Was this just a game to you? Do you enjoy the death of innocents? Couldn't you have just sent a letter? I followed the path of bloodshed and devastation knowing it was you and I'm finally here to…" he paused, his mind too slow to match the speed of his words, "On behalf of all you have robbed of a future, I am here to put an end to you once and for all. Is there anything you would like to say before it is over?"

North looked once more at South, her face tired and indifferent. "You're right, my old friend, my time is at an end. I've been waiting for you for so long. Sat on this very spot. Waiting. For hundreds of years I have waited. Waiting for you to come back so we could talk. You must forgive me, but I don't know what you're talking about. Death? I've killed no one. I have sat on this spot since you were washed away."

South was halfway around the volcano's brim. "Liar! You lie. I have seen your corrupting force the world over. All that harm you did. Don't take me for one of those foolish mortals."

"Not I, dear brother. Has it not occurred to you once over all these years that the humans brought their own evil into the world?"

South shook his head. He swung his hands out and gestured as if toward the world beneath them. "This is all your doing. It has to be. You did it."

"Is that how you've chosen to remember the past, South? I may have given them a nudge in one direction a long time ago, but that was it. Their brutality is all their own. All I did was give them tools. Am I to be held responsible for their improper use?"

South stopped walking. He resisted the urge to sit. Staring at North, he saw no trickery in her eyes. He lied to himself. "I don't believe you."

North stood, her body frail and withered, energy drained from it as if she was searching for death's embrace. "You can believe whatever you choose, but my truth won't change. I thought I was helping them, from a distance, and then I realised as you fell into the river I was wasting my time. To be honest, I never understood why you were so concerned about that race. Is it because they look like us? Apart from that minor similarity, I don't see why you didn't champion the cat, the eagle, or the cow. At least those animals don't have the same capacity for malice. Except maybe the cat. But still…"

"There are two animals with that capacity for malice, North, or have you forgotten what we've done?"

"We were farmers. Does the shepherd rue the culling of his flock?"

"There is culling and then there is a legacy of death. You—"

"Even if that's true, my role in this planet ended a long time ago. And you? You've been running from yours for centuries." She turned to look down at the world below as if seeing it for the first time. Her eyes glistened. "My intentions, while you might not believe me, were pure, but they corrupted my message all the same. They've been on their own path for millennia now. If you think this legacy of death, as you put it, is bad now, just wait. I can promise you one thing: they are going to get worse. Trust me, my brother, my friend, my love. This experiment failed the moment The Creator abandoned us all. The whole world is forfeit, and I have watched with despair while they perverted any lesson. I tried to give them. If we hadn't been left alone so long ago, maybe things would have been different. But we will never know now. I'm so sorry you won't find the absolution you seek here."

She staggered toward him and embraced him as a brother. She kissed his lips. He stood motionless, robbed of a fantasy. Finally, he spoke, "We could have saved them together."

"But we didn't. We didn't." She stepped back and took one last look at the darkening sky. "I wish the history you have written for yourself could more closely match the reality of the world. The animals you are trying to protect have been damned since they first invented the coin. Before The End comes, they will eat each other, mark my words. They cannot be saved. And now you're the last of our kind. I wonder what you will do with that knowledge. Goodbye."

At that, North fell backward into the maw of the fiery abyss beneath them. She disintegrated before contact, becoming one with the dust and the ash and the fire.

South sat and waited for whatever was supposed to come next. He had no idea. She had robbed him of his destiny and future. But worst of all, she was right about everything.

The Emperor Suite, Château Rothschild - 20__ CE:

"Of course, a lot of us thought he was back then."

"The Black Dahlia killer?"

"No, honey, a homosexual."

"There must have been a lot of secret identities back then."

South didn't expect to hear Nell's voice when he entered the gigantic hotel suite they were staying in. A penthouse larger than some mansions, three floors of sickening opulence. Their voices echoed through the mahogany halls and into the foyer. South tiptoed toward them, wanting to hear the conversation. Alexandra and Nell were talking like old friends. It made him smile.

"Yes, the passé blanche, the secret gays, the especially secret communists. Then you had the dope fiends, rapists, mobsters, murderers. It was all a big secret. Now the rapists get rightfully expunged unless they've made some very good films and you have a chance at making it regardless of your ethnic background, so long as your auntie puts in a kind word. Then you've got executives adhering to things they don't understand. Like the Bechdel test. And it's all just another ham-fisted way to make money, that's the sad truth; they'll go along with anything so long as it makes money."

"I don't think the Bechdel test is anything more than a vague litmus test, but if it gets more perspectives out there, I don't see what the problem is."

"It's fine, but us talking about the Bechdel test right now passes the Bechdel test. And what does that mean? Maybe it does offer fresh voices a chance to speak, but it's also become another tool for cynical rich people to commodify diversity while maintaining the status quo."

"But so long as people are getting their stories heard, that's a pretty decent compromise, right?"

"It's great, but it's also an illusion. I don't think anyone with a real story to share is going to get heard without a thick coat of white paint. You must look at who is really benefiting from it all, namely the executives. It feels sometimes like the studios have co-opted righteous causes as a marketing gimmick.

Part of me wishes I were born thirty years later so I could enjoy some of this action as my true self. But here's the sad truth: the same fifty guys are still making most of the money. Or their grandkids are. So, is there really any progress or have the suits just gotten smarter? Is it truly a fairer system or have they just trawled with larger nets?"

The conversation drifted just as South was about to approach the stairs. His foot hovered in place while he waited on them. The windows were open. Outside, the group of people were growing in number.

"It'll be one giant company by the end of the century," Alexandra said.

"If we make it that long. I guess I don't have to worry about that though, do I?"

"Oh, you're tougher than you look."

"Damn straight. But come on, I'm flirting with a hundred. And more to the point, do I really want to keep going?"

"I'm sure you've got a lot to look forward to."

"You don't really think that."

"No, I suppose I don't. Are you scared of death?"

"No. It's just another stage of life. I'm far more terrified of living too long. When my eyesight or my mind goes, that's when I'll be ready to die."

"I think I'd end it once I started to forget the important stuff. I'd hate that: to be a prisoner of your own mind."

South slammed his feet on the floor as he walked up to meet them. Death was one topic he would never understand, one that tugged at him in a multitude of unspeakable ways. He had seen the last moments of countless people yet could never comprehend it. Things had not improved since the skirmish in Iceland. Often, he discovered the deaths of those he was closet to by rumour or gossip if he ever learned of their deaths at all. For all he knew, Detective Blight was still running around with a group of misfit children somewhere. The thought of either Nell or Alexandra no longer being alive was the closest South would ever come to contemplating his own death; a vast black horizon too painful to glean but too all-encompassing to fully ignore.

"Hi," he said to the two women. They were sitting near the open doors to the balcony. Alexandra had ordered up some room service water and had mixed it with black currant Ribena she'd smuggled through multiple airports. Nell looked gaunt and tired everywhere but her eyes, reminding South how long it had been since Cullercoats.

"I'm so glad this worked out for your, Claudio," Nell said, her face resembling her headshots of old.

"Takes me back to the days of hanging out with Howard, how about you?"

"Howard had way more class than these old country hoodlums, and I'm saying that knowing full well what a creep he was. But anyway, how are you feeling?"

South sat down between them. "How am I feeling? How are you? I'm still not completely convinced you're here. The flight must have been a nightmare."

"It was fine. The resurgence in Claudio Sud films netted me a nice royalty cheque so I can't complain." She paused, "So this is it, huh?"

Alexandra poured herself more drink. "I can't believe they're letting you go on television. Do you have anything prepared?"

"No, I was hoping I'd get inspiration when I got back here."

"And here I am," said Nell.

Outside, the growing number of people were dancing. Someone had brought a sound system, and they had closed off the street.

"Sometimes I think I should have stayed hiding out in chip shops," South said.

"But you didn't. Now you have a chance to make a difference."

"I don't think one man can save the world any more than he can be responsible for all its past ills."

"But you're not one man, you're a sum of your parts. You've got us two, and so many others watching out for you. So many who would if they were still alive. There must be people who've influenced you in the past. You're a living part of history, just like the rest of us."

South sat in silence, which the two women took as a sign to return to their earlier conversation. They talked of their hopes for a brighter future and shared stories of their lives as women with hidden pasts. Outside on the streets the party was in full swing, with even the local authorities joining in. Some of them had no idea what they were celebrating or why they had gathered outside the old hotel, but their never-ending quest for release had led them all there to that spot, and for that night at least their sins and worries were expunged.

The Theatres of War – 1939 – 1945 CE:

Quite why they called them theatres was something South refused to understand. He had paid little mind to the world since North evaporated herself. Instead, he had taken to walking across continents in a vague attempt to prove her wrong. He first realised she was right about the same time a bomb went off beside him. He stood there nonplussed as the shock waves and explosive force obliterated everything around him. Sheep guts, gizzards, and a ruined wall all flew at him with enough force to convince him something bad had happened. He lay there for some time, listening to yells and the unrelenting sounds of gunfire, not sure what he was supposed to do. Help. He was supposed to help.

But there would be no helping the world this time, not even if he wanted to. Which he supposed he did, despite the ennui.

He had the sense that perhaps they were called theatres because the people behind them weren't there. They were in bunkers and palaces and surrounded by armed loyal supporters. Gone were the days a king would lead from the front. Or even from the rear. Yes, to the men in charge, and they were all men from what he could surmise, the battles were theatrical. From a distance, most things are. Up close, for South, and for millions of people less fortunate (i.e. not immortal), things weren't quite so quaint and charming. Watch a man drag the limp, half-gone remains of his best friend down a field, or the bloodied remnants of a happy family buried under five floors of rubble, or stand powerlessly by a person trying to staunch the arterial bleeding, knowing for certain that you can do nothing but prolong their terrible, inevitable end, or any of the countless other horrors he witnessed, and words like "theatre" feel like an insult. Even words like "good," "evil," "justified," and "slaughter" lose all sense of meanings. The world South found himself in was far worse than the future he envisioned during his last conversation with North.

He tried to run from the horrors, but they were everywhere. From the middle of Europe to the coasts of Asia. Death was omnipresent, industrialised, and easy to find. South thought he knew the capacity of human cruelty, but he had underestimated it by some margin. In earlier stages of his life, he would have tried to help those around him. But he did not know where to begin. If he were to save a small unit of men, say, he knew elsewhere a village, or a civilian ship would be destroyed. The fear froze him. Fear of saving the wrong people, of making the wrong decision, of costing more people their lives. Liberate prisoners in one camp, and it was a certainty the others would be executed wholesale on the whim of a paranoid man in a starched uniform. No. It was useless. Even heroics would beget more horror than he ever considered imaginable.

He was trapped by depression and uncertainty, even while all around him cried out, died, begged for mercy. And this depression meant nothing. What was an immortal's feelings of inadequacy when compared to the annihilation of an entire family legacy, a town's future, the uncountable unmarked graves of unnamed victims of human cruelty? It was nothing. And that did little but compound the depression, adding layers to it. For all his bluster and talk of saving the world, he was a charlatan, a selfish clown, a performer. He couldn't stop the war any more than he could stop the illusion he spent centuries chasing. No, he was a fraud and a coward. The only saving grace was the knowledge that for all his many failures, people would continue to die whether he tried to help or not.

Fading away from the battlefields and ruined regions of the world, South took his despair and bleakness to the coast. He found many cities filled with people just like him. People who were stuck in place, acting like the planet was not on fire, as if it all were just a matter of a difference in opinions. Away from the horrors, people did what they could to keep moving forward. South tried to ignore them as they turned his stomach, a crude reflection of his own failures.

He hid away in a sleepy coastal town and wiled away the war, watching the tide come and go. Few spoke to him. Some who talked to him thought he was a coward because he was not prepared to kill other people, others agreed with their enemy in principle but thought their approach to murdering their fellow man lacked the nuanced decorum of the English speaking world. South paid neither such person much heed, except to remind himself that North was right. Had been. People were their own undoing.

One day, in 1945, South was sitting outside a diner overlooking the Pacific. He'd been there for days. Somewhere on the other side of that ocean, someone had dropped a bomb. A big bomb. The radio was saying as much. He turned to the only other person outside that diner.

"Turn that up, please," he said.

The other person obliged, and the radio said, "It is an atomic bomb. It is a harnessing of the basic power of the universe. The force from which the sun draws its power has been loosed against those who brought war to the Far East." It continued, but South ignored it. He'd received all the confirmation he needed.

The stranger tutted and shook their head, turning to speak to South. "They didn't need to do that, did they? I thought they'd already surrendered. Seems like they just killed a bunch of civilians for nothing." They looked around, as if expecting to get hauled away by MPs for not showing enough patriotism.

South nodded at the stranger and tried to think of an appropriate expression to give. His face had been set in stone for decades. The strangers shuddered and returned to their drink and the radio. South looked out at the sea. The sun shone so brightly it made the waters seem like a blinding mirror. A second star. A cold west wind kissed his cheeks as he continued to stare. Until that moment, the smallest part of him remained confident things would change. "It is people being people," he said to the stranger who was no longer listening. A long held secret had been revealed. "Nothing changes. Nothing ever changes."

Chateau Marmot, Los Angeles – 1955 CE:

"Nothing changes! Nothing changes!"

The voice was coming from the bungalow across from the swimming pool. Nell hesitated. A couch was floating in the deep end of the water, bobbing as if keeping rhythm. The ground was littered with shattered glass, torn pages of library books, the burnt remains of suits and ties. A small fortune of loose bills wafted in the wind and concerned onlookers eyeballed the bounty and each other, money already acquired and spent in their minds.

The bungalow's door was wide open, hanging off the frame by a single intact joint. The entryway was blocked, stuffed with a mattress and a broken chest of drawers. A plate smashed inside. Nell looked back at the producer, unsure what to do.

"It's Claudio," the producer said. "He's been like this all day. We've bought some time with the police, but the concierge wants this resolved before the Rockefeller checks in or they're going to call it in."

"Why me?"

"You two have always had a rapport. We thought about calling the rest of his friends, but… It's a short list."

"Nobody else answered?"

"Nobody else was on the list."

Nell bowed her head and rolled her tongue in her mouth machinegun style. "Fine, fine. I'm not sure what good this will do. But…"

"Fine?"

"Yeah. Be right back."

She crossed the red stone pathway beside the pool, climbing over tossed deckchairs and manoeuvring herself around the broken ashtrays and margarita glasses on the floor. From the edge of her vision, Nell thought she saw someone approaching the bungalow's window, realising at the last moment it was the refrigerator unit. It crashed through the pane and buried itself in the manicured lawn outside. She ducked instinctively and turned to look at the producer, who could only muster a concerned shrug.

"Men these days," she mumbled to herself, pressing forward.

Reaching the door's barricade, she first knocked the mattress and then realised it made little sound. Instead, she coughed. She could hear stamping and walls being hit. "Claudey, baby, it's me, honey, I need you to calm down, OK? I'm not about to die today."

The stomping stopped and became a soft padding of feet. Nell thought she could hear ice cubes clatter against the inside of a glass. Then silence. Nell took this as an invitation to enter and pressed her shoulders beneath the side of the mattress to lift it up. Kicking one leg over the broken dresser, she forced a gap open and shimmied through the wreckage one limb at a time. The inside of the bungalow was ransacked, which came as no surprise considering. Claudio at least had the grace to smash objects against the walls, so there was a trail to follow on the centre of the floor with only a few wayward shards of broken wood and glass. The walls had been decorated, or rather, perforated, with a peppering of fist-sized holes. Claudio's face was indented in the far wall.

The man himself sat hunched over a radio. Empty bottles of scotch and the remains of a hundred history books surrounded him. He had built a firepit on the floor, made of snapped shelving and a porcelain bathtub. He swirled his drink and tossed another book into the fire.

"How are you doing, Claudio? Everything OK?"

He laughed. "Oh, definitely."

"What's this all about? Nothing changing?"

"Pretty much."

"But you knew that already. What set you off?"

He turned to face her. His face was red, eye bulging, nostrils flared. Then he tossed a book on the rise and fall of the Roman Empire into the bathtub and returned to his drink.

"Honey, if only you could show this much emotional range in the movies. Come on, though, big guy, what's the deal? And what did those poor books ever do to you?"

He stood. Nell stepped backward, lamenting the fact she hadn't pulled the mattress down from the doorway and then chiding herself for not using the hole where a window had once been. She watched him pace the room, trying to find his words. And they came all at once, in a blur, the words of someone trying not to lose track of his thoughts.

A decade ago. A decade ago, we were burying people en masse. Entire bloodlines gone, whole cities burnt to the ground. A decade, Nell. And now we've all just forgotten? Again. It keeps happening. It keeps happening, again and again, and nothing ever changes. The radio man says it's already happening. I just didn't pay attention. And those are my two choices. To pay attention and be powerless to do anything about it or ignore it and hope it goes away. It never goes away. It's just going to keep… and I'm in a fantasy land making films so that other people can keep pretending everything is fine? Is that what I've become? Propaganda? Anaesthetic? Is that all I can aspire to? To distract people until they die or until one war ends and another begins?"

"People need comfort to endure the suffering, love."

"Oh, I bet. But if you're in a burning building, would you rather have an extinguisher or another detective movie?"

Nell didn't know how to respond to that. The truth was the industry was a waving hand, distracting you while the other one picked a pocket or sank a knife in somewhere. Even as she stood there in the broken bungalow of a high-end hotel, there were whispers of the Vietnam situation spiralling further out of control. And that was just what she'd been paying attention to. She was about to say something when Claudio tossed his glass against the wall.

"Claude, stop. This is pointless. What is this going to accomplish besides scare me?"

A twang of empathy hit Claudio and he paused, mood altering almost at once. He fell crumpled to his knees and howled. "I just don't understand the point of all this. You never learn anything. I've been waiting for you all to get your act together since you were living in mud huts and worshipping trees. On an individual level you're fine, good even. And you'll all live as best you can for as long as you can. But the bigger picture, the bigger picture, makes no sense. How can one person be so loving and yet as a whole you're rotten to the core?" He paused, "Not you specifically. You know what I mean."

"Gee, thanks. But you haven't answered my question. What is this tantrum going to accomplish?"

He looked at the debris filled room, the jagged edges of former furniture sunken into the seams and ceiling and plaster, the sparkling sea of broken windows and bottles, the bonfire of the vainglorious. "I… I don't know. I just want it to stop. Used to be at least I could pretend I was doing something important. Now all I am is another court jester."

"Then do something about it."

"I can't. It's not how the world works. You're hard-wired for self-destruction. Again, not you specifically. Nothing I do or try works. It's always the same result, just more well-honed, precise, and automated as the years go on."

"Maybe you haven't tried the right thing, then, Claude. Maybe you've been too busy making it about you to realise it takes more than one person to save a planet. While you're in here burning library books and waiving your deposit, there are mere mortals out there making a difference. So. I don't know. Try harder."

"I'm just so tired."

"Look, you can wallow in your misery or you can be proactive. But right now, you're exactly what you're complaining about. Maybe you need to get out of town. Educate yourself. Reach out. See the world for the good, not just the cornucopia of suffering you've decided it is."

Claudio stood and looked at the window. "There's no going back from this. Not for Claudio Sud."

"Then be someone else. Go slip out the back door. I'll smash a few more things, say I saw some robbers or something. Buy you some time."

"You'd do that?"

"It's what friends are for. Now scram. And next time I see you, you better have things figured out."

"I promise. Nell, I…"

"You don't need to say anything. Just run. See you when I see you."

They shared a smile before Claudio Sud slipped out the window. Nell eyeballed the few unbroken objects in the room and considered which one she wanted to break first. She'd always wanted to ransack a room. Shame the heavy lifting had already been done.

Television — 20__ CE:

South stood facing the camera, an impossibly painted skyline behind him. He spoke. He spoke a thousand times. Using every language known to man, he relayed the same message from Mandarin to Persian to Navajo. It was his wish for every living person to hear what he had to say. To talk only in the requested five languages would have destroyed the message itself. Rebuilding Babel one diphthong at a time.

And the television channels of the world acquiesced as best they could, emitting his message to a billion people. People would be too busy to watch, perhaps. Political announcements had rarely been ratings winners ever since they'd introduced a third and fourth channel. He spoke regardless. Some channels saw this as a chance to advertise their own programming, which only further helped to drive away viewers. Others would interrupt his message to give their own opinions, yelling "wrong!" at every opportunity or else talking about their endless blather as they had done since their first day of media training. And so, the message was diluted somewhat.

And yet, in the six-by-six booth with the fake blue sky and the out-of-date vista of a dying city, South talked as best he could. While he knew perhaps, some would not hear his words for a multitude of reasons, if he could inspire just a handful of people to cast themselves back out into the lake of life, their ripples may yet revive a thanatoid planet. So he spoke. And he spoke thus:

"Oh, hi, this is only my second time being in this kind of recording studio. The last time I had some irate chipmunk screaming at me to shut up the whole time. It feels weird talking and not knowing if anyone is out there listening to me, and I have forgotten half of my notes, so you must excuse me if I get a bit tongue-tied while talking. I'm a little unaccustomed to public speaking. I don't know if you'd count this as public speaking, but… let's get down to it. And if you speak multiple languages, I promise this will be more succinct the second time around, so please stay with me. And sorry for speaking in English first. I wanted someone close to me to hear this as close to first as possible. But, yeah…

"Whatever else I was, I wasn't very good for most of my life if I'm honest. I wiped out the dinosaurs and killed proto-humans and maybe inspired a few too many philosophies, which didn't amount to much. But even then, even two hundred thousand years ago, I felt a kinship for your species. I wanted to belong. Never quite got there. Still, though, I tried to observe you all to learn.

"And then the bad stuff started to happen. You thrived in new ways, but with that you went beyond primitive anger and territorialism, and began to conquer and kill in the name of gods and kings and masters who have long since died. I blamed some invisible force for all of that, a malicious version of myself spreading hate and greed through your cities and cultures like a plague. For a long, I tried in vain to put a stop to a virus from killing you all, and in the end, it turned out, it never existed in the first place. I was looking for and blaming the wrong thing. If only things could have been so easy, some tangible end boss to punch in the mouth, with obvious answers and solutions, everything black and white and binary. But it's not and never has been this way. It was you who killed each other, you who idolised wealth and land and possessions. You who turned away from your neighbour and retreated into your own minds. Everything I tried to excuse away was your own doing. Just as my sins are all mine.

"Or that's what I thought for a long time. I regretted ever caring about your species at all because you were all so irredeemable. This was also a fantasy. The truth is most of you are if not good, at least inherently decent people. Always have been. Probably always will be. But you're being misled by systems designed to govern and enslave, and I don't know why you put up with this. Have you not noticed you outnumber them? They grind gears and try to preserve a dying status quo because they know the future is yours. Fearing this, they would rather you live in the past while they buy up land and pretend to be better than you.

"I've seen what happens to all emperors and charlatans. They end just as abruptly as everyone else. They do not realise they are living in a book that has not finished yet, one in which they are not a main character, one without a linear plot or a single protagonist. The book is about all of life. And they're scared of that because they've deluded themselves into thinking they're special, just as a lot of you have convinced yourselves you don't matter, or your enemy is an abstract concept, or the ills of humanity are categorically the fault of some unfamiliar other. And this breaks my heart, has broken it for ten thousand years now. Don't you know a happier future is waiting for you? Don't you know it doesn't have to be like this? It's only gotten so lousy because you've given them permission.

"Some have accused me of not doing enough to save humanity in the past. The truth is, I can't do that alone. It's this self-serving combine milling you all up you need to destroy to progress. Until then, it will keep spinning. I could kill a hundred thousand despots and all that would happen is another hundred thousand would take their place. Because the system has failed you and yet you allow it to keep running. You're living in a world of design, not a world of reality. You've isolated yourself and divided yourself and accepted your invisible prison because you've forgotten you surround them. But that's not enough. You need to recognise you're all in this together.

"And for those watching who are in a position of power, I hope you have a moment to reflect on your legacy. Do you think you'll wind up as myths? How many Caesars can you name? Kings? Bankers? Local officials? All their corruption was for nothing. Choose a different path, my friends, because soon the people outside will remember who they are, and they will engulf you for your crimes. Think of your end and think of how you will be remembered and ask yourself if you're truly happy.

"And please bring back Firefly. I know it's a bit late for that in a lot of way, but just, I mean, please. Anyway, that's all I wanted to say to you. We have a world to save. Not for me, but for all of you. Good luck out there. Et maintenant, pour mes amis…"

He talked all day, never fully knowing what impact his words had on the world outside. Even as he talked, he replayed his words back in his head and wondered if he had chosen the right things to say. Had he come off too preachy? Too judgemental? He worried for a long time about that. Longer than humanity itself survived.

Alexandra and Nell, however, thought he'd done OK when he found them in the hotel bar. They'd watched from English all the way to Italian before the bartender put on a banking channel. Apparently five currencies had tanked the day before, but nobody seemed to care.

The Invisible Hand — 20__ CE:

The following was recorded in a subterranean bunker by our anonymous friend Hugo Khrushchev. Hugo sought out South several years after the hearings to hand over the tapes and then promptly disappeared. Their meeting was an interesting one, but it's a little too late in the day to add a spy subplot into a novel that is already feeling too chaotic. Hugo never explained why he recorded so many conversations, or why he was handing them over to South. All he said was "People deserve to know why they've been sentenced to death."

A: What are you doing?

B: Looking around. I don't want anyone jumping out at us this time.

A: We're in a secure facility, who would jump out at us?

B: It could happen. This is why I said we needed spaceships. You all said you liked spaceships and yet here we are down here like rats.

A: There wasn't enough time for decent spaceships. You know that. The technology isn't advanced enough to sustain fifty years up there. Besides which, I get motion sickness.

B: Who cares about fifty years? I just wanted to spend some time in space before I died. It would have been fun. I could have made myself space admiral.

A: Isn't it enough we already have all the money?

B: What good is that going to do down here? If that's the only metric you're using for success I've been winning ever since mummy left me all my hard-earned inheritance.

C: Except you're both forgetting about the people up there.

B: Where in the blue hell did you come from?

C: I hid up in the vents. My bunker is around the corner. We're going to have to do something about that man now. People are waking up.

A: If you say so. But jeez, man, would you stop jumping out at us?

B: You snuck all the way into this bunker for that?

C: Well… yes.

B: You're worrying about nothing, my friend. They'll wake up for a minute and go right back to sleep. And even if they stay awake, we won't be there, anyway.

A: We've already won. Don't you see? They can get angry at figureheads and try to change the world around them, but we've got our bunkers and we've got all the money. Who needs them?

C: So that's all this was to you? A race to hide down in the dirt like worms.

B: Uh, yeah.

C: All the… things we've done, and this was your end goal?

A: I mean, we were all pretty clear about that at the meetings, weren't we?

B: Yeah, disrupt the world, hoard wealth, move to sweet bunkers with our own security task forces and a bunch of beautiful women.

C: At least you've opted for adult women, I guess.

B: Yeah, some of those other bunkers…

C: But no! I thought there was more to our plans beyond just hiding around.

B: We'll all be dead in thirty years, so really what else was there to do? Make a difference?

A: Space travel is still out fifty years and no way am I funding something I won't be able to enjoy myself.

C: I just thought there was more to our machinations than this, man. It's… I'll be in my bunker. Call me if you need anything.

B: You're leaving already?

C: Yeah, I've lost my appetite. Bye lads.

B: Wait, stay, have some cake at least.

A: Let them be. So… what should we do first down here?

B: Table tennis? And when are the guards showing up?

A: Oh yeah, speaking of, how are we going to pay them when they get down here?

B: With money.

A: But won't money be worthless once we're down here?

B: …

A: I'm sure you have some fail-safe in place on the off chance they decide to kill us and take over the bunkers for themselves.

B: …

A: …

B: …

A: Right?

Isla del Sud — 20_9-20_7 CE:

And everyone was free forever. All the world's problems were resolved without bloodshed. Some of the corrupt and the incidentally evil were cast out into the abyss, the rest went into hiding. Food and wealth and housing were all distributed evenly. People smiled at each other on the street and, strange still, on public transport. Art, music, and literature were judged on merit and not on marketability. Proper education and medical assistance were made available to all, not just the fortunate few. Dating apps banned people who took photos of themselves holding fish, or used dog filters in every picture, or referred to US sitcoms as their litmus test of choice. All was good. Or so some people said there for a few years.

Not that South and Alexandra would know. They had been gifted a private island by a rich benefactor who "didn't need so many." It was a rich, verdant land full of luscious life, both flora and fauna, and pearl-white beaches. In the centre of the island there was a jagged mountain that loomed over the land below. The infrastructure was adequate.

South could not relax on the beaches. He kept expecting a public challenge from a duplicitous coward looking to make a name for themselves. "Well, if you've got it all figured out, how come you're not creating a utopia on your little island there, huh, mister?" he imagined them saying, perhaps on their nightly television show. And it was a tempting prospect, to be sure, but one that would require time and help. Otherwise it would be like expecting a loose set of farming communities to become technocratic utopian cities overnight.

The challenge never came. Life had moved on. Pundits were focused on whatever was trending on the internet. The surviving politicians did their bare minimum to prevent a complete worldwide revolution. The world kept on spinning.

People, though, came on boats and hot air balloons, guided by the daydream of a better life. To them the island represented a world they often talked about on lunch breaks at bad jobs, but never believed was a real possibility. All their lives they'd been denied the simple life they so desperately needed. Instead, they had been birthed into an indifferent world and forced to adhere to imbalanced rules, all of which was decided long before they were born without their consent. All their break room chats about moving to a commune suddenly felt like an all too real prospect. South's island promised a life beyond pointless drudgery. Drudgery, yes, but with a sense of purpose. Like proofreading your own material despite being the only thing left in the universe knowing full well you've used the passive tense far too much.

And some pilgrims were allowed to stay. The good ones. The happy majority who weren't trying to recruit a cult, get laid, or create a country in their image.

The others were sent packing.

South was reminded of the pirates of old, his friends of the seven seas. Some, to be sure, were horrible people capable of all kinds of terrors, like eating the still-beating hearts of enemies or wearing velour. Others drew up charters most would accuse of being too progressive even in the 21st century. With them in mind, he drew up a charter. He didn't want the island to become a cautionary tale or evidence that people needed a hierarchical capitalist structure to survive. He also wanted people to leave, eventually. The rules he laid out were simple enough. To wit:

1. We all drink from the same cup.
2. If you don't help, you don't eat.
3. Anyone harming another will be thrown into the sea.
4. Barring these rules, everything will be decided democratically.
5. No vlogs, acoustic guitars, or attempts to otherwise commodify the experience, and especially no long-form improv without the appropriate certification.

Alexandra had the idea of encouraging people to leave once they'd seen how more gratifying a pared down life could be. They'd leave, she hoped, happy and confident enough to set up their own self-sustaining communities. To spread the message. Plus, she didn't like all the people milling around the whole time, poking their sunburnt heads in and getting chummy with her all hours of the day. It was all well and good, she postulated, to have your own private Idaho, but universal change was impossible if trapped inside a bottle. Who cares if Patti and Tommy are happy on the island if ten million people a year were dying because of destabilised agriculture and dirty water? The world needed empathy to spread like a disease before it was too late.

But it was too late. Bit by bit, fewer people arrived at the island. While it was true, the world had changed a degree or two into the direction of positive progress; it seemed people were once again starting to forget. They were becoming complacent all over again, falling back into the boredom trap. It was mostly because of Yap Stanson.

Yap Stanson was a talking dog. Nobody knew where Yap Stanson came from, but there Yap Stanson was. On television, talking to reporters, making cameos in films, hosting self-help seminars. Yap Stanson was a border collie with a red collar. Yap Stanson really enjoyed buying electronics and cosmetic goods and wanted to make sure everyone else bought things too. As many things as they could fit in their homes. You couldn't say no to Yap Stanson's face. If you couldn't afford to buy a lot of stuff, Yap Stanson also had weekend retreats to help you figure out how to get more money to buy more things. There were rumours Yap Stanson was an experiment from Area 51, a last ditched ploy to stall capitalism's inevitable demise, but Yap Stanson had a Boston accent and Area 51 was in Nevada. It made little sense. Yap Stanson, on the other hand, made perfect sense.

People were quick to forget a boring immortal with a "hey, let's just not kill each other and the planet" schtick when Yap Stanson showed up. Sure, people would say, you may have seen first-hand the folly of man's inhumanity to man, but are you a dog who talks? No? I didn't think so. Now get your goody goody jambalaya bullshit out of my face. The Yap Stanson Consumer Advice Hour is starting.

When the last of the people on the island left, citing an incurable need to buy designer sandals, South and Alexandra sat on the coast. For the first time, South noticed Alexandra's hair was showing small patches of grey, her skin was becoming loose, and her eyes, while still emitting a resilient glow, seemed tired. The water from the ocean had all but consumed the edges of their island. The tide would never go out again, not how it did at least. They sat on the last parcel of sand the island had and looked out at the ocean. Behind them, the farms had been left untended and overgrown. Creeping vines were reclaiming the wood huts. Their time on the island seemed illusory.

"I want to go home," said Alexandra.

"We are home," said South.

"This is a prison. I'm seeing that now. It's the best kind of prison, I guess, but it's still a prison. We were so caught up in hubris we didn't notice the cage around us. I want to go home."

South put his arm around her and held her close. "We did some good here."

"Yes, we did. And now it's over."

"If that's what you want, I will go pack out things."

"Not just yet."

They stared at the sunlight bouncing off the ripples of the ocean, that indifferent monster. Above them storm clouds drew near, planes flew oblivious to what was beneath them, the sun glowed as it ever did. South made to stand up. Alexandra pulled him back down.

"Just one more hour before we go." She paused. "Do you think the store where we met is still there? Can we go visit?"

"Anything for you."

People's (Formerly Royal) Infirmary, Edinburgh - 21_3 CE:

The basement museum was no longer there, the book store instead a combination of eateries and pod-based micro apartments. Wherever the statue of South and North had gone, it had gone there for good; his last, irreplaceable tie to his first life tossed out to make way for a pho/taco fusion restaurant. South was not a man to see omens, but in that moment he should have been.

His time in Edinburgh had been brief, all things considered, but returning for the last time was more bitter than sweet. Alexandra, who in comparison had spent most of her life there, agreed. Gone were the lesser landmarks. The views, the basement comedy clubs, the old pubs and homes, had all become capsule hotels and data storage facilities. The hills all engulfed in a multi-coloured blanket of tents. While the castle remained, a copper wiring mogul had bought it and turned into a boutique hotel. Old David Hume was no more, replaced by a morphous statue that could change from one unheard of celebrity to the next on a weekly basis. It was a technological marvel, the statue, as were a lot of the recent additions to the city as banal as they were. But miraculous advances in data science and alterable statues don't keep away acid rain or put food in mouths.

South stayed there with Alexandra for as long as possible. Venturing out into the world when the fancy took them. They would see friends, what few remained. Attend funerals. So many funerals. Watch in disbelief as piece by piece the world unravelled. Refugee crises from English-speaking countries got a lot of traction. The media seemed intent still to blame someone for all the world's ills but could never consider maybe their own drive for ad revenue had something to do with it. New, incurable diseases showed up. Wars began and ended over trivial things. And it seemed most days the people around them didn't care.

So South and Alexandra moved to another island of sorts. An island all their own. A small house on what was once the outskirts of Edinburgh. If they could not save the world, at least they could save their own small home. And they did, for a time. They grew vegetables on the roof, purified water in rain barrels, learned to make their own clothes out of hemp. Their bookshelves were stuffed with finished books and completed puzzles. They did not live in the promised future where people burnt books, but one where few cared enough about them to notice they'd all gone out of print. In their home, at least, they tried to cling to the waning promises and potential held by those who came before. A shrine to dead hope, Alexandra would say.

This tranquil paradise for two carried on even as the world outside unravelled and even the least astute observer was starting to suspect something was wrong. In time, though, Alexandra grew old and feeble. She would walk from one room to the next without her feet leaving the floor, shuffling to already-forgotten tasks and then back to her room. South, of course, did not age. But a lot of him died in those years, watching his rescuer, his confidant, his love. Not so much strut but shuffle her last hours upon the stage.

The time came for them to enter the hospital for what would be Alexandra's last time. In that moment he realised how many of her moments had been last times. Her last smiles, her last mornings in their bed, her last dance by candlelight. Her last. Her last. Her last. He tried not to dwell upon the homes he could never return to, the times far behind him, the knowledge that Alexandra's life, as generous and as tender as it had been, was no more than a whisper in the wind.

"Don't look so sad," she told him in her hospital bed.

"Then don't die," South said before he could stop himself.

A smile. "I'll try not to. Do you ever regret it?"

He looked at her, all the many hers she had been, and said "Hm?"

"Asking me for a coffee that first time. I don't know if we made things better or worse."

"Of everything I have done, meeting you is the one thing I couldn't begin to regret if I tried."

"You're just saying that because I'm a dying old woman. I know you built the pyramids, darling. Don't placate me."

He held her as closely as he could and looked at her in the eyes; her fire still burning despite it all. "There is so much I have done for the wrong reasons. But asking you for coffee, helping you with those translations, everything with you was something I did outside of myself. And for that I'm thankful."

Well, thanks, I guess," Alexandra pried herself loose from South's embrace and rested on the bed. She closed her eyes as a single tear formed. "Do you… think there's an afterlife?"

South frowned. "Whether there is or is not, that's one place I can't go with you."

"Finally, some peace and quiet."

They laughed. They talked for some time about their memories, their hopes, their unfulfilled dreams. Through it all, Alexandra never lost her optimism in humans figuring things out. Even with all evidence to the contrary, even as her breath became shallow and her heart rate dropped, she maintained things would work out just fine.

"Just remember there's no future in the past and there's still hope so long as someone who cares is around," Alexandra said.

And then you died. My sweet. This was not the dramatic death I'd feared, a sputtering and desperate few final moments. Nor was it a stoic display of wisdom in the face of your own mortality. You spoke. Took in a breath you never let back out. And you died. I must have stared at you for an hour before I knew. But you were gone, never to return, and I to this day I cannot talk about it.

I miss you.

I love you.

Always.

2137 CE:

Fade in on a CGI Amsterdam back before the incident. The Rijksmuseum has been put next to the Anne Frank house by mistake and the streets are full of cars instead of bicycles, and palm trees surrounded the canals, but it was the Amsterdam of old. The brightness has been dimmed to hide the flaws and errors from the less attentive members of the audience, not that they remember what Amsterdam looked like. A camera follows a canal straight into a floating bar filled with wooden monkeys. And handsome computer-generated actor sits at one side of a bench and faces a less conventionally attractive computer-generated actor with red hair. They are sipping absinthe out of separate bottles.

"You're a good man, Vincent, but you'll never make it as a painter," the more attractive of the two says with a tinny, robotic voice.

The audience laughs. He's talking to Vincent Van Gouge the famous painter man. It says as much at the bottom of the screen in a bright yellow impact font so the audience can get the joke. The scene pauses to ensure everyone watching gets the joke. It does this for every joke, of which there are allegedly many.

It was a two-hour film, not counting the pauses, with a joke told exactly once every two minutes. The metric decided that was the perfect amount of time between gags. It was the same joke every time, but with the names and verbs changed each time. "Oh, come on, Adolf is not such a bad chap, what's he going to do? Start a war?" Laughter. "I don't know about you guys, but King George seems a bit mad to me." More laughter. "If Julius Caesar gets murdered by his own senate, I'm the king of Sheba." "Well then good morning your majesty." So much laughter South had to put his hands to his ears. By the end of the film, people were laughing whenever the film paused, whether or not they got the joke. Anything to move on to the next movie.

The outside world had become so hot, and the remnants of the film industry so desperate, people could live in cinemas. The idea being, in exchange for air conditioning and nutritional yeast infused popcorn, the inhabitants would watch sixteen hours' worth of films a day. With most professions at that point performed by a single computer, there was not much else left for the public to do except consume media and food, typically at the same time. The cinema gig was one of the most lucrative and sought after positions the average person could hope to find.

Film itself, all film, was written for one mega corporation by a writer called AI. The director was also AI. All the scenes were made through old satellite scans of famous landmarks and fractal geometry. The actors were little more than composite faces generated from a slew of dead hopefuls who had signed their life rights away at some audition or another. They lived forever on the screen, photorealistic ghosts of themselves, with soulless acting ability and flat delivery, which in some cases was an improvement.

The corporation was a self-regulating network of computers, pumping out precisely fifteen new films a day except during what used to be winter, in which case they would produce twenty-five a day as per the algorithm's demands. Scripts were created through deep learning and access to the public domain. Everything was public domain, and the AI owned the rights to it. Their fanbase had no other option, and for many it was their only means for survival. The corporation had no competition. No real auteurs remained. Print died years earlier, to the surprise of no one. Music had become bite sized fifteen second dopamine pills. There were no supplies left for art. Sport of all kinds was considered a lethal venture which was just as well because with no ad revenue or capable participants, it wouldn't have garnered much attention, anyway.

Over the years, the wealthy corporate heads of the few remaining corporations overreached and fazed themselves out of usefulness, their responsibilities governed instead by unfeeling digital neuro-networks programmed to think like an idealised version of an unscrupulous boss. And since the smug bosses were considered useless by the computer, they were all kicked out into the street, abandoned, their money useless, left alone in the wilderness with nothing but a vague sense of overdue karmic retribution. The jobless CEOs and their cronies had neither the skills nor the personality to survive in a world they didn't have complete control over. They survived just long enough to realise their lives had been one long calamitous spiritual debt they could not pay, and they died en masse one blistering January day, like so many of the forgotten dead they'd trodden underfoot during their long and parasitic careers. The computer networks didn't care because they were computer networks modelled on those very same scorched corpses left on the side of the road for the weekly automated corpse collecting vehicles.

Too far gone now, the world was consuming itself as fast as it could, like a glutton with a defrosting freezer. The rudderless AI corporations followed their instructions to the letter, not knowing or caring what was happening to the humans beneath them as per their coding's instructions. Media_Corp1, Social_Image_Corp1, Food_Corp2, Consumer_Corp1, and Clothes_Corp2, the Big Five, were focused on earning what little money remained in the real world, pursuing goals they were unable to care about or accomplish.

South had stumbled into the cinema after seeing a giant holographic poster outside Cinema City advertising The Immortal Idiot. Stumbling was South's favourite activity since about three hours after Alexandra's funeral. He briefly considered spending the rest of eternity in the ocean, but remembered it was crowded with waste and plastic, and that he'd have a less depressing time rolling around a mass grave. Which, when he thought about it, was something else the ocean had become.

The rest of the audience seemed to enjoy the story that was both his and not. So much of his life was changed and warped for mass appreciation. He barely recognised it as a film about him. Everyone in the chilly cinema applauded the credits, mainly because there were told to and had no better options. The credits were:

Everything
By Media_Corp1

The credits were accompanied by one of those fifteen second pop songs. It was upbeat and sung by a voice lost way down deep in the uncanny valley. It went like this:

You have just watched a movie, baby
Thank you, customers, maybe
Remember, you are scheduled for six more, baby
Then you can sleep, maybe
Yeah baby, I want you inside me, baby
Feel your body next to mine, yeah, yeah, yeah

It was the most popular song of the year, perhaps because the coding had failed in the last two lines and almost hinted at real, genuine emotion, which was a rarity in music even a hundred years earlier.

During intermission a five-minute trailer played for all the next day's new films, including *Yap Stanson: Sex Pest, This Person's Life was Worse than Yours So Get Over It,* and *Marcel Proust versus Godzilla.* Media_Corp1 had bought up the rights to all dead people and animals and were making them all into films. Most historians considered Yap Stanson's horrible descent into self-destruction to be the moment the world lost all hope.   Or at least that's what historians would have said if any were left standing.

The next film was another two-hour film. They were all two-hour films. This one was about how buying more things from the last remaining website (everyone's homepage) made everyone happy. The protagonist was a single parent who lived in a cinema and it was only through running up a massive amount of credit that they were able to win the love of a penthouser (a rich, unemployed former webcam model and programmer who lived, you guessed it, in a penthouse). They fell in love, the impoverished single parent and the computer-generated approximation of the perfect partner, because of debt and consumption. There was a simple moral to the story which is what people enjoyed. It ended with a freeze-frame jump shot of everyone smiling. The audience, mostly single parents, their partners dead or lost to the wilderness of a neighbouring cinema complex, collectively cried during their allotted one-minute crying break. If they didn't cry at the end when instructed to do so—and only when instructed to do so—they would not get another ration of popcorn.

The film after that was the nth gritty remake of a famous superhero franchise, and even facing the near destruction of humanity, South couldn't bring himself to watch it. He stumbled outside.

The ground level of the domed city was full of cinema-homes, clothing stores, and insect-based restaurants. Nobody else walked the streets. If someone appeared, they would sprint from one building to the next. Above them were the conical penthouse buildings for the social elite. The remaining few who still lived in those buildings liked to pretend they weren't waiting for death, that they were somehow better than the survivors in the cinemas and cubicle hostels below.

From the sidewalk, South could see a couple of flecks up in the penthouses trying to maintain their sanity. What was left of the influencer class, trapped in their former success. South had lived in a similar building himself for a while, but left the moment there was a surge in suicides. With no wealth to accumulate, and each resident more concerned with getting attention than giving it, they soon became insular, tribal, wary people, hiding in corners away from the others. Truly the beautiful ones. Liberate te ex inferis, those specks were saying to South. To the common cinema dweller and the other inhabitants of the lower levels, those who did not know what bleak existence waited up above, those buildings were their last bastion of hope, something to aspire toward, like parched nomads staggering toward a mirage, except in this case it wasn't a mirage but a poisoned well.

It was around this time South had an impulse to stand in front of a train. For all his talk of being unkillable, it had been centuries since he last put tested the theory. Years of walking from city to city, no hope, no future, no Alexandra made him yearn for the void. If nothing else, it was a new experience. The last time a train came close to hitting him was the launch of Stephenson's Rocket.

Bullet trains of that era were without a crew, passengers, or cargo, designed to ship empty containers from one abandoned warehouse to another. The AI calculated this was one of the few remaining ways to generate a profit. Every day, empty planes, trains, and automobiles would move from one place to the next, propelled by a few lines of code. They'd cross over the burning planet and all they would accomplish was a 0.0001% increase to the AIs balance sheets.

So South stumbled in front of a train.

He braced himself when one approached. It slapped him with a metallic wallop before the high-velocity lead carriage crumple in on itself. The rear carriages buckled, jack-knifed, flew into the air, their near-weightless frames carried off some distance, landing in the dust of the planet. South staggered, notices a line in the dirt where his feet had been pushed back some three yards, and that was it. The wrecked train all around him the only proof he'd just tried to feel something. He was inspired with the vision of all the other deadly activities he'd missed out on when he was trying to be human.

For months, he would track down fresh ways to hurt himself, or at least try to hurt himself. He would cling to the wings of automated planes, sometimes jumping face first into their turbines, or else plummeting down into the wastelands below. In the storm-wrecked continents, he sought hurricanes and tornadoes, doing his best to recreate scenes from Uzumaki, riding violent weather over counties and ragdolling himself across bedraggled plains. He would build trebuchets in the graveyards of old cities and fire himself into leaning skyscrapers. He did all this with the stoic detachment of a bored professor with tenure. It wasn't helping. Nothing was. No amount of hurling, falling, or smashing through the planet fixed the emptiness inside him.

Once he knew self-destruction was by definition impossible for him, he climbed up what remained of Everest. It smelled of death and faeces. The thawed remains of adventurers and retired dentists alike would never be frozen again. The rocks were littered with the bloom of countless neon jackets, bright boots, aluminium bedding, an orchard of wasted life. The rutted and grey ascent a shadow of the mountain's former majesty. From the peak, South could see the damage the world below sustained. Everything, even the seasons themselves, lost to endless heatwaves and inclement weather.

What anger he felt years earlier rescinded like the ice caps of old, another emotion he would never feel again. Looking at the debris of the world, all he knew was loss. Loss of a future, of hope, of a life worth living, all so machines could push around theoretical money for dead shareholders. And so South wept.

He wept for twenty years up on that mountaintop, lamenting all the things gone forever. There would be no shrine for what was taken from them, the world itself the memento mori. He wept for the billions who had dreamed of brighter days, who spent lifetimes striving toward a better tomorrow for their children, for all the countless citizens of Earth who died with the conviction things may just accidentally get better still, maybe, in their hearts. There was no future, no dreams, no chance for the humans below, Progress had finally won.

"Excuse me?"

South turned. Standing at the base of the peak was an implacable figure. They were both there and not, wearing a cheap Hawaiian shirt and cargo shorts, white socks and sandals. They stood looking up at South, legs akimbo, hands on hips, a crumpled letter in their front pocket. A dim hum came from their vicinity.

"Uh, yes?" said South.

"Have I caught you at a bad time? Are you done crying? I can come back."

"It's bad times from here on out."

"Ain't that the truth, mister. I have a message for you from an old friend. They want you to have this," the figure handed over the battered envelope.

It read:

HELLO OLD FRIEND,
IT HAS BEEN TOO LONG.
HEARD YOU'VE BEEN IN SOME TROUBLE
IN RECENT CENTURIES AND
THOUGHT WE SHOULD TALK.
COORDINATES ON THE BACK.
YOUR CREATOR. XOXO

South reread the letter several times. "Who gave this to you?"

"No idea, mate, I'm just an astral projection."

Odawara, Japan — 2203 CE:

Around a hundred years earlier, there had been a quaint town named Kamakura not too far from where the pilgrimage to Fuji-san began. There were surfer bars and guest houses, a cute vegan sandwich shop tucked away in a back street, a monorail, a giant, hollow Buddha statue, and a group of shrines built on the side of a cliff. And people–there used to be people too. South hadn't visited the area in many years and was the only person on the bullet train to notice the entire region was now part of the ocean. Commuting over a sprawling metropolis, the other passengers knew, for sure, but had numbed themselves to their country's past.

It was the same wherever people still lived. A few megacities tried to pretend things were as they always had been. Communes of shacks and tents tried to adapt to a new world. Still more cities were submerged almost completely. New York, Rio, Alexandria, Shanghai all lost to the sea, their metal limbs still jutting out of the water like the fingers of a drowning sailor. But wherever there were people, there were people in denial. They sat with vacant stares, seeking out distraction or death, anything to avoid the dreadful truth the world was over.

When the bunkers of the absentee world leaders were discovered, and those inside were pulled out into the streets and strung up from the lampposts of the cities they'd destroy, people expected things to turn around. It was too late, of course. But at least they had their moment of revenge. South looked at the passengers and wondered how many fought for their future. It was hard to tell; each person was as dejected as the next. Despair, it was revealed at last, was the true great equaliser.

And yet, despite it all, they pretended there was never a Kamakura to begin with. South couldn't understand that much.

Odawara, too, was unrecognisable in its own way. For one thing, it offered seafront property. For another, a network of mass-produced box homes, created with the surplus of recyclable materials in the oceans, had built up around the city's edges. Each home, a near-identical plastic box, could be set up like a child's play blocks, creating a wall of tiny domiciles that filled in all available spaces. They housed refugees from sunken or sundered countries, the poor, the trapped. Even isolationist nations could no longer turn away the suffering, displaced masses. There was no one left to stop them from entering.

The city, then, was a patchwork of old buildings and recycled, repurposed homes. It was all smog and decay and depression. People from all corners of the planet hung over burning tires for warmth. Stray cats were hunted down by hungry children. It was a place ready for death.

Even as South walked from the train station to the road to Hakone, people were dying in the street. He walked by five people who just gave up and died right next to him. As living became even more difficult, dying had become significantly easier. They distributed free packs of suicide pills at the clinics, but people seemed capable to die at will. Their bodies were stripped, flayed, sterilised and repurposed with a level of detachment once reserved for fish.

He had walked to Hakone once before, unwilling to spend any more time in what was once considered a crowded train. It didn't feel like the same walk the second time. He could envision how it had been, the wide shallow river, the red trains packed with camera-toting gaijin riding uphill, the crawling cars, the greenery, the view of upcoming hills. No such things accompanied him on his second walk. Smoke smothered even the nearest hills.

He looked at the map the spectre had given him and did his best to follow its directions. Up through the hills and the cicada-like remains of old trees he walked, pushed on by limp fury. In time he reached a cave on top of a hill, a mossy hole where flowers somehow grew; he'd forgotten what flowers looked like. An unnatural green light emitted from the depths. Inside, he found a replica of his apartment in Whitby. The light came from all directions. He walked over to the bed and pulled it to one side. There was a hole in the ground. A ladder too, so it wasn't an exact replica. South looked at the room and wanted to pretend that was where it all started for him. If only life had a singular genesis point. He knew that whether he left Whitby or not, met Alexandra or not, was exposed as an immortal or not, he would have eventually found himself in a world with close to nothing in it, standing in a replica of an old memory and looking down at a hole in the ground. These were inescapable truths.

He climbed down into the darkness because there was nothing else left to do. A faint glow waited far beneath him. The walls pressed against him as he lowered himself into light. In time he was in another room, it looked much like he remembered The Creator's workshop, but without the glowing orb in the centre of the room. Instead, a small floating pyramid spun above a pedestal and glowed while it did so. The floor had been engulfed with thick vines. They climbed up the walls of the room, searching for fresh space. The source of the vines sat in the far corner of the room on what was left of a throne.

"Ah, so you've decided to show up finally. Where's the other one?" said the tree.

South looked closer at the clump of wood on the throne. Remnants of a face still haunted the upper edges. He could make out the outline of a humanoid figure. A slow, rhythmic throbbing came from the centre of the figure. The wood creaked like an old home in a storm.

"Well?" the tree said.

South wasn't ready to talk. He remembered The Creator as a tall person, not a tree. There was so much he wanted to say and to ask. All the countless times over the years he'd imagined how he'd talk when he finally met The Creator again. But it all slipped from his mind except for South's oldest thought.

"You abandoned us," he said at last, "And now everything is ruined."

"What do you expect me to do about it? And where is the other one?"

South walked around the room like a man searching for a lost wallet. For a man who commanded all language, he was at a loss for words. "She had the courtesy to annihilate herself when she knew she couldn't do anything."

"Oh, that's a shame. I always liked that one. Anyway, pleasure to see you again, even if you have that look on your face. Who taught you how to look like that? What are you hoping to accomplish now, after so many wasted moments?"

"I just want to know why all this happened. Why you abandoned us."

"Do you honestly think my being around would have made any difference?"

"You could have stopped all this from happening. It was all your idea in the first place."

"And then what?"

South stopped moving. He couldn't answer that.

"I've done this experiment innumerous times, and the result is always the same, my very good friend. I'll tweak and tinker and experiment and it just never works out. So I retired. And what do you know? The exact same thing happened, anyway."

South walked to the tree in the throne and punched what he thought was a face. "You don't get to retire! You had a responsibility! All those people. All that suffering."

"Oh yes, tell me about my responsibility. I created it all, that is true, but it was that or nothing. And I seem to remember you taking part in the early stages without question. You could have stopped it any time. What about the dinosaurs' suffering? The protohumans you wiped out? The millennia wasted feeling sorry for yourself? Hiding in the darkness like a fugitive."

"Don't talk to me about hiding."

"I'm not hiding, I'm retired, big difference, buddy. But please, do not pretend you wouldn't have wiped out all life on earth if I'd have asked you to." The tree opened its eyes, misty swirling ancient orbs, omnicoloured spirals. "I set you free to make your own decisions in this world. If I didn't, you'd still be doing what I demanded."

South looked down into the eyes. He could not speak.

"Think about that. Think about what would have happened if I stayed. Could you live in a world without an Alexandra knowing now she existed? Could you have killed her for me? The others? All those you helped? Would you have wiped them out at the sound of my voice?"

South shook his head. An eternity of sins and an infinite other versions of himself revealed themselves to him.

The tree tried to smile. "You should thank me. I retired because I wanted something different to happen. And maybe it did there for a while. I'm sorry it didn't turn out how you wanted it to, but think of the alternatives."

"I just wish I could try again. Maybe if I did things a little differently, the world out there would be far better. At least I'd get to see her again."

"Can't really help you there, what with me being a tree and all." The Creator sighed and its vines slithered and buckle as they returned to him. The floor beneath them was clear again. In front of the throne was a second ladder. "But, you know, you can help yourself, if you want. Down there. Down the ladder."

"What's down there?"

"Nothing and everything. Think of it as a reset switch. A little apology from me to you. It'll get you to where you need to be."

With little thought, South began his final descent.

Exact Time and Location Unknown:

Down, down, down South went, on ladder unending. The glow from The Creator's workshop becoming a pinprick far above and no sign of an end below. No sign of anything. He could hear whispered echoes pass through the abyss like a gentle breeze, voices of all those he had known. North in their palace, laughing at an ancient joke. The people of the plains and jungles he watched over, their songs and ceremonies. Bartholomew and his crew of progressive pirates, with their drunken shanties. A world of workers and the free and those seeking freedom, each just as ambitious as the next. Detective Blight and his ragtag band of mercenary investigators keeping London safe. The children he had entertained for a month on the SS Lapland with their questions and fears of a darker tomorrow. All those lost in battlefields, to sickness, to slavery. Nellie with her elite friends and unflinching honesty. Jimmy, Dean, the volunteers he'd met, the call centre employees, the customers at the hundred jobs he'd worked in secret, all just trying to be heard in a world full of screaming. But most of all, he heard Alexandra.

South thought back on her smile, her laugh, how she would cry sometimes at night without wanting or needing to explain why, the way gentle wrinkles claimed her face, her indomitable spirit even in the face of Death. How fortunate he had been to feel Fortuna's blessing that first day in Edinburgh. There was no going back, he knew, all was faded and irreplaceable, yet he could still touch those cherished memories.

As he climbed down further into darkness, he thought of how much the world had come to mean to him. Regrets and guilt were abated at last. All he chose to remember was the good. Was this how the release of death felt to mortals? Was this how clear it all became for Alexandra in her last moments? Had Nell died happy? The others? He hoped so.

His thoughts were interrupted by a loud voice far above. "There are three stones down there. If you move them all to the pillar, everything will turn out just right."

South could still see nothing below. "What, you mean like a time machine?"

"Uh… sort of. Don't worry about the technical side of it. You'll see what I mean when I get down there."

"In what order do I place the orbs?"

"I just told you not to worry about it. Just get down there and I'll handle the rest."

"And what happens if I don't do anything?"

A cough echoed through the nothingness. "Yes, about that. If you mess this up even a little, everything will die. Everything. Even the amoebas and cockroaches. Even the nothing you're climbing down right now will die in time. Oh, and time. Time will die. You'll be stuck here alone for all eternity until… but you wouldn't like that, matey, not one bit."

"You'd still be around. We could hang out."

"Perhaps I would. I don't know. It's never happened before. But even if I did stick around, I'm incredibly boring. I'm so boring I became a tree. By choice. Who chooses to become a tree? And do you really want to spend a timeless forever chatting to a tree?"

"I guess not."

"You guess not. All you have to do is climb the rest of the way down and move those tiny stones for me, OK, buddy?"

"Whatever you say, boss."

The climbing was taking too long. South reminded himself he was immortal, thought back to the days of shoulder charging trains and leaping face first of jets, and let go of the ladder. He plummeted downward for hours. A speck of light grew below him, transforming all at once into a levitating platform. He tried to stick the landing, but his face rammed into the pillar.

"I see you found it," said The Creator from nowhere.

"Gesh uh fnd duh pwuluh," South replied before tearing his face from the side of the slab.

He looked at a platform. It was circular with zigzagging black and white vinyl flooring. Three spherical stones lay on the outer rim, forming an invisible equilateral triangle. There were no walls, no ceiling, and the ladder hovered above him, suspended in impenetrable blackness. Each of the stone orbs was a different colour, one red, one green, one blue. They pulsed in sequential order. The pillar in the centre of the room had the outline of his face on it.

"Um, mind telling me where I am?"

"It's the centre of the universe. It's funny, in a way. The humans you so loved often thought they were the centre of it all, and they were so close to being right."

"It looks more like an unfinished kitchen from where I'm standing."

"Of course, it does. You're a three dimensional being, so you're not seeing the whole picture. There's more there than you will ever know."

Pride appeared out of nowhere, a feeling South had forgotten about. "You're forgetting I'm an immortal."

"Yeah, yeah. A *three-dimensional* immortal. Even you have your limitations, which you'd have discovered if you tried a bit harder like you were supposed to. Take my good friend Mavis, for instance. Mavis is a six dimensional being, and she'd see twice as much down there as you. And even she wouldn't have the whole picture. And you don't catch those sixers whining about lost love or mortal animals, neither, let me tell you, buddy."

"Have I ever met this Mavis?"

"Bits of her, probably. But you wouldn't know it if you did. None of this matters, though, please place the stones on the top of the pillar."

South strolled to the first sphere. He liked the red one, and put it onto the pillar. It disappeared, and the platform shook. The nothingness shook. South could see a plethora of outlines around him, faint ghosts all reaching out for the pillar at once.

"Uh…" he said.

"Don't worry about any of that, it's supposed to happen. Just ignore them."

South hesitated as he reached for the green sphere. The outlines all around him did the same. He placed it onto the pillar, and it vanished like the first one. This time the void around the pillar glowed, running a spectrum of every conceivable colour and some forgotten ones like sberv. A thousand million images flashed on the hitherto unseen walls of the abyss. He was inside a giant sphere. The pictures flashed at incalculable speed and seemed to show his life and also not his life. The outlines around him took on a form. They were him and not. Different South's, some rail thin and depressed, some vascular slabs of muscles. Some weren't him at all, but North, and she too took on a multitude of forms. Possibilities surrounded him. He could see but could not touch. He tried talking to him and they tried talking to him, but they were all lost in their own space, the shortcomings of the third-dimensional immortal made flesh. Or not, as the case appeared to be.

"And this is supposed to happen too, huh?" he said to The Creator.

"Oh, yes, very much so. You're all converging. This happens every time."

"Every time what?"

"Every time one of you hits the switch. You've had infinity journeys, all different, but they all end here sooner or later."

"And you convinced each of us to put these balls into that block?"

"Yep. It was easier than you think."

South nodded. He thought about the universe, about the ball, about what The Creator was asking. There was more going on than he could comprehend. It took him three hundred years to come to this conclusion. He picked up the blue sphere and held it over the ledge.

"No, South, put it on the pillar. We just got done talking about this."

South edged closer to the side of the platform. Amidst the flashing images on the sphere's wall, he could see his past laid out before him. "You're not telling me everything."

"Would I lie to you? All you have to do is put that miniscule pebble onto that wee slab of rock and you'll see her again."

Somewhere in among the images on the wall, Alexandra's face flashed. She was smiling as she had done. The image pulled at South's... whatever South had for a heart. He felt it in its entirety, throbbing, beating, yearning. The sight of Alexandra, her smile, recalled an eternity of happy memories. Some connected to her, others not, but all worth remembering. Of preserving. Even the saddest of them reminded him of being alive. Which is what he had become. Alive. It had taken too long for him to appreciate that simple fact: he was alive, he existed, as had everyone else.

"You'll have another chance, South, maybe next time it will work out the way she wanted."

"How? What does moving this thing into that thing actually do? Why should I trust you? You abandoned us."

Silence.

South raised his pinky and index finger, the orb making a slow descent from his fingers.

"No, wait, stop. I'll tell you. I'll tell you."

South stepped away from the edge and held onto the orb.

The Creator, wherever they were, hummed an old song before talking. "If you put that in the pillar, this universe is cancelled. Erased. Gone. I'm scrubbing it all. One by one. I'm sick of it. I'm sick of existing. Do you get it? You think you've had it rough? You start from scratch every new universe; I've had to sit through all of them for infinity. Can you even fully comprehend infinity? Infinity, South! Just think about it, except wait, you can't, can you? I've endured infinity infinity times over infinite plains of existence in dimensions you can't even see. We have had this conversation infinity times and I have to have it infinity more if I don't cancel the whole thing. Most of the time you agree, you know."

"Why?"

"Because you're usually a lot smarter than this."

"No, why erase everything?"

"It's so boring, man. I want some time off. For once. So please, I'm asking you this one little thing, and please oh please put the little blue thing near the little monochrome thing so everything will stop existing and I can maybe get some rest."

"And how does that get me back to Alexandra?"

A tut. "You're so selfish."

"You said this would help me."

"And it will. In a way. Technically. You'll be reborn another time in another universe where you see her again."

"But in this one?"

"In this one it won't matter because this one will have never happened. But in a way you'll always be with her somewhere or another. Just, this version of you will have never existed. That's all, old chum."

"I'm not worried about alternate mes. Me. I want to feel something again. I want to exist."

"Are you telling me you don't have any regrets? After all the death you've seen you'd want to do it again? What about the suffering? Existence is suffering. You could make that all go away. Wouldn't never existing in the first place be so much better for you? Is seeing a mortal you only knew for a few decades really worth all that pain? Come on, you're smarter than that. You're six feet away from making all the terrible memories go away."

South took a step toward the pillar, then stopped. "But the good ones too. All the good things would go away too. I could do better if I had another chance, and if not, every moment would be worth it for the hint of joy I felt."

"You're not thinking rationally. We're talking about a complete absence of suffering here. That's what I am offering you."

"I suffered, though, and I don't think I'd want to change that."

"I can't promise you anything. The truth is, you've started now so you have to finish. I'm sorry. If you don't, even I don't know what will happen. You might reset the universe; you might just wind up stuck in this room forever. All alone. The only solution is to do what I want, can't you see? End your suffering and set me free. Please, mate, you don't want to wind up in a different part of the multiverse by mistake. Just take a few steps to the pillar and wipe out your timeline. For me. For your Alexandra."

The other shadows had long since put their respective orbs into the centre of the platform and South alone remained. Upon hearing Alexandra's name, he hurled the orb over the edge into the depths of the sphere. "I'd rather she had lived and died than never existed. Sorry I can't help you out."

Silence.

One small problem with the incomplete reset sequence was the world outside was warping. South could not see what was happening, but knew his decision had immediate consequences. In scientific terms, what happened was this:

$$\text{☺} = \int_i^f \sqrt{\frac{Fm^2}{Eg}}$$

But in simpler terms, South done goofed. Each atom in the known universe was hit by a million identical copies of it plus a million and one anti-copies of it. Except for South's atoms as they had been erased from all other known universes. This mass deletion rippled out across the planet quite quickly, taking its time to extend to the far reaches of time and space. Bit by bit, the universe was eaten away by interdimensional termites, leaving South alone. He didn't know what had happened while the planet was dissolving as he still had the ladder to climb back up.

When he reached the workshop, the last thing on Earth to disappear, The Creator was gone, leaving only a few stray brambles as proof of their presence. All that remained was a gift on the throne: a crankable flashlight, a bundle of notepads and a pack of pens. There was a small card, too. It said:

RISKY BUSINESS DOWN THERE.
YOU'RE THE FIRST TO GIVE IT A GO.
THESE ARE FOR YOU IF YOU GET BORED LATER.

By the time South reached the mouth of the Cave, outside was gone. He was shocked, of course, to discover Hakone had been replaced by the absence of anything but did not mind so much. Behind him, the caved closed its maw like a sleeping babe before yawning itself out of existence. He was alone. A quick puff of a laugh escaped his lips.

"Well shit," he said. His words didn't carry.

It was about that moment he realised he was flying.

So here I am at the end of the universe. Hopefully, this would have made it to your bookshelf in another life. I know it's not your preferred genre, but if it helps, just pretend I was a Templar space pirate. Obviously this will not be the big seller you always envisioned me writing, what with everyone else being dead and all, but it is the most well-read book in a few billion years, so you know what, I'll take it. Now I just have to worry about film right. I will play myself. And everyone else.

When I think of you I consider myself extremely lucky. I am now more than a couple of billion years old, but the handful of years I spent knowing you were among my most cherished. Life, I suppose, offers a lot less when you're looking inward, shut off from the world around you. You wind up chasing dreams and phantoms and ideas which may never have existed in the first place.

Sometimes up here I wonder if my inactivity was the problem. I wasn't a saviour, that much is true. No, I spent far too much time being complacent to really save anyone. Hiding in the trees or blaming a woman for all my problems accomplished nothing. A neat distraction, though. Pretending I was saving the world wasn't the same as doing it for real. It's a common mistake.

The UN was right in their way. Would things have turned out different if I put myself out there? Went outside? Stopped hiding earlier? Never hid at all? I suppose we all suffer our own shortcomings. I just got to live with them for longer.

It is like you told me once a long time ago: you create your own reality. If you live in a world where you believe everyone around you is selfish, stupid, enti-

tled, lazy, and if not outright evil than at least
malicious in their indifference, that becomes the world
you live in. Nobody will ever be good enough for you,
nothing will matter. I wasted so many centuries believing only I could make a difference, living in that fantasy box I'd made for myself. We all did. North's contempt for the failure of humanity led her to destroy
herself. Our Creator was so tired of life, the life
they had complete control over, they gave up on infinite chances to do better.

You stopped me falling into the same trap. Or
better yet, you grabbed me just as I was about to fall
in.

But here we are, all the same. It's dark out. And
cold. There is nothing around me except my notepad and
pens. My wind-up flashlight has sputtered after a few
minutes. It's amazing these things last this long,
really. The last sentient lifeform I met out here disappeared around a billion years ago. It was a talking
gas giant who fed off pure energy. You'd have liked
them. Name was @~{>@~@{}!"£.

In the end, it would be seductively easy for me to
float around and reminisce about all the myriad bad
things I've experienced, or else wallow in a pit of if-
onlys. But what good would that do now, Alexandra? What
has happened has happened. I can comfort myself with
the good memories and learn from the bad. Nothing can
touch me. Focusing on a minor injustice now of all
times would drive me mad. Basically, what I want to say
is thanks: you've saved my sanity.

I don't know what happens next. The story was my last
idea for passing the time. Too late now, but a lot of
things I've always wanted to tell you just came to
mind. Real interesting stuff, too. But I'm down to my
last pen. I suppose I could write about the extra-ter-
restrial sex cowboys I hung out with for a while,
except you wouldn't want to read that, would you? There
was the… no, that was a hallucination. What else? What
else?

My hope is it turns out all time and space is cyclical, and I wake up at the dawn of time, all memories intact, and get to try again somehow. Yes, that's what I hope for. We were so close last go around to making things work out. I would gladly wait around another twenty-three billion years to see you again, maybe try a little harder. Perhaps all these experiences I have could be used to create a better world. I could save North from herself. Stop as much of the bad stuff as I can. Introduce Nell to Kubrick. Head off the East India Company and whoever else before they get their roots into the world. Get in the way of a few sniper's bullets. Invest in tech companies. Meet you. Try not to smile when I see you again. A second chance. Same as last time but with empathy, connectedness, less of the greed and obliviousness. A world you deserved. You all deserved. Were all secretly crying out for.

But would you be the same person if I did all this?

I'd like to hope so. I'd like to hope you're an unchangeable positive constant in the universe. An intangible limb of a pandimensional entity, spreading love and connectedness through infinite universes. It's a stretch, but then so is a naked man floating around the unknowable emptiness of time and space. But I hope you're there when I get back all the same.

Hope. That word again.

I was a lot of things in my life, Alexandra. A god, a warrior, a demon, an actor, an underpaid fry cook, a pirate, a cowboy, a prisoner, a minor celebrity, the, uh, the person responsible for destroying what was left of the universe. I was never good at the whole "hope" thing, though. Apathy? Did you read the book? Contempt, pity, admiration, resilience, compassion, pride? You betcha. But hope? Hope was something that eluded me right until the moment you agreed to get coffee with me. That's the human gift, right there: hope. It's not your thumbs or your electronics, your weird pornography or your history of bloodshed. It's Hope. Capital H.

Look at me now, I'm lost in space wishing for another chance to see you. It defies logic or rationality, but

I'm doing it. I'm doing it, anyway. All common sense and evidence to the contrary. What is that if not hope? A little hope in my life made everything more better.

What comes next? I've got my theories. We won't know until we get there, whatever there turns out to be. Will it be that psychedelic 2001 shot or just an abrupt resurgence of light like you're leaving a dark water-slide? I'll let you know when I next see you.

And with that, I wait for the end. It may be tomor-row, it may take another billion years, but it's com-ing, and I'll be waiting. Waiting and hoping. And I cannot wait to see where this takes us, Alexandra. All thanks to you, my love, my guiding light, my rescuer. Thank you for everything.

Actually, you know what? While I'm waiting, I might as well get started on that screenplay.

See you soon,

South.

Thank you for reading!

About D.D. Williams:

D.D. Williams thinks novels should speak for themselves and refuses to write a bio. We have respected this decision.

About Ixtab Media:

Founded by an international, rag-tag group of creatives and disillusioned media types, Ixtab Media was developed to explore new content, develop under-represented voices, and provide fresh, interesting works in industries that refuse to take many chances. We are a non-profit who invest heavily in writers and artists alike, paying significantly more than the industry average by fusing a cumulative six billion years of experience with guerilla publishing techniques. We are currently releasing new works as often as possible and will expand with your continued love and support. But mainly support. As in, financial. Thank you again for reading.

More from Ixtab Media:

The Cursed and The Dead, *Avi Llio*

Four strangers sit around a poker table in a remote desert town. They're all bluffing about more than their bad hands. Cryptids, cowboys, and chaos in this supernatural Western anthology.

Abel High's Least Wanted, *Angela Fuentes* (Coming Soon!)

When all of Abel High's attractive students and faculty are devoured by an unspeakable ancient terror, only a few outcasts, loners, and unwanted teens remain. But if they hot ones couldn't survive, what chance do they have? A YA horror debut that celebrates diversity, inclusivity, and demonic monsters.

Beneath Eldritch Lake, *David X Reiver*

Returning home for the first time in years, Oz Caduca wants only to attend his father's funeral and get out of there. But when the body disappears and the town's population begins to show signs of madness, it is clear something is afoot. A surreal, experimental exploration of madness and family.

Master of my Domain: A Nick Carraway Mystery, *Gaby G Seratt*

Celebrating The Great Gatsby's inclusion into the world of public domain works, Master of my Domain is a fast-paced, jet-setting cash-in. Uncovering an evil conspiracy to kill US president Tom Sawyer, Nick Carraway must team up with Dracula and Sherlock Holmes before it is too late! Oh wow!

Dane Morris: Rise and Fall of an Ubermensch; Or, An Intellectual Derp Derp, *Lazarus Tooms* (Coming Soon!)

Dane is a bad writer who seems doomed to live in anonymity until he brutally murders a local publishing executive. Becoming an overnight success, Dane has to ask himself if fame is what he really wants. A satirical look at fame, masculinity, and a world that will commodify just about anything if it makes a quick buck.

Diapsalmata, *Various*

A collection of short stories from the Ixtab Media family. Near-future dystopias, pop culture favourites gone feral, and the perils of advertising, this series explores everything from suicide and depression to survivalism and reality. A must read for everyone on the planet. Please and thank you.